I0760580

MALICE

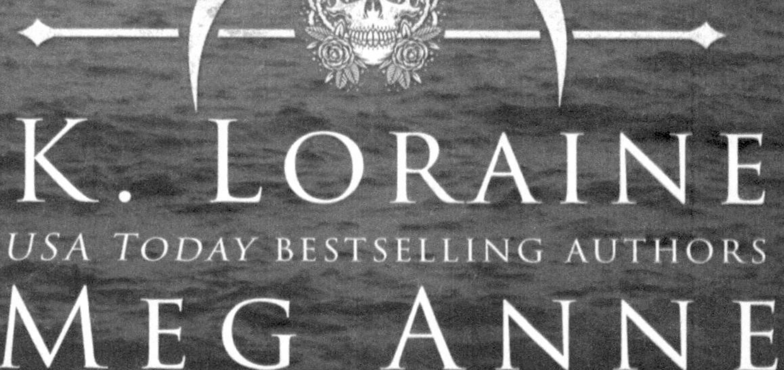

This book is a work of fiction. The names, characters, places, and incidents are products of the author's imagination or have been used fictitiously and are not to be construed as real. Any resemblance to persons, living or dead, actual events, locales, or organizations is entirely coincidental.

Copyright 2025 © Ravenscroft Press

All rights reserved.

ISBN:

978-1-961742-54-3 (Paperback Edition)

978-1-961742-55-0 (Hardback Edition)

No artificial intelligence was used in the creation of this work of fiction.

You may not copy, distribute, transmit, reproduce, or otherwise make available this publication (or any part of it) in any form, or by any means (including without limitation electronic, digital, optical, mechanical, photocopying, printing, recording, or otherwise), without the prior written permission of the author.

NO AI TRAINING: Without in any way limiting the authors' [and publisher's] exclusive rights under copyright, any use of this publication to "train" generative artificial intelligence (AI) technologies to generate text is expressly prohibited. The author reserves all rights to license uses of this work for generative AI training and development of machine learning language models.

Permission requests can be sent via email to: authors@themategames.com

Edited by Mo Sytsma of Comma Sutra Editorial

Cover Design by CReya-tive Book Design

Photographer: Wander Aguiar

Model: Jack A.

This one is for those who unapologetically wear their hearts on their sleeve.
It takes true strength to own that kind of vulnerability.

"Hope confronts. It does not ignore pain, agony, or injustice. It is not a saccharine optimism that refuses to see, face, or grapple with the wretchedness of reality. You can't have hope without despair, because hope is a response. Hope is the active conviction that despair will never have the last word."

— CORY BOOKER

MALICE

AUTHORS' NOTE

Malice contains mature and graphic content that is not suitable for all audiences. Such content includes scenes of dubious consent, sex work, role playing, disasters and more. **Reader discretion is advised.**

As always, a detailed list of content and trigger warnings is available on our website.

OPERATION PFFN SUPER SECRET VIDEO CORRESPONDENCE: #7

Shot opens with Remi up close and personal with the camera.

Remi: Mmm, looking good, Mercer. I'd fuck me. ***kiss noise***

Remi blows himself a kiss and preens a bit more for the camera. After fixing his hair several times, he settles back into his seat and peers into the lens.

Remi: So I guess if you're watching this, you might be wondering if you've died and gone to heaven and whether I'm the angel sent to usher you through the pearly gates. ***snickers*** Have no fear. You're very much alive, just blessed to find yourself on the receiving end of a special message from yours truly. Finally, am I right?

Remi rolls his eyes.

Remi: I don't know why Asher insists on being so selfish with who gets to film these. I am an excellent anchorman. And, between you and me, he's all doom and gloom, and honestly, the world is hard enough, so I figured why not add a little fun to this apocalypse stuff? I'm sure you'd all appreciate it a hell of a lot more.

Remi casts a glance at something out of frame and adjusts his position on the couch.

<<rustling clothes>>

Remi: It's really fucking messy outside. Have you guys looked out the window lately? Fire in the sky, earthquakes . . . Shit's going down, and I don't know if you've gotten our previous messages, but we really need you here, like . . . ASAP. I'm holding everything together for us as it is. Asher's told me more than once that I'm the glue, but you guys . . . a handsome wolf can only do so much. We need you—

Remi strikes Uncle Sam's iconic finger-point pose and holds it for several seconds.

Remi: To prevent forest fires. Wait, wrong PSA. ***chuckles*** Seriously though, we do need you. I don't think any of us are going to make it through what's coming without some epic firepower.

<<door opening>>

Asher: Remi? What the fuck? Are you in here recording?

Remi looks sheepishly from Asher, standing out of frame, to the camera.

Remi: I'm just giving the people what they want, babe. I can't help how the camera loves me.

<<footsteps coming closer>>

Asher comes into frame and sighs.

Asher: *heavy sigh* Some days I still can't figure out why *I* love you.

Remi: Ouch. Shots fired, babe.

Asher: Please. You're a pain in my ass and you know it.

Remi: But like the good, sexy kind of pain.

Remi winks at the camera.

Remi: You heard it, folks. He loves me.

Asher sits next to Remi.

<<couch creaks>>

Asher: So how far did you get before I caught you?

Remi: Just the essentials. The world is ending, I'm still handsome as fuck, come help us. You know, the highlights.

Asher: Couldn't be bothered to read the notepad with the bullet points I wrote out, could you?

Remi: Um, this is *my* super secret special puffin bulletin thankyouverymuch. I'll say what I want. I don't need any notes, m'kay?

Asher shakes his head and mouths "I'm sorry" to the camera.

Remi: Uh . . . so, what else is there to tell them?

Asher: Oh, I dunno. Maybe something about the ice house that was recently erected outside of Aurora Springs.

Remi: Shhhhhh. Ixnay on the Aurora Springs-ay.

Asher: That is not how you pig latin.

Remi: We aren't supposed to talk about our location. You're breaking your own rules. How can we have a fight club when you are over there talking about fight club like it doesn't even matter? What are we going to have next? Mass hysteria? Dogs and cats living together???

Asher: That's from Ghostbusters.

Remi: It still stands. Also, that's a great movie and you know it.

Asher: If you say so.

Remi: Rosie says so, and she's a Queen, sooooo . . . do with that what you will.

Asher leans forward and focuses on the camera.

<<rustling clothes>>
<<couch squeaking>>

Asher: The Novasgardians are our most recent arrivals. They have set up camp outside of town alongside the fae. It's finally starting to feel like we've got some numbers on our side. And not everyone has arrived yet. The Blackthornes are coming, and they've gathered as many of the most powerful vampire families they could.

Remi: Mmm, those Novasgardians are something else. But of course Alek and Tor's daddy would be so hot he could melt the polar ice caps.

Asher gives Remi a healthy dose of side eye.

Remi: And don't forget all our wolf friends. Kingston really showed up when he rallied the Farrell pack, and now we've also got the rest of the packs in the Pacific Northwest. So many alphas . . .

Asher: *clears throat* You've got a little drool on your chin, you horny fuck.

Remi: Do not!

Remi turns away and wipes at his face. Then he turns back around and sticks out his tongue to an amused-looking Asher.

Asher: *chuckles*

Remi: I do like that you still get jealous, though.

Asher: Keep it in your pants, Mercer.

Remi: Fine. For now.

<<knock on the door>>
<<door creaks open>>

Hades: Am I interrupting? You said you needed me.

Asher: Hades. Yes. I need you. I mean, we need you. We. All of us. Uh . . . we need you to get us up to speed about your meeting with the horsemen.

Remi: Now who's drooling?

Hades walks into frame but doesn't sit down.

<<footsteps coming closer>>

Hades: The Horsemen are aware of how deeply involved they have to be in stopping the apocalypse.

Remi: But are they good witches or bad witches? Personally, I wouldn't mind if they were sandwiches. Mmm, we do love a sandwich.

Remi elbows Asher and winks.

Hades: They aren't witches at all, you twit.

Remi: It's called a sense of humor. I think you need to get one.

Hades: I can't say that I find much amusing about the world ending.

Remi: I'm just saying, if ever there was a time to laugh, it's now. Humor heals, my friend. It's how humanity copes with the darkness. We're just one boiling sea away from extinction.

Asher: Allow me to get us back on track. What he was trying to ask you was, are they on our side or not?

Hades: As far as I can tell, they aren't working for Lucifer.

Asher: That doesn't mean they're working with us.

Hades: They've always maintained neutrality.

Remi: Which means what, exactly?

Hades shrugs.

Hades: It means I'm as confident as I can be that this time they're going to help us.

Remi dramatically swoons on the couch.

<<couch squeaks>>

Remi: *swoony sigh* Thank God. Okay, but real talk, how hot are these guys? I need to prepare.

Asher: You know, Rem, a less secure guy would take offense at the way you blatantly ogle other men.

Remi: Aw, baby. You know you're the only guy for me. It's you and Rosie. The rest is just window shopping.

All three men look away from the camera and toward the door.

<<distant footsteps growing closer>>

Rosie: (off camera) They'll be out in just a moment.

Lilith: (off camera) This can't wait.

<<door slams open>>

Lilith and Crombie walk on screen, an apologetic Rosie trailing behind them.

Hades: Lilith? What are you and Crombie doing here?

Asher: More importantly, how did you find us?

Remi: See! This is why you can't talk about fight club.

Lilith rolls her eyes and grabs Rosie's arm to hold it up and show off the red demon mark on her forearm.

Lilith: Rosie still bears my mark. I can always find your sweet little mate if I need to.

Crombie: My Lilypad is so resourceful.

Remi: There's something different about you . . .

Remi looks between the two of them, his eyes growing wide.

Remi: What happened to your chain?

Lilith: Drystan broke it.

Asher: Are we happy about that or . . .

Lilith: Or. But we'll have to get into that later. I have some rather urgent news.

Asher: Good timing, I guess. We were just wrapping up one of our—

Lilith: This is a private matter, I'm afraid. Drystan, darling. Would you mind?

Crombie: It would be my pleasure.

Crombie holds up his hand and sparks fly from his fingertips toward the camera.

Asher: Wait! That's expensive equipm—

Blinding light consumes the screen before it goes black.

End of transmission.

CHAPTER ONE

LILITH

Five minutes earlier

“If you want to leave this room alive, you will tell me everything there is to know about one Meredith Deveraux.”

My blood ran cold as the devil I knew far too well stared me down. The last thing I would ever do was betray Merri to the likes of Lucifer Morningstar. I’d outsmarted him before, but there was no way out of this one. He had me cornered, quite literally.

I met and held his stare, my heartbeat erratic but my face expressionless. I knew better than to give myself away. Even a twitch of my eyelashes could be used against me.

“Well? I’m waiting.”

Drystan threaded our fingers and gave my hand an almost imperceptible squeeze.

“Oh, how sweet. He’s not only a pet, he’s an emotional support faerie.” Lucifer’s taunt—as lighthearted as he made it seem—had a thread of steel running through it. "I think I'll make him watch me take you apart piece by piece."

Lucifer shoved away from the desk, his eyes flashing with the promise of agonizing torture. The chair toppled backward, and it was all I could do not to flinch from the anticipation of what was sure to be a future filled with misery now that he'd come to collect.

A hint of ozone was my only warning before Drystan's palm burned against mine.

I didn't have the opportunity to consider what that meant before it occurred to me that I had yet to hear the clatter of the chair against the floor.

"Lilypad, let's go," Drystan urged, giving my hand a tug.

My gaze drifted to Lucifer, who, by all rights, should already have his fingers around my throat. He was still as a statue, his luxurious mane swept back from his face and held in place as though he'd been carved from wax. In fact, everything in the room was frozen aside from my fae and me.

"What did you do?" I breathed.

"Is now really a time for questions? We have to go. I can only suspend time for so long before I'll be forced to release him."

"You've been keeping secrets, pet."

He tightened his grip on my hand. "So have you. Now, darling, take us to safety."

If this were any other situation, I would have corrected his insolence and reminded him of exactly who was in control, but he was right. We needed to get out of here.

My gaze flicked to the broken chain dangling from his neck. Then again, perhaps I wasn't in charge at all any longer. Now that the one thing connecting us was severed, I had no say over what he did. Our deal was all that had ever given me the upper hand. He'd just effectively ended it, and there was no way to know if he'd continue to cede his control to me.

The thought was as terrifying as it was thrilling.

"Lilith!"

I blinked, knowing that shock was the only reason I was operating so slowly.

Where the bloody hell could we go that wouldn't endanger us or Merri? She was my first thought, but if I attempted to find her, I'd likely lead Lucifer directly to her. Gabriel had been unreachable and would be no help, even if I could locate him. The few other souls who bore my mark were either dead or useless—except for one perky little Blackthorne princess.

"I hope you're up for company," I muttered, closing my eyes and homing in on the connection between Rosie and me.

"Ouch! Cheese and rice, that hurt." Rosie's sweet, lilting voice hit my ears before I opened my eyes.

Relief flooded me as the unfamiliar room came into focus. I honestly didn't give a twig where we were as long as Lucifer wasn't in the room.

"A-are you o-okay, sugar?" Bentley Mercer asked, his large form protectively curling around his mate. "I-is it th-the pups?"

"No. It's this blasted mark from . . ." Rosie's amber eyes lifted to meet mine. "Oh my stars. Lilith?"

"Yes, it's me. No time to explain. I need to speak to Asher."

"And you had to hurt my mate instead of calling like a normal person?" Ben growled, his voice pure alpha wolf and lacking his usual stutter.

The air grew heavy with Drystan's power, his palm coming to rest on the small of my back as he let out a low, "Watch yourself, wolf."

A growl rumbled in Ben's throat before Rosie got between them.

"Ben, I'm fine," she insisted, pressing a hand to his chest. "It mostly startled me, to be honest."

I could have apologized, but what was the point? It wasn't like I wouldn't do it again in a heartbeat if the need arose.

"We don't have time for posturing. Where is Asher? I need to speak with him."

"He's in the den. He should be done soo—" Rosie began, but I turned away from her and stormed into the hall.

"This way?" I belatedly asked, not knowing exactly where I was going but trusting that the soft murmur of voices was a good indication.

"Well, yes, but—" she called as she chased after me. "They'll be out in just a moment."

"This can't wait."

All right, poppet. Now that you're up to speed on what happened to me, we can pick this back up where we left off. No need to rehash a conversation you've already witnessed. Make sure you're comfortable, darling. Things are about to get intense.

"Wait! That's expensive equipment," Asher protested as the camera fell to the floor and let out a pathetic burst of sparks before smoke curled into the air.

"I'd say I was sorry, but that would be a lie, and the fae don't lie," Drystan drawled.

I waved a hand. "Just send me an invoice, Asher. Or, if you'd prefer, I can make a donation to one of your beloved penguin sanctuaries."

"Puffin," Remi corrected, his confidence faltering on the tail end of the word as I locked my eyes on him.

"What was that?"

"It's . . . uh . . . You know what? Penguin is fine."

Asher snorted. "If you were in wolf form, your tail would be between your legs. You sure you're an alpha?"

"Fuck you, man. She's terrifying."

I smirked. "Thank you."

Striding across the room, I took a seat on a leather club chair and let my gaze roam the room. The decor seemed very out of place for Asher Henry. Everything in here screamed old money. Old conservative money at that. There was a ship's wheel mounted over the fireplace, along with taxidermied animals displayed on shelves and hunting trophies staring lifelessly back at us. The bookshelves were filled with tomes about the Alaskan wild and explorers who'd ravaged the land but glamorized it as heroism. History is always written by the victors. Human nature at its finest.

"Sure. Go ahead and make yourself at home. We can wait for you to get comfortable, and then maybe you'll do us all the courtesy of telling us why the fuck you finally decided to show up."

I raised a brow at Hades's tone. "Is that any way to speak to an old friend, *Cain*?"

"I love it when she gets like this. Her voice goes all . . . *Yes, Mommy*," Remi whispered to Asher.

"My voice is always like this, pet. You just haven't had the pleasure. Now be a good dog and shut up." I trained my gaze on Asher, the need to understand exactly how much they'd achieved burning a hole in my belly. "Lucifer is gaining ground. Drystan and I barely escaped with our lives, and you're all sitting here making ridiculous videos and having a campout. What is going on over here?"

Asher's chin lifted defiantly. "That's rich coming from you. You've been almost as MIA as Gabriel. I understand you two can't interfere and all, but the world is fucking ending, lady. It's a little too late for you to ride in like the cavalry now."

My temper ignited, and I knew the mortals could tell because they all collectively flinched. "Once again you prove just how little you know, hacker. That's actually the exact reason I'm able to be here at all. Now that the apocalypse has begun, the rules of engagement have changed."

"Oh yeah? So where's leather feathers, then?" Remi challenged.

That was a brilliant question. Alas, it was one I didn't have the answer to.

"We have bigger fish to fry. I'm sure he'll make an appearance when it suits him."

Asher snorted in disgust. "It's probably never going to suit him. The angels have been so uninvolved if I didn't know he existed, I'd think they were nothing more than a myth."

"And, you know, you're one of them," Remi pointed out. "Go, go Lavender Lantern!"

"So not the time, Remi," Asher muttered, squeezing the bridge of his nose.

"What? Every hero needs a name."

"Lavender Lantern?"

"What's wrong with that? Your hands get all glowy, and you pew-pew your purple lasers—"

A heavy sigh came from beside me as Drystan's hand found purchase on the small of my back. "This is already exhausting. Someone gag him so the grown-ups can get this conversation over with."

Remi ha the good sense to blush. "Sorry. The higher the stress of a situation, the worse my ADHD gets. I'll be on my best behavior. Scout's honor." He gave us a little three-fingered salute and then sat on the edge of the sofa.

"Humor is his defense mechanism," Asher grumbled. "Have you seen the videos? That should tell you everything we know so far. We've kept them really up to date."

Disappointment settled inside me. I'd hoped they knew more and were prepared for a fight sooner rather than later. "Well then, you'd better make yourselves comfortable because if all you know is in those videos, then you are woefully uninformed."

Asher raised a brow but did as I asked. Hades, the insufferable arse, purposefully ignored me. He was lucky I was in a hurry, or I would have forced the issue. With the heel of my stiletto.

"Go on, then. We're listening," Asher said when I hadn't looked away from Hades's challenging stare.

"Oh bloody hell, where do I even begin?" My thoughts were scattered in a way I wasn't used to. I always had it together. I was strong and composed even on my worst days, but seeing Lucifer and nearly being caught by him had put me off balance.

"Where do we have it wrong?" Hades asked, gentler than I've ever heard him. Hmm, it seemed being a mated man had softened the god of the underworld. I'd have to keep that in my pocket and use it to my advantage at a later date.

"The horsemen. They're not looking for their partner. They have found her and are with her right now. I made certain of it."

"That's a good thing, right? Means things are further along than we thought," Asher asked, glancing between Hades and me.

"Yes and no," I allowed.

"Is this about the child?" Remi asked.

My brows raised. Perhaps this wasn't going to be as hopeless as I'd originally thought.

"You know the one from the Book of Ted?"

I scowled. So much for that theory. "You clearly don't understand the book."

"Yeah, well, that's because it's written in some ancient as fuck form of demonish. You try reading it," Remi retorted.

"I don't have to read it. I wrote the bloody thing."

They stared at me as though I'd just whipped off my clothes and started prancing about like an elephant.

"And you couldn't have mentioned this sooner?" Asher asked.

"No," Drystan answered for me, challenge radiating through him.

"How did we misinterpret it?" Asher conceded.

"Lucifer isn't looking for a child. He's looking for Merri so that he may conceive one."

"Fuck," Hades muttered. "He's going to use that sweet little succubus to make the antichrist."

"The horsemen are currently trying to beat him to the punch and ensure her womb is already occupied."

"How's that supposed to work?" Hades asked. "Merri is a succubus, and succubi are notoriously infertile."

I smirked. "Not if they're bonded to their partners."

"Bonded? Succubi don't have bonds," Hades said, his disbelief palpable.

"Don't we? Just because it's something you haven't witnessed doesn't mean it was never so. One could argue the lord of the underworld had never bound himself to another until Persephone."

Hades made a sound somewhere between a huff and a snort. I'd take begrudging agreement over further protest.

"When you say bonded, do you mean like mated?" Asher asked.

I raised one shoulder in a shrug. "It's complicated."

Remi threw his hands in the air. "Of course it is. Why change things now?"

"Mate bonds are like a strike of lightning. Instantaneous and irrevocable. Even without a mating mark, the call to be together is stronger than anything else. For us, a bond is woven slowly, the threads creating a powerful connection over time. Fate is still at play, and a sense of . . ." I trailed off, waving my fingers through the air as I searched for an appropriate word, "magic."

"Magic?"

I nodded. "Put simply, once a bond has started to form, it will not be denied. Not without great cost."

"What do you mean, it won't be denied?" Hades asked.

"Exactly that. It will force the issue if it feels it is being ignored."

Remi cleared his throat, but Asher spoke first. "How?"

A wicked smirk spread across Drystan's lips when I flicked a glance toward him as I worked to find the right words. "Uncontrollable desire for one's bonded. Physical pain that can only be assuaged by contact with her chosen. A withering away of body and mind the longer the bond is left incomplete."

"Sounds fun," Remi said with a grimace.

"And if the bond isn't satisfied?" Hades asked, his eyes shrewdly narrowed.

"Then all parties will perish. As I said, the magic of the bond refuses to be denied. Succubi magic is parasitic at its core. Our bonds are no different, at least until they are fully formed."

"So it's the old fuck or die trope."

Asher rolled his eyes at Remi's assertion, but the wolf wasn't wrong. He simply wasn't as eloquent as I.

"Does this remind you of something?" Asher asked Remi.

"Sounds a helluva lot like a feast."

Asher nodded.

"Feast?" Hades asked.

"Sort of like a heat," Asher explained, "but the vampire version."

"Fuckfest," Remi confirmed. "Doesn't stop until she gets enough, if you know what I mean."

"We're forgetting a vital piece of this puzzle," Hades interjected.

I slid my gaze to him, knowing exactly what piece he was going to mention. "Go on."

"They can fuck her until she's boneless, but if she's not fertile, that doesn't help. And that brings me to another point. Why would Lucifer's vessel for the antichrist be a succubus? It seems counterintuitive to me."

Shaking my head, I sighed. "There's a lot about my kind that has been lost to the ages, and some of those secrets best remain hidden. Suffice it to say that Merri is absolutely capable of bearing a child under the right set of conditions."

"And are the horsemen aware of those conditions?" Asher asked.

"They don't need to be. From my last conversation with Merri, I have nothing but confidence that things will sort themselves out in that regard."

"And as to the Lucifer part of the equation?" Hades pressed.

I fought the impulse to fidget. Generally, I was very guarded about the secrets I revealed, preferring to offer crumbs as needed rather than laying everything out in the open. But given that we were all staring down the barrel of the apocalypse, I suppose this was one truth I could part with.

"Merri is part of Eve's bloodline."

Remi let out a garbled noise. "Eve. Like . . . Eve of the garden and the apple?"

"For fuck's sake, yes. Do you know of another?" Drystan snapped.

"Well, I mean, there are about a million Eves . . ." Remi stopped talking when the rest of us pinned him between our combined gazes. "Right. Zipping it." Then, under his breath, he muttered, "Eve is a really common name."

"And I'm assuming, given that correlation, that something about her bloodline makes her more susceptible to Lucifer's seed?" Hades asked.

I nodded. "Merri may not be a reincarnation of her many times removed great-grandmother, but her blood calls to Lucifer just as strongly as Eve's did. He's been obsessed with her since the garden, and the infatuation only continued through the ages. Eve was the first mother. Her line has always been blessed in that regard. Lucifer will always be drawn to her descendants."

"Because of his obsession with her?" Asher asked.

"Because Eve's line is the only one who can create his antichrist."

"So your plan was to what, throw her at the horsemen and fill the oven before Lucifer could?" Remi asked.

As much as I loathed the cocky wolf, he was quite astute. "Yes."

"It's not terrible, as far as plans go."

"How confident are we that they're going to be successful?" Asher asked.

"As confident as we can be."

"Correct me if I'm wrong, but even if they are successful, wouldn't that just piss Lucifer off even more? You know, give him an even stronger reason to carry on with his war?" Hades asked.

"Perhaps, but it also creates a more even playing field. If Lucifer gets his antichrist, then it's game over for all of us. If he doesn't, there's still a chance we can win."

"So what do we do in the meantime? I, for one, don't intend to sit around and wait. If I learned anything from Mommy Dearest, it's that the only person who gets to decide my fate is me."

I smiled at Asher. "I hope that's true. And to that end, if you intend to be on the front lines of the upcoming battle, then you need to get to safer ground."

"What do you mean?" Asher asked.

"Darling, you're shacked up on the edge of the hellmouth. Do you really think this is the smartest place to gather your army? This is one of the first places hell's army will break through. You'll be overrun before the battle begins."

Remi leaned closer to Asher and whispered, "She's mean."

"Can I kill him?" Drystan asked, not bothering to lower his voice.

I bit back a smile. "No, pet. We need him."

"Lilith is right," Hades said, ignoring Drystan. "We are running out of space to house everyone. Lilith found us, which means Lucifer will be able to as well."

"How? There's no reason for us to be on his radar at all. And even if we were, he doesn't know where we are."

I sighed. "Lucifer can trace me at will. He won't do it until he's exhausted all other options, and I can only hope he's too preoccupied with finding Merri to give chase, but when he decides to, he will come for me."

"Wait, are you telling me you brought war to our doorstep?" Remi asked, jumping out of his seat. "What the hell kind of ally are you? Why didn't you just pick up the phone and call instead of putting us all in danger?"

"Now can I kill him?" Drystan tried again.

I shook my head and sighed. "Remington, war was already on your doorstep. It's only a matter of time before you all find yourself in the crosshairs once more. And I stayed away as long as I could."

Asher's sigh joined mine. "She's right. We were just giving her shit for keeping her distance. We don't get to be pissed now that she's here. And really, it doesn't change anything except the timeline."

Remi pointed at me. "You aren't invited to the new fight club."

"Fight club?" Drystan asked.

"He means their next hideout, my darling."

My fae prince huffed. "As if we'd want to spend any more time with these miscreants than absolutely necessary."

"Well, do you have any suggestions on where we should go next?" Asher asked. "I'm all ears."

If I was honest, I wasn't sure where they could successfully settle their army. No place on earth would protect them indefinitely. But I knew one thing: the final battle loomed ever closer, and we all needed to prepare for the worst.

"I don't know. Until we figure something out, we must hope the horsemen are successful."

Remi stood and stretched. "I've never been so excited for someone else to get laid."

"Oh, I don't know if that's true," Asher said with a smirk. "Remember that one time . . ."

"I stand corrected. I've never been so invested in someone other than us getting laid."

Rolling my eyes, I looked to Hades. "Show us to a room? Drystan may actually kill this one if we have to hear him speak another word. My protection only goes so far."

With a laugh, Hades strode to the door. "Follow me."

CHAPTER TWO

MALICE

The soft click of my kettle turning off coincided with the blue light snuffing out. That was my water ready. Without missing a beat, I began the ritual of preparing my cuppa.

It was a shame we didn't need to eat because this beautiful kitchen was mostly wasted. Out of the four of us, Chaos and Sin were the most likely to work their way down here and make something, but that was more force of habit. Muscle memory, if you will. Food provided no nourishment or essential function for our kind, but it didn't harm us to partake either. If anything, I think it was probably some sort of self-soothing behavior.

"I know why *I'm* here. Why are *you* lurking in the kitchen?" I asked Grim as I removed my tea bag and set it aside.

Grim released a low hum more akin to a growl, his eyes never leaving the window and the view beyond. "Something is on the horizon. I can sense it. This is the best view of the drive."

I gave my tea a few stirs before lifting it to my mouth. "And you really think our enemies are going to slowly parade their way up to our front door?"

"I think they are unpredictable, which is why they've gotten the drop on us twice already. Can't you feel it in the air? There is something electric running through my every cell. Intuition perhaps. Either way, a storm is about to break."

He wasn't wrong. I could feel it as well but had chalked it up to the continued peril the world was in. I flicked my eyes up to the sky, which was still a fiery blend of red and orange. Before I could reply, Chaos barged into the kitchen, his large frame tense as he gathered ingredients for yet another one of his smoothies. His movements were jerky as he slammed cupboards closed and grumbled to himself without paying the two of us any mind.

"Something bothering you, Chaos?" I asked, finding it odd that three of us were all on edge.

"I need to fuck or I need to fight. I'm on the verge of exploding, and it's only getting worse." He ripped open a banana so forcefully the fruit broke in half and fell to his feet. "Fuck!"

Grim simply offered me a raised brow before saying, "Exhibit A."

"I'm not sure a hankering for violence is really that much of a—"

Sin's panicked, albeit muffled, shout rang out from the direction of the stairs. "Guys! Come quick, something's wrong."

Grim didn't bother uttering *I told you so*. Before I could blink, he was gone. I followed suit, materializing right beside Sin as he stood in Merri's doorway. That feeling Grim spoke about hit me harder than Chaos wielding a sledgehammer and nearly sent me to my knees.

"Fuck me," I whispered.

A quick peek showed that my brothers were no less affected. Chaos gripped the door so tight that the wood cracked beneath his hold. Sin was pale, hands shaking as he stared at Merri writhing on her bed.

"What the bloody hell happened?" Grim bit out, the veins in his neck distended as he visibly fought to keep from going to her.

I couldn't blame him. The way she whimpered and moaned woke that same need to care for her inside me. That, coupled with the intense arousal permeating the room, had me achingly hard in my jeans.

"Sin?" I asked, just the formation of that single word entirely too difficult.

The incubus had to tear his eyes away from Merri before he could respond. "I don't know. I found her like this. She's been unresponsive. I don't think she's all there right now."

Merri's back arched as she traced her fingers along her inner thighs, then up the length of her body. Dammit, I could see how wet she was even through the fabric of her leggings. She gasped and locked eyes with me, her pupils eclipsing those beautiful blue irises along with the sclera, making her appear more demonic than she ever had before.

"She's not," I whispered, the first tendril of understanding beginning to form in my mind.

"But this is her power," Chaos argued, his muscles straining as he physically held himself in place.

And it was her power. It was attempting to lure all four of us to her side like willing captives. But why? What had happened that sent her into such a state?

"I think her hunger is in the driver's seat right now," I finally said.

Chaos grunted and shifted on his feet, clearly unsettled. One glance at his tented joggers told me everything I needed to know. He needed to fight or fuck. He'd said it himself. It looked like fuck was the best option. "Is this what it felt like the first time this happened? When you found her in the wine cellar?"

"No," Grim ground out. "This is worse. That time she was just weak. This feels like she's gone completely feral."

"And she's trying to take us with her," I added.

"Why is she this bad? She's been feeding," Sin said, sweat beading across his forehead.

"It's like an addiction, remember? We've watched her go from snacking, to regular full meals, to insatiable. Her hunger has only grown with each passing day." I ran a hand across the back of my neck in an effort to relieve some of my tension.

A look crossed Sin's face, and if I didn't know better, I'd say it was recognition.

"Something must have triggered this."

Grim's soft intake of breath was the only sign that Chaos's words affected him.

Focus entirely on Merri, Chaos continued thinking aloud, "Is it a trap? Did someone get through the wards?" He stormed across the room and began searching the windows for something to prove him right.

Sin audibly swallowed. "I don't think this is a trap. I think it might be part of her Famine heritage."

All three of us turned to him.

"What do you mean?" I demanded.

"Well, we've all been at a loss as to why her hunger only seems to grow, but we've been focusing on her succubus nature."

"That's because we didn't know Famine was her mother until Hades told us," I pointed out.

"Right," Sin said with a nod. "If there's one thing I know better than sex, it's how famine works. One thing Sabine loved to remind me was that it always came down to feast or famine. And it's true. Our nature is extremes. We take and take, leaving nothing behind, but still never manage to fill the void inside. Think of Merri's hunger right now like a black hole. A supernova. She's consuming herself because there's nothing else to feed her."

"But we're right here," I said.

"Exactly. We're in her orbit, and she needs us to fill that emptiness before she burns out."

"And if she burns out?" Grim asked, but I was pretty sure the question didn't need an answer.

Sin stared us down, expression grave. "She dies."

"How do you know that?" Chaos asked, eyes burning with an unnamed emotion.

"I've experienced it myself. Not like this, obviously, but the precursor. Remember that time Malice dared me to go a month without feeding?"

We all nodded.

"You broke after two weeks," Grim reminded him.

"Right, well, it was more like my power forced the issue. I started feeding on people without even realizing it. I took out that VIP group in five minutes. They were all dead before I even knew what happened."

Merri began a new chorus of pained moans as she tore at her clothing, rubbing her thighs together and murmuring unintelligibly.

"We have to do something for her," Sin said.

Grim turned away, making for the door. "I can't take this. I'll kill her before she has the chance to burn out."

I understood his plight, and fear stabbed through my heart at the thought of giving in and letting myself have her as well.

"No." Sin's protest was loud and strong, causing Grim to turn and face him. "We do this together. We have to. Remember the library? It works best when all four of us can share the burden."

"What if there are side effects, even if we do split them?" I asked, thinking of Merri's current state as some sort of super virus the four of us were coming into contact with for the first time. How were any of us supposed to survive this?

"There won't be. We've all experienced it. She might take from us, but she gives as well." Chaos returned to our group and wiped the sweat off his brow with the hem of his shirt.

"Yeah. He's right. She fucking supercharged me." Sin's proud grin was almost boyish.

Still uncertain, I looked back to Merri. She was still squirming on the bed, though she'd managed to remove her shirt while we'd all stood here debating our best course of action. Her skin was flushed as though with fever, and long strands of her hair stuck to her glistening skin. I'd just lifted my gaze to her eyes, only to falter. The black orbs had been replaced with her robin-egg blue irises.

"Please," she rasped, the word only for me.

That was all I needed.

With a gasp, she arched her back unnaturally, and when her eyes returned to meet mine, they were black once more.

I began unbuttoning my shirt even as I strode toward the bed. Merri had asked me to help her, and I would not leave her to perish.

With each step I took toward her, Merri grew more still until she was frozen on the bed. If not for the rapid rise and fall of her chest, I would have thought her a statue. Her gaze was fixed on me, and I could sense the calculation taking place in her mind. She was a predator assessing her prey.

"Merri," I whispered.

In a flash, she was on me, pulling me to the bed and tearing at my clothes.

"Christ," Sin whispered harshly.

"I don't think he's involved in this one, Sinclair." Grim's voice filtered through the room, but I hardly had the attention to spare, not with a ravenous succubus atop me.

A feral claiming wasn't exactly what I'd pictured for my first time with Merri. Not that I'd allowed myself to think on it at all. Or at least not much. She raked her nails down my bare chest, the slight sting radiating long after she'd reached my open fly. My shirt was nothing but tattered fabric, barely hanging on to my shoulders, and though my jeans were still intact, the button fastening them was long gone.

A low growl radiated from deep in her throat as she made to remove the offending denim, but I stopped her with a hand on her wrist.

"Allow me, hellcat."

I was already moving, wriggling my way free of the obstruction.

Merri practically purred, one soft hand running along my length before she sheathed me inside her. Hot, wet, and impossibly tight, her cunt enveloped me all at once, and the sensation was so intense I nearly came then and there. Which was to be expected, honestly. I hadn't been inside of a woman in more years than I could currently count. But even for me and my situation, the rapid approach of my climax felt fast.

"S-slow down," I begged, not ready to lose the sensation of her moving over me as quickly as I'd found it.

"No."

Her hips rolled with no regard for my request, the lust-crazed look in her eyes only serving to bring me perilously closer to falling.

"I won't last."

Before I could say anything else, her fingers wrapped around my throat and she squeezed. "Good."

The curl of her fingers mimicked the tight squeeze of her cunt, and my eyes rolled back in my head as a wave of euphoria crested. The fact that I'd thought I'd had any control of this situation was laughable. I was completely at her mercy. A pawn for her to use or destroy at her whim. There was no choice left to make but to surrender.

It shouldn't have been possible, but my dick hardened even more, and there was nothing I could do now to stop the orgasm she drew from me. And it was her who did it, make no mistake. My eyes opened and found her face hovering over mine, lips parted, eyes fully black, cheeks flushed.

"Now," she whispered, tightening her grip on my throat.

I was lost. To pleasure. To pain. To her.

Distantly, I heard the startled cries of the others, whatever sensual magic Merri had woven over me affecting them just as deeply. I spilled myself inside her, giving her everything there was of me and relishing in the fact that I was seeing to her needs. She'd chosen me, and there was no denying that something between us shifted.

Without warning, she rested on top of me, the soft puff of her breath fanning over my skin as she tucked her face into my neck. It was so unexpected there wasn't even an opportunity for me to consciously decide how to react. My arms cradled her protectively, my mind memorizing the happy sighs that escaped her. She was, for all intents and purposes, a contented cat seeking out a cuddle.

My heart thundered in my chest, and my mind emptied of everything except the feel of her against me. Clarity and reflection would come later. For now, I simply existed. With her. For her.

She shifted in my hold, and I turned my head toward her, curious what I would find this time. Merri blinked as our gazes connected, the brilliant blue of her irises a welcome sight.

"There you are," I murmured as the woman I knew returned to the forefront.

A soft smile tilted her lips, and something happened to the walls around my heart. I felt them crack ever so slightly. Fuck.

"Is she back?" Chaos asked, his deep voice rumbling through the room and startling both of us.

As if a switch had been flipped, black stole over her eyes, and her entire body stiffened as her head snapped in his direction.

"I'm going to take that as a no," Sin drawled. "Guess that means it's time for round two."

CHAPTER THREE

SIN

Merri hadn't said a word. In fact, she hadn't moved from the bed where she straddled Mal. So the phantom sensation of her hot little hand wrapped around my wrist and luring me closer was quite the surprise. I didn't hate it. If she wanted me, she was going to get me.

I reached behind my head and began tugging off my shirt.

"What the hell are you doing?" Malice asked, his hands tightening on Merri's hips in a rare show of possession.

"Tapping in, duh."

"I'm more than capable of doing this myself."

There was another, more insistent tug on my arm.

"That's not what Merri thinks."

Malice's violet gaze drifted between her and me, his brows furrowing. "What do you mean?"

Glancing to my left at Chaos and then to Grim, who stood off to the right, I asked, "You guys feel that?"

Grim frowned, as usual. "Feel what?"

Chaos took a ragged breath before shifting from foot to foot, clearly uncomfortable. "The lust?"

"No, the way she's pulling us in."

"I don't feel a pull," Grim admitted. "Beside the usual kind."

I flicked my gaze back to Chaos with a question in my expression. "Me either."

"She hasn't moved," Mal pointed out. "And she's still clenched around my cock, so I'm pretty sure I'd have noticed."

I quirked a brow at Merri, a smirk playing on my mouth. "Is it just me you want then, kitten? I'm honored."

Merri licked her lips, her body shifting like she was preparing to crawl off Malice and straight toward me.

"You were saying?" I taunted, hand dropping to my fly and making quick work of my jeans. Without ceremony, I took the denim and tossed it in Chaos's general direction. "Hold these for me, will ya?"

His annoyed grunt told me he'd caught them. But I was more interested in the way Merri's obsidian gaze seemed to trace over each newly revealed part of my body.

I'd never admit it out loud, but I felt Malice's tortured groan as Merri slid off his dick as though he'd reached over and grasped mine. Jesus, the sexual energy pumping through this room was so potent I'm pretty sure I was high. In fact, we probably all were. We were trapped in our very own sexy little hot box of Merri's lust.

Goddamn, she was pretty as a picture. A slightly terrifying one, but still. Her skin was glowing from exertion, cheeks still flushed, lips swollen, nipples hard. I was always ready to let her have her way with me, but I couldn't deny there was a sense of danger coming from her right now, and that thrilled me.

She took her lower lip between her teeth, and a soft whine escaped her as she rocked those shapely hips back and forth. Merri was ravenous for me. My dick gave a twitch, the persistent throb impossible to ignore. I needed inside her just as much as she needed me. Maybe more.

Usually this was the part where I'd ask how she wanted me, but she was practically nonverbal at the moment, so I guess that meant it was dealer's choice. Malice currently possessed the majority of the real estate on the bed, and the last thing I wanted to do was waste energy fighting to get him to move. All I could focus on was sliding my cock deep inside her as soon as possible. You know what they say, "The quickest way from point *A* to point *B* is a straight line." I closed the distance between us in three long strides and scooped her into my arms.

Merri must have been on the same page as me because she slid down on me in one smooth glide. Then she locked her ankles around my back to keep me there. As if I had any intention of ever leaving. I'd fucking move in permanently if that was an option.

"Fuuuck me," I hissed as her slick walls clenched around me.

Whatever half-formed plan I had in mind went straight out the window. This was happening right here, right now.

I staggered a step or two until Merri's back was pressed firmly against the closest pillar of her bed. Thank fuck for this ostentatious four-poster frame, because whatever magic Merri was throwing at me had my incubus powers rendered obsolete. My knees were weak from the pleasure of being joined with her alone.

"She needs you to fuck her, not stand there," Grim chastised. "Don't tell me you don't know what to do with her."

"Listen, Granddad, you can chime in when you're able to participate. Until then, zip it. You have no idea how hard it is not to blow my load right now. This is unlike anything I've ever felt before."

"Glad it wasn't just me," Malice muttered.

Fire raced across my back in the form of deep scratches made by Merri's nails. It was all I could do not to cry out as the burning pain pulled my focus from the conversation to the woman in my arms. I returned my gaze to her and whispered, "Hold on tight, kitten."

Her eyes were locked on mine as I slowly pulled out and then drove back inside her. She made a soft mewling sound, which I took as approval, so I did it again. Her eyes closed as pleasure flitted across her features.

"Fuck yes, you take me so well." My voice was a harsh rasp as I continued pounding deep into her, loving the way I could feel myself nudging her cervix with every thrust.

The tips of her nails pricked my back as she tilted her head and inhaled deeply. I could always tell when she fed on me, but this was so much more intense than usual. As if she'd been drowning and finally got her first full breath. My reaction was no less intense. Merri had reached inside and found some inner dial, then turned it all the way up. I could hardly bear it, so powerful was her hold on me.

She took, and I gave. Willingly. Desperately. Because right now, if she asked it of me, I'd let her suck every ounce of my essence from my cells into her. As it stood, I wasn't fully convinced that the fate of my existence wasn't in her greedy little hands. She just might kill me, and I think I would thank her for the experience.

It was a good thing I couldn't actually be killed. But this might be the closest I'd ever come to testing the theory.

The bed creaked and shook as I pounded into her, and Malice let out a harsh bark of laughter. "Who knew you could get seasick in a bed?"

"You could always get off," I gritted out, my eyes fleetingly finding him lying on his back, hand furiously shuttling over his length.

His answering smirk was as cocksure as my own. "Oh, I intend to."

I grunted as Merri's teeth sank into the meat of my shoulder, and although I'd never been one to enjoy receiving love bites, something about my girl leaving marks on my skin sent pride rushing through me.

God, it felt like she was claiming me. Like she'd wound our souls together or something. But how could that even happen? Horsemen didn't have souls, right? Not in the traditional sense, anyway.

Her nails scored up my back again, ensuring once more my focus was solely on her as she removed her teeth from my flesh and growled, "Mine."

The orgasm I'd barely held at bay roared forward, and I came with a startled shout of her name. I'd swear on my life that she'd just single-handedly triggered my climax. No one had ever had such control over me. I was completely and utterly under her spell.

I had to reach out and brace one hand on the post behind Merri to keep myself from falling and taking her with me as I pulsed inside her until I had nothing left to give.

As I came back to myself, breaths heaving, limbs shaking, I found her gaze on me. It wasn't the pools of blue I'd grown to crave, but the demonic black. I knew what she was going to say before she opened her mouth.

"More."

CHAPTER FOUR

CHAOS

Merri's voice, though only a whisper, filled the room with such powerful lust magic I had to bite back a groan. Sin was already turning his body, preparing to indulge her request, no doubt. But I wasn't about to be looked over a third time.

"I've got her," I said, striding forward and pulling Merri out of his arms.

Cradling her, I allowed myself a glance down at the state of the woman who had us all at her mercy. Here and now, I'd do just about anything she wanted. I couldn't even blame it fully on the fact she was a succubus. I couldn't pinpoint when exactly she'd assumed such control over me; it felt like only yesterday that I despised her presence in my life. Now I couldn't imagine it without her.

"Hi, Red," I murmured, hoping to coax the snarky, playful woman to the surface.

She responded by reaching up and gripping the nape of my neck, forcing my head down as she took my lips with hers. The kiss wasn't sweet or tender. It was painfully starved.

A fleeting thought gave me pause. What if she might never be sated? Had we all been the victims of some trap set by our enemies, doomed to spend eternity in an endless cycle of lust and feeding?

As quickly as the thought took shape, the press of her warm body against mine sent it fleeing. We'd deal with it if and when we had to. For now, all that mattered was her.

I nipped at her lower lip, drawing a breathy sigh from her. I started to pull back so I could better navigate the room with her in my hold, but she didn't appreciate the distance. She hissed and writhed in my arms, the grip she had on the back of my head tightening as she pulled my face back down to hers.

Depositing her on the bed, I took my time shedding what was left of my clothes. I'd discarded my shirt while Malice was taking care of her, the arousal in the air too strong to keep my body from reacting. Just the brush of fabric on my skin had been too much to take. It had been a show of great strength to leave my sweatpants on. As it was, the inside of them was a mess of precum, a dark stain spread across the front.

Merri's eyes seemed to lock on the patch, and a wicked smile curved her lush lips. She knew what she did to us, and she was proud of it.

"Hungry, Red?" I asked, taking hold of my aching length behind the cotton and squeezing hard.

She licked her lips and surged forward as if I was denying her her favorite snack.

I stopped her with a hand around her throat, lightly collaring her and holding her in place. "Not so fast, Red. You want me, we're playing by my rules."

Anger flashed across her face and she fought me, reaching for the waistband of my pants.

"The two of you aren't playing the same game," Grim muttered.

"Hell, you're not even on the same court." Sin's words were laced with amusement.

"I put my money on Merri bringing him to his knees before the minute's up."

I glared at Malice over Merri's tousled hair. "You've had your fun. Get the fuck off our bed."

"Since when is this your bed?" Malice countered with a lift of his brow. Then, like the arrogant asshole he was, he made himself more comfortable among her pillows.

"Fine. Enjoy the show."

Merri's nails scraped along my abs. Not gentle, playful scratches, but hard, insistent ones.

"Enough of this," I barked before flipping her onto her hands and knees, ass in the air, pink pussy on display.

The swollen folds were glistening with cum.

"She's dripping," I murmured for the others' benefit.

"Allow me," Grim said, the inky phantom shape of a hand appearing between her legs for a brief second before scooping up the milky fluid and pushing it back inside her. "There. Now it's where it belongs."

She whimpered and arched her back, begging for more without words.

My cock was a throbbing, aching thing, desperate to be freed. "Out of the way, Death. She needs me." I shoved my sweats down and palmed my dripping length.

Grim's shadow retreated, leaving Merri bared to me. I reached out and grasped the full globes of her ass in each hand and spread her wide, just as I had in my dream. She was every bit as glorious as I'd remembered.

Positioning myself between her legs, I fed my cock inside her welcoming body in one long thrust. She cried out and arched again.

"You like that? You like the way I fuck you, Merri?"

Her answering moan had my balls tightening. She shifted her weight, rocking her hips back and forth as she tried to bring me to my finish far too soon for my liking. That wouldn't do. She wasn't in charge here. I was.

And I would come when I was ready.

Releasing her ass, I reached forward and grabbed her by the

wrists, pulling her arms behind her back and forcing her face down onto the bed. It wasn't a gentle transition. Her chest dropped to the comforter, the move angling her hips up and back and forcing me to slide deeper than I thought possible inside her.

We both groaned at the unexpected shift in our position.

"You might act like you want control, Red, but you fucking love when I take it."

She thrashed beneath me, like she could deny the truth of my words.

Adjusting my hold on her wrists so I held both with one hand, I reached forward and threaded my fingers through the hair at the base of her skull, tugging until she was upright.

"Admit it," I growled into her ear.

"Yes," she hissed.

Lowering her back into position, I kept my hold in place and began thrusting in long, languid rolls of my hips. She wanted my orgasm, but I also recognized the distinct lack of her own climax. Merri might be focused on feeding from us, not giving the others a chance to bring her off, but I wasn't one to leave my woman unsatisfied. Every drag of my cock along her G-spot had her walls squeezing me, a flood of wetness following.

"More," Merri gritted out.

I was already pounding into her with enough force I knew she'd feel the memory of me inside her for days. Sin must have registered the conflict in my expression because he said, "I don't think she means you."

"What?" I grunted, carrying on a conversation with him while balls deep inside her. Not the easiest feat to manage.

He moved until he could meet my gaze and gave me a droll stare. "She wants another cock, Chaos."

The bed dipped as Malice came to his knees in front of her. "Let go of her hair."

Muscles trembling from the effort it took not to find my release, I slowed my pace and looked to the man who knelt naked at Merri's head.

"You already had your turn with her."

I pulled harder on her hair, making her cunt flutter around me, and a whimper escaped her lips. But I also saw the way she looked at Malice, specifically his straining cock. Sin was right. She wanted another.

Malice challenged me without words, leaving the decision up to me. But Merri had already made it for me. This was all about her and what she needed. My pride would heal.

"Fine." I released her hair with a soft snarl. Malice was quick to scoop the long strands up into a sort of ponytail so he could take over, guiding her movement from that end.

"Fuuuck," Malice groaned as she engulfed his length in what had to be the perfect heat of her mouth.

Jealousy spiked inside me for a fleeting moment because I wanted to know her in that way. I wanted to know her in every way possible.

"Not gonna lie, guys. This is a really pretty picture. Our girl all trussed up, getting spit roasted."

Any other moment and I'd have socked Sin right in the mouth, but I was a bullet train on the way to my climax. Nothing was going to stop me now.

The grip on her wrist and hip tightened until I could see my fingers digging into her skin. The thought that I might leave my mark on her again sent me over the edge. Merri might be pleasuring both of us, but she was still fucking mine.

"I'm coming," I panted, my voice tight and desperate. Merri tilted her hips back so she could take me deeper, but I wasn't sure if the move was hers or if it was a result of the hold I had on her hip. Either way, our bodies seemed to be completely in tune with what the two of us needed in this moment.

She moaned as my thrusts grew erratic and pleasure overtook my senses. Her answer to me losing the rhythm was rolling her hips in sensual circles, which only prolonged my orgasm. Somewhere in this suspended sexual fog, I could feel the tug of her energy pulling on mine. Not like she was feeding, but like she was drawing part of me into her. Like we were linked in more ways than simply physical.

Malice grunted, his breaths coming in sharp pants as he must've also reached his peak.

"You look beautiful taking us both," I whispered as I came back to myself.

My palm skated up her back, rubbing soothing circles between her shoulder blades. I needed her to know she was so fucking good to us.

"Perfect," Malice agreed, his thumb stroking her cheek as he slid out of her.

Arms free once more, Merri pushed herself up and looked over her shoulder. "More," she demanded.

"Jesus," Sin said with a laugh. "I've heard of an insatiable appetite, but this is next level." Shaking his head, he climbed up on the bed. "Catch your breath, boys, I'll tap back in."

Merri gave a slight shake of her head, her pitch-black eyes landing on Grim.

I smirked, knowing exactly how this was going to go. "You're up, old man."

Grim swallowed hard, concern etched into every line on his face. "It can't be me."

"It's you she wants."

"There's nothing I can do for her." Panic replaced the concern on his face as he took three rapid steps backward toward the door.

"No!" she shouted, her voice cracking through the room like a whip.

"I'll ruin everyth—"

Merri screeched in frustration, throwing out a hand before making a fist and yanking at something none of us could see.

Grim grunted, then his eyes went wide, and, for a beat, everything fucking stopped. I had to blink to ensure I was really seeing what I thought I was seeing. Then I blinked again, because I still didn't believe it.

"Did she just—" Malice started, shock rendering his voice barely above a whisper.

"She did," Sin confirmed.

"Holy shit," I breathed.

Where Merri had been holding nothing but air now stood a very discernible shadow form.

Grim's shadow form.

CHAPTER FIVE

GRIM

Merri's enraged cry drew me up short, and I froze just as she threw her hand out. For a heartbeat, I couldn't tell if she'd made me stop or if I'd consciously decided to do so. Before I could land on an answer, my breath caught in my throat and a foreign weight sat in my chest. Not on top of, but *inside* the very marrow of my bones.

There was a tug, like that weight had somehow latched on to something tangible, and then the strangest sensation of being peeled away from myself washed over me. I didn't have any other words to describe the feeling. I'd never experienced it before, nor had I ever heard someone else mention it.

I released an audible gasp as I struggled to process what I saw before me and marry it with the sensations I could feel in my physical body. Warmth encircled my wrist. It was undeniably Merri's soft skin against mine, but she wasn't touching me. In fact, Merri wasn't within reach of me. She was perched on her knees on the end of the large bed, eyes trained on me, fingers wrapped around the wrist of a fully manifested shadow figure.

I'd seen my shadow enough times to recognize it as my own. But never like this. Never when it was completely severed from me, as if it was now its own unique entity.

A sudden pang of fear had me instinctively sending a testing bolt of my will its way. Merri made it manifest. Did that mean it now answered to her? Or was I still in control?

My relief was potent when the shadow form moved as I'd intended, the fingers on its right hand flexing. Her reaction was immediate, a tightening of her grip that sent a shiver of excitement chasing away any residual fear. She could touch me this way and not suffer the consequences. More than that, she could feel my touch every bit as much as I was experiencing hers.

"I didn't know you could do that," Malice murmured from the bed.

I shook my head, reaching up with my shadow hand and cupping Merri's face. Her skin was just as soft as it had been in my dreams. I'd never imagined this was possible. After things failed so spectacularly with Hel, I'd completely given up on the possibility of knowing a lover's touch again. Of being able to touch her in return. And then Merri had stumbled her way into my dreams, teasing me with a loophole.

But this? This was *real*. This was her and I, awake. Together.

A disbelieving laugh escaped me. "Neither did I."

"He didn't do it," Chaos added belatedly. "Merri did."

Malice frowned, his eyebrows furrowing. "How?"

"Horsewoman power," Sin answered, shocking all of us.

"And how do you know that?" Malice demanded.

"I've seen Sabine do something similar. She has the ability to interact directly with her prey's life force. Usually she chooses to drain them instead of feed. She calls it her deadly kiss."

"Are you trying to tell us she can suck someone's soul from their mouth?" Chaos asked.

Sin nodded. "We can both do it. But she loves to feed on fear more than lust."

"That's not what Merri is doing now." I knew it as surely as I knew my own name.

"No," Sin agreed. "Our girl is a problem solver. She wants you, Grimsby. She just ensured she can have you."

In a handful of long strides, I was beside the bed, aching to be as close as was safe so I could revel in the noises I was about to pull from her, the micro-expressions that would flit across her beautiful face, the scent of her desire. I didn't want to miss a second of what was sure to be the single best experience of my immortal life.

"Move back," I snarled at Chaos, who'd disengaged from her body but remained close enough to touch what was mine.

Chaos, to his credit, didn't argue. He simply backed away from the bed, and I sent my shadow to claim our rightful place.

My attention turned to Malice, who was still kneeling in front of Merri. "You as well."

I half expected him to refuse, like he did with Chaos, but he also surprised me by complying.

"We're going to stay in the room, all right?" Sin murmured soothingly, as if talking to a feral creature. "Just in case you need us. But this moment is all yours."

"I won't need you."

Merri let out a soft moan before spreading her knees apart and bringing my hand between her legs. I felt her touch mirrored on my corporeal flesh. Something about it seemed . . . thinner, as though she was holding me through a veil of fine chiffon. It wasn't true contact, but I'd take what I could get. And right now, that was her perfect pussy. Needing no further direction, I slid my fingers inside her and groaned at the sensation. She was slick and hot, and even though it was my shadow playing with her, I could tell how much she wanted me.

"Fuck," I grunted, the word practically dragged out of me as my brain struggled to process all these new stimuli. Not only was I essentially in two places at once, I was feeling all of it. Merri's arousal, my own, the wonder that such a thing was even possible, the anticipation of sinking into her and making her cry out in ecstasy. You'd think already it was too much to handle, but no. I wanted more. I wanted every-fucking-thing.

No one ever said that Death was altruistic.

I was greedy. Insatiable. And I'd just been given free rein.

"What are you waiting for, Grim? Give her what she needs." This from Chaos as he watched on, his gaze locked on Merri's glistening cunt, still visible through the shimmering darkness of my shadow.

My teeth ground together, the urge to shut him up with a punch to the face almost uncontrollable. Instead, I simply moved my shadow limbs to spread her thighs wider before sending my form climbing atop her.

She clawed my shadow's torso, the slight prick muted but still sharp as I felt its echo down my abs. My cock gave a happy jerk, likely offering itself up as tribute.

A gasp escaped me when Merri reached between my shadow and herself to grip the length desperate to get inside her. If there'd been no danger of me killing her and she'd touched my true form like that, I may have spent myself then and there. Did she know the effect she had on me?

The wicked curl of her lips told me that she did.

Of course she did.

She was hardwired for exactly that. Merri was a creature born to read every subtle shift in our moods. That it was sexual only meant she was more interested than ever.

"Relax for me, wildflower. I'll make sure you have everything you want."

Her little whine of protest as I batted her hand away with my shadow's had me grinning, but soon all pretense of play was gone. I moved my shadow into position, placing the tip of my cock at her entrance with my gaze trained on her face.

"Look over here, Merri. Look into my eyes as my shadow fucks you for the first time."

Those dark orbs snapped to mine, and I had a brief moment of protest at the wrongness of them in her angelic face. Thankfully, I'd had enough run-ins with demonkind over the centuries, so I knew how to spot the spark of emotion and intelligence behind the black pools. Her demon might be front and center, but our girl was in there too.

With our gazes locked, I sent my shadow sliding forward, sinking down into her sweet heat. The ripple of sensation along my actual shaft was a torturous tease.

"God in heaven," I groaned, the words tight and guttural.

Even though my logical brain knew it wasn't my body inside hers, there was no denying what I was feeling—or its effect on me. I'd never fucked wearing a condom, but perhaps this was similar. My shadow was akin to one—the thinnest barrier keeping us apart. I knew from my limited experience with Helene that had I actually been buried balls deep inside my sweet little wildflower, everything would feel exponentially *more* than it currently did. It'd be hotter. Wetter. Tighter.

That said, I had zero fucking complaints. For one such as I, who'd spent the greater part of his existence not touching at all, this was practically the equivalent of a nuclear bomb going off inside of me. I wanted to commit every second to memory so I could relive it ad nauseam. I wanted to collect every possible interaction available to me so that if I woke and found this all to be another fantastical dream, I wouldn't walk away empty-handed.

With that thought center of my mind, my shadow form bent over so it was pressed torso to torso with Merri. Her warmth tingled along my chest, a tantalizing glimpse of what it would be like to hold her against me.

Kiss her, I thought.

The brush of lips was like a drop of rain in a drought. All it did was leave me wanting more.

As my shadow savored her in slow, controlled thrusts, I opened my trousers and freed my cock, needing to add that last bit of missing friction.

Unlike me, Merri wanted nothing to do with a long, drawn-out affair. She squirmed beneath my shadow, letting out a snarl of frustration as she bit down on its lower lip hard enough that I'd have sworn she drew blood from *me*.

"Naughty girl, wildflower," I grumbled, but there was no heat in it.

She wrapped her legs around my shadow's hips and rolled her pelvis upward, searching for faster, deeper, harder thrusts.

"She needs more from you, Grim," Sin whispered, his voice breaking through the haze of desire that had enveloped me.

"And she'll get it. But not just yet." I wasn't done taking her all in.

I pushed back just far enough with my shadow form to begin kissing my way down her neck and collarbone. Merri bucked against me, wordlessly demanding more.

"Not so fast," I murmured, using one of my shadow's hands to pin her down by the throat while the other glided down her belly and dipped between her legs. "You wanted me, *demanded* me, and you've got me. But it's going to be on my terms."

My shadow was stronger than her, even with her demonic power holding the reins. But she struggled nonetheless. She wanted me to feed her, to give her my orgasm, but I wasn't ready yet. And even though I'd give her exactly what she asked for, I was in charge here.

"I didn't realize we were allowed to have terms," Malice grumbled.

"You sure weren't complaining." Chaos's deep voice filled the room even when he spoke under his breath.

I forced their voices into the background, keeping my attention locked on Merri. She might be protesting against my methods, but she was responding to my shadow's touch all the same. My shadow form took her nipple into his mouth, sucking on the tight bud before paying her back for her earlier assault on my lip with a sharp bite. Merri yelped, her back arching off the bed as her inner walls flexed around my shadowy shaft, followed immediately by a flood of wetness.

"You're gushing, beautiful," I whispered, my fist tightening over my length as I lost the battle to keep my strokes slow and measured.

I let go of control, let my shadow rock into her in time with the pace of my hand as it shuttled along my cock, moving ever faster as her body squeezed mine. Precum dripped from my crown, my balls drawing up, signaling the inevitable.

"Grim, she needs your cum inside her."

Sin's unwanted interruption buzzed around my mind like an annoying gnat before it fully registered.

How the bloody hell was I supposed to manage that?

"Can his shadow actually do that?" Chaos asked softly.

"Doubtful," Malice replied under his breath.

"No, it has to be him. If the goal is to fully sate her, she needs her partner's cum."

In my periphery, I could see Chaos nodding. "It's true. Her demon clearly took hold because she wanted more than Merri was willing to provide and got tired of waiting. This won't end until she's satisfied."

"Just get as close as you can and let your shadow take care of the rest," Sin offered.

He didn't need to elaborate. I knew exactly what he meant. But if I was going to do this, I needed to take every precaution.

Spread her legs wide, I thought, ensuring she was safe as my shadow did my bidding.

Her legs were splayed in a wide V, the sight of her cunt taking my shadow cock reinvigorating the orgasm that had been waylaid by my brothers' unwelcome voices. She let out a keening cry when a shadowy finger began rolling her clit, making her thighs tremble. There was no sound of slapping skin to accompany the act, but Merri's moans were the only soundtrack I needed.

"We do this together," I grunted as I positioned myself as close as safety would allow.

My cock wept for her, and I could feel the heat of her pussy from proximity alone.

She detonated with a harsh gasp and an arch of her back, a pleasure-filled wail coming from deep within. I followed. There was no way to stop it, and there wasn't a single part of me that wanted to.

"Fuuuck, Merri," I groaned, spilling my seed onto her plump pussy lips.

Tingles raced across every nerve ending, chasing along my skin as my orgasm seemed to go on and on. When it finally began to dim, my chest was heaving and sweat dotted my brow. My vision blurred for several heartbeats before things returned to focus.

The sight that greeted me was straight out of my filthiest fantasies. Merri was still splayed, her chest rapidly rising and falling as she struggled to catch her breath, her belly and swollen sex coated with my release.

"Put it where it belongs," I whispered harshly, my order for my shadow, but I wanted her to hear it too.

Merri's eyes snapped open as my shadow obeyed, two thick digits swiping through the mess I'd left and pushing it deep inside her. Her mouth formed the sweetest *O* of surprise, and I caught the exact moment the obsidian orbs shifted back to blue.

For good measure, I curled those shadow fingers up and rubbed against her internal walls, making her gasp as her eyes fluttered closed.

She returned her gaze to me with a satisfied smile on her lips.

"Are you back with us, kitten?" Sin asked.

A slight nod was her only response before she sighed dreamily and fell into a deep sleep.

CHAPTER SIX
MERRI

The antique wardrobe's door creaked as I pulled it open, once again making me yearn for the walk-in closet at Grim's penthouse. It was so much larger, with a wider variety of camming outfits. Reaching inside, I trailed my fingers over a few options but cast them aside. I needed black, lace, and over-the-top.

I shoved several hangers to the side, on the hunt for the perfect teddy/robe combo, when the scent of the ocean hit my nose. I paused, checking behind me to ensure the window was still closed. We were on an island, but this was the first time I could recall being able to smell the sea.

Another waft of salty air overtook my senses, but this time it was accompanied by a decidedly cool breeze . . . from *inside* the wardrobe.

"What the heck?" I muttered, pushing the hanging garments out of the way so I could see the back of the large piece of furniture. Or at least, I tried to.

Instead of finding the back of the antique wood, I was met with a second row of clothing. Then a third. At this point, I was literally inside what was arguably a wooden box. Except it wasn't a box. Not anymore.

"What in the Mary Poppins bag of furniture is this?" I grunted, pulling a coat sleeve off my face.

The cry of a seagull pierced the air, followed by the unmistakable sound of waves. Oh. Oh, I understood now. This was a dream. I'd never had a portal to Narnia dream before, but that had been one of my favorite movies as a kid. I didn't know why my subconscious was choosing this precise moment to bring it back around, but hey, might as well enjoy it.

I pushed through the last of the clothes until I was standing in a field of swaying grass. The sun was high overhead, but it wasn't hot. The cool ocean breeze was more than enough to mitigate the powerful rays. Seeing a normal sky after a week of one filled with fire was incredible. That alone was worth the price of admission.

"Stop fighting me, you menace." The male voice floating through the tree line sent my pulse skyrocketing. I didn't recognize it. Normally in my dreams, I recognized the people and places. Well, except that first time I met Luc.

I guess, come to think of it, it wasn't that unusual to have randos show up in our dreams. It certainly happened now and then. Usually it just meant they were some sort of amalgamation of traits used to represent something—or someone—else.

"Well, let's see what all this is then," I murmured, heading off toward the voice.

A strange sound, low and almost cow-like, grew louder the closer I got.

"You guys are ridiculous. Stop complaining." That voice again.

As I snuck through the trees, a figure came into view in the distance. A tall man with shaggy blond hair was crouched over a large box, from which more of the weird cow-chainsaw sounds were emanating.

"How are there so many of you? You're only supposed to have one egg at a time, you know."

He scooped something out of the box, a little fluffy black bird who squirmed in distress as the man chick-napped him or her.

"All right, Staypuft, you're up." The birds in the box squawked in protest. The man gave the box a glare. "Listen, you know we have to do this. You'll all be reunited in a matter of minutes. Just let me live, broskis."

Oh my God, what was my brain making me witness?

"This hurts me more than it hurts you. Believe me," he grumbled before winding up like a pitcher and hurling the flailing little bird off the cliff.

"What the hell are you doing?" I shouted, rushing up to the man and his potential victims.

He spun toward me, his face set in a scowl. "The job I hired *you* for," he snapped. "Nice of you to show up, by the way. Do you have any idea how hard it is to do all the testing and returning by myself? It's not like we're trying to save the world or anything."

"I'm sorry? What are you talking about?"

He stepped closer, his white lab coat flapping in the wind. Then he pointed at my chest. "Operation PFFN. It's right there on your shirt. God, where does Remi find these people? Mars?"

I looked down my torso, and sure enough, the logo he'd indicated was splayed across my tits. Well then. He was still looking at me expectantly, so I shrugged. "Must have mixed up the start time." Because seriously, what the hell else was I supposed to say to my dream boss?

"These puffins aren't going to catalog themselves, lady. Grab that clipboard and start checking off their names, would ya?"

Before I could irritate him further by asking where I was supposed to find one out here in the wild, I noticed a table on my right. A table that definitely hadn't been there a minute ago.

"Dreams are so fucking weird," I muttered, heading over to pull on a lab coat of my own and grab the aforementioned clipboard.

The man picked up another bird, this one looking to be a full-grown puffin. "Dragon, Puff the Magic."

It took me a second to realize he was talking to me. "Huh?"

"That's her name. Mark it off."

"You named a puffin Puff the Magic Dragon?"

"No, I named it Dragon, Puff the Magic."

"That's the stupidest thing I've ever heard."

"Likewise."

I found the name on the paper and marked it with a little check. Then screamed as he hurled little Puff off the cliff.

"Why are you murdering them? Are you a puffin serial killer?"

He could not have been more offended. "Exqueeze me? Murder a puffin? Are you out of your mind? Lady, do you have any idea what we're doing here? We are *saving* these puffins. If it wasn't for me"—he forcefully pushed a finger into his chest before flinging his arm back toward the box—"these absolute badasses would all be dead. That's why we're testing them. The puffins are the key to the vaccine."

I had officially lost my mind. The words coming out of this dude's mouth barely made sense.

"The vaccine. Riiight."

"We are trying to stop the . . ." His face contorted in confusion as the words died on his tongue. "Wait, where did they go?"

I looked over the edge of the box, and sure enough, nothing was there, just brown cardboard. Not even a stray feather.

The man whipped his head from left to right before focusing on me once more. "What are we doing here? What the fuck is going on?"

Oh great, was this about to turn into a nightmare? Had my subconscious gifted me an encounter with a crazed puffin enthusiast?

I held up the clipboard. "Uh, saving the puffins?"

Confusion swept across his face. "That does sound like me, but . . ." He dragged a hand through his hair, leaving several strands sticking straight up. His gaze was unfocused, and he was muttering under his breath. "Nope. No. This isn't right."

"Operation PFFN?" I offered.

His eyes went wide as he jumped on the name. "Right. Operation PFFN."

"Save the puffins."

His eyes latched onto mine. Fierce and clear. "No. Save the world."

I shot up in my bed, eyes wide, gasping for breath as I looked around my bedroom. What the fuck had that been about? Puffins? A handsome weirdo on a cliff? I could still hear the echoes of the waves and the odd sounds those birds made.

Strange as it was, I should have been thankful that it had been just a normal run-of-the-mill dream and not a dreamwalk. Small mercies, I supposed.

Not that the dream could erase what had happened leading up to it. My cheeks burned with embarrassment. I hadn't lost control like that in a long time. Actually, I'd never lost myself so completely I'd ended up in a full-on fuck fest with a bunch of hotties. The last time I'd lost control, my succubus decided to start a sex riot so she could feed. Stupidly, I'd thought that I finally had a handle on her, but boy did she prove me wrong.

Gluttony, thy name is Merri.

Standing, I stretched my pleasantly sore muscles and gasped at the sensation of warm wetness running down my thighs.

"Ugh." I grimaced.

I didn't have an issue being marked by their cum, but there was nothing fun about the sticky aftermath.

"Right. A shower is a must. Then we face the music," I muttered to myself as I awkwardly shuffled to the bathroom.

No one talked about the effect of gravity after sex without a condom. Add three extra dicks to the recipe, and the mess required more than a simple wipe-down.

I started the water and took stock of myself in the mirror as it heated up, muttering as I did, "Fellas, we're gonna have a little chat about aftercare."

I wasn't upset that they'd left me to sleep it off, but a warm washcloth went a long way.

A moan slipped out as I stepped under the hot spray of the shower, memories of last night surfacing in flashes every time I closed my eyes. My succubus had been in control, forcing the issue of my hunger and giving me what I needed, but I'd still been a willing participant. I mean, sure, I'd been attempting to keep my distance from the horsemen because of the whole manipulating them into wanting me due to a totally accidental bond. But it was never like I didn't *want* to sleep with them, so I could hardly complain about getting to enjoy the ride.

The problem was, I hadn't truly understood my hunger or seen it as a living, breathing thing. I'd gone so long doing the absolute bare minimum to keep myself going, but now that I was actually feeding myself properly, I'd gotten a little addicted to the power that came with feeling truly full. Camming had stopped being enough pretty much the second I'd joined up with the horsemen. What used to last me a couple days was barely sustaining me for an hour. I needed it regularly.

Oh, fuck. Would it eventually reach the point where I had to feed three times a day to stay healthy?

But how could that be the case? Lilith didn't live on her back in a bed with people fucking her multiple times a day. Did she?

Iniquity *is a sex club, dummy.*

Lilith may not be actively fucking twenty-four-seven, but she was certainly surrounded by sexual energy all day, every day. And then there were Lilith's demon marks. Any deal done with Lilith was in exchange for them bearing her mark and allowing her to siphon lust magic from them when she chose. Which meant that Lilith was feeding nearly constantly.

I paused mid-soap-up as realization dawned. I couldn't keep acting like things were business as usual. My life was seriously going to have to change if I didn't want more episodes like last night springing up on me.

Assuming, of course, the world didn't end first.

A shiver that had nothing to do with apprehension raced across my skin when I ran the loofah over my breasts. Grim's shadow hands cupping them as he moved inside me took the spotlight in my thoughts. God, I could almost feel him even now.

What a revelation that had been. I didn't even know I could do that. Manifest a whole-ass shadow person, I mean. Was that something I could do to anybody? Or was it unique to Grim's deathiness?

It was probably a question for Sin. Or maybe Malice. The first knew the most about being a sex demon, and the other was an expert in the mental side of my power. Surely one of them could tell me what the hell I'd done.

I shampooed my hair with deliberate slowness, taking the time to make sure every inch of my scalp was clean. The slight ache at the base of my skull reminded me of Chaos's firm grip on my hair as he drove into me. Then I recalled the sensation of him and Malice both working in tandem.

I licked my lips at the memory of Malice's taste on my tongue. As far as first times went, ours was certainly memorable, but not perhaps the way I'd have chosen for us if necessity hadn't won out over all else.

His voice whispered through my mind. *"Allow me, hellcat."*

Fuck. My whole body clenched in response, and I licked my lips again.

My heart gave a pained throb for what he and I could have experienced without the cloud of my hunger over us. Honestly, I wondered if all of us would have more than lust.

Immediately, I remembered Sin's anger when I'd tried to convince him sex was all that existed between us. When he'd all but asked me to be his girlfriend. I smiled to myself as I thought about him asking if I'd deleted my apps or wanted to wear his ID bracelet. Those weren't the words of a guy who just wanted to get in my pants.

My sweet Sin wanted more with me. And it wasn't just because of the bond I'd unwittingly created. At least, I didn't think so. It certainly felt real when he'd let down his mental walls for me to peek inside. But was that just because my magic made him think so?

I groaned in frustration as I worked the conditioner through the ends of my hair. Those stupid dreamwalks had ruined everything. I couldn't trust that any emotions they showed me now truly originated from them. But what about my own feelings? Could I trust those?

I craved them. Not just physically, but emotionally. Each one of them called to me in a way I'd only experienced once before. With Jimmy. And the way I'd wanted him in my life didn't hold a candle to the magnetic pull between me and these four horsemen.

What is wrong with you? They're literally having a secret contest to see which one can knock you up fastest. That should be a deal breaker, Meredith. Where is your feminism?

I snorted. "Joke's on them. Pretty sure it's never going to happen anyway. No matter how hard they try."

As I rinsed the last of the conditioner out of my hair, I couldn't help but wonder why they would even want to get me pregnant. What the hell were the four of them going to do with a baby? Was it just a game? A way to pass the time while they hid me from the denizens of hell? Some inane display of their virility?

Getting out of the shower, I wrapped a towel around myself and rolled my eyes as Chaos's obvious breeding kink replayed in my mind. Even veritable gods could be victims of toxic masculinity.

I should be angry. Honestly though, the connection I felt with each one of them dulled that flame of outrage into nothing but an ember. Why?

We had a lot to discuss, the five of us. Their plot. The bonds they didn't know about. And whatever else they've been keeping from me.

Mind made up, I beelined for the wardrobe. It was time to get some answers. Whether the horsemen wanted to give them to me or not.

CHAPTER SEVEN

MALICE

Silence sat heavily in the room where my brothers and I had gathered post Merri's . . . whatever the fuck that was. The sunroom had never been so filled with tension, and what typically created a serene and comforting atmosphere only underscored how on edge the four of us still were.

"You'd think after that many orgasms, we'd be more relaxed," Sin joked, playing with an antique tea set and causing my left eye to twitch.

"That is not a toy, Sinclair. I've had it in my possession since Marie Antoinette got a permanent haircut."

Sin smirked and held one of the delicate cups to his lips, one pinky out. "Are you and Grim competing for fussiest Brit? I've gotta say, you're gaining on him, Mal."

In a brilliant display of stealth and finesse, Chaos snuck up behind Sin and cuffed him on the back of the head. Sin jolted, the precious china tumbling out of his hands. My breath caught in my throat, but I needn't have worried. Chaos caught the cup and replaced it on its shelf before the rest of us could do more than register the action.

"Ouch, man. Careful with the goods."

"We need to talk about what last night means for all of us," I said, striding toward the wall of windows and training my focus on the arc of flames streaking across the sky.

"Why?" Sin asked, idly rubbing the back of his head as he made his way toward an overstuffed sofa.

I slowly spun around to face him, one brow raised. "You cannot possibly believe that what happened last night is normal."

"Only you three could turn a fuckfest into something bad," Sin complained, sitting down with a plop.

"Careful," I gritted out, worried he was about to ruin yet another piece of my furniture.

"I mean, sure, it's not normal, but is any of this normal?" Swinging his arm wide, Sin gestured to the world at large.

"I have no issue with sating her hunger and seeing to her needs, but we nearly lost her to her power last night," Chaos said, his voice grave.

"What are the odds something like that happens again?" Grim asked.

We all turned to Sin for an answer.

He startled, eyes flicking between each of us. "How am I supposed to know?"

"You are the resident expert, are you not?" Grim pressed.

"When it comes to fucking, sure. But the rest of it? Merri's part succubus, part horsewoman. There's only one other being like her in existence, and that bitch kept her cards close to her giant tits, if you know what I mean."

"Famine doesn't even feed on lust. She prefers fear wherever she can get it."

Sin's gaze met Grim's as the eldest horseman's statement landed.

"There's plenty to go around. I'm sure she's well-fed these days."

Chaos grunted his agreement as he replaced me by the window and stared up at the blazing sky.

"Do you have something to add, Chaos?" I asked.

"Not really," he murmured, crossing his arms over his chest. "Seems like the only thing we can count on right now is the unknown."

"Helpful as ever," I grumbled.

"Hey, c'mon, guys. Perk up. We should be celebrating what we did last night." Sin sauntered over to the bar and began working on some sort of cocktail. "Malice, you broke your chastity and got your dick wet for the first time in, what . . . three centuries?"

"Longer than that," I muttered.

"Chaos had his first threesome. And Grim. I mean, wow." Sin began a slow clap before mixing up what I could now tell was a pitcher of Bloody Marys. "Did you know you could do that? The whole *shadow man* thing?"

Sin kept talking before Grim could answer.

"I mean, clearly not. Otherwise you would have been doing that all over the place. No way you would have been living your monk-like existence all these years knowing there was an alternative readily available to you."

Grim shot Sin a pointed look. "Are you quite done?"

Sin took a sip of his cocktail, eyes closing in pleasure as he smacked his lips. "Don't get mad at me for calling it like I see it."

"Do you have a point? Or are you just being crass for the hell of it?" I asked.

"Yes. I thought you'd never let me get there. You're all standing around sulking like we just got back from a funeral when we should be happy about last night and any future opportunities like it."

The thought of Merri so ravenous for us again had arousal flooding me, but then apprehension quickly chased it away. She hadn't been herself. She'd been in danger.

"Why would we want that to happen again?" Chaos asked.

"Because we all got the chance to knock her up last night. We were probably already successful. Bingo-bango, baby." Sin's expression twisted and he looked at Grim. "Well, maybe not you. The viability of sperm once it hits the air isn't, you know, great. But we can pretend you're still a contender. Don't want to leave you out of the celebration."

"Thanks so much," Grim deadpanned.

Sin winked. "I'm a giver."

"You're an asshole," Chaos countered.

"That too. They aren't mutually exclusive."

"For once, the issue is not whether we got Merri pregnant. It's whether we can prevent her turning feral," Grim said.

"Not so fast. Maybe her going feral is a good thing. I mean, can you do the shadow man magic without her being feral?" Sin wasn't going to let the topic of Grim's additional form lie, and I didn't blame him. It was quite fascinating.

Grim didn't so much as twitch an eyelash, but I could tell his attention had turned inward. "I don't know," he eventually murmured.

Sin waved an arm dramatically. "Why don't you test it out, buddy?"

"I am not a puppet who will perform for you on command, Sinclair."

"Chicken shit," Sin mocked, pushing to his feet so he could flap his arms and paw at the ground with one of his feet.

"Don't. You. Dare," Grim warned.

Sin began to squawk and peck at the air.

An irritated grumble preceded Grim's heavy sigh as he closed his eyes and concentrated. As I watched on, Grimsby's shadow spread outward onto the floor, then rose in front of Sin, slowly taking shape until it was a man.

"Hey! Great jo—ow! Motherfucker."

While Sin had been congratulating Grim, the shadow form had cocked back its arm and nailed Sin straight in the nose.

"Why do you have such a hard-on for breaking my nose?" Sin muttered, his words thick and distorted from the trauma to his nose.

"Because it hurts, shuts you up—"

"Does it?" Sin mocked as he dabbed at the trickle of blood rolling down his lip.

"—and feels really bloody good," Grim continued as if he hadn't been interrupted, pulling his shadow back into himself and adjusting his cuffs.

"Nothing ever really shuts him up," Chaos groused.

We needed to get back on track. Sin was a runaway railroad car, and if none of us took control, we'd never get to where we needed to be.

"Now that we've established Grim isn't beholden to Merri if he wants to use his shadow form, can we address the other major issue?"

Sin turned to me and shrugged. "I don't know what you want me to say, man. I already told you this is way out of my wheelhouse. Best guess is we just have to keep her fed."

"If she lets us," Chaos grumbled.

"I believe the answer lies in the dreamwalks," Grim added.

"So we're back to those again," Sin said, slumping back down onto the sofa and tipping his head forward to stanch the bleeding in his nose. "Dammit, man, you really got me good this time. It's taking forever to heal."

"They're the most viable way to make sure she gets what she needs." Grim ignored Sin's complaint, choosing to focus on the topic at hand instead. Good man.

I trained my gaze on Death, a knowing smirk curling my lips. "And what *you* need."

"It has nothing to do with me."

"If you say so," I intoned, my disbelief evident. "So you've found your solution. Now all we have to do is get her to agree to it. Should be easy. Will only take us, what? An entire bloody apocalypse?"

"Get me to agree to what?"

We all flinched in unison at the sweet and unexpected sound of Merri's voice from the doorway.

"Hey! You're awake!" Sin called from the couch.

Merri frowned at his blood-streaked countenance. "What happened to you?"

"He earned it," Grim said under his breath.

"Oh, this? I'm fine. Nothing for you to worry about, kitten." He still sounded stuffed up and ridiculous, but the bravado was strong as he stood and puffed out his chest.

Chaos strode over to Merri and leaned down to peer into her face. "How are you feeling?"

Merri jerked her head back. "Ever heard of personal space?"

He pinched her chin between two of his fingers and tugged her back so he could continue his inspection. "Answer the question."

"Fine."

"Fine is not an answer. You were hardly yourself only hours ago."

She removed herself from his grasp and stood taller. "I slept all night, woke up, showered, and here I am. Fresh as a fucking daisy. What more do you want from me?"

"That's a loaded question," I muttered under my breath.

"Everything, Red. I want every-fucking-thing."

He was posturing, trying to intimidate her into compliance, but my little hellcat was having none of it. She placed her palms on his chest and shoved at him, not even answering as she waltzed past him into the room.

"Let's try this again. You four were clearly scheming and talking about your plans for me. So why don't you go ahead and say it to my face? Feels like I should probably be a part of the discussion, right? Since it's about me and all." She crossed her arms over her chest and chose me as her target, leveling those blue eyes on mine.

I had a moment of relief at the sight of the clear blue instead of the solid black we'd all witnessed last night. But then she spoke again.

"Tell me."

Chaos answered before I could. "What do you want to know?"

Her head whipped to the side so she could stare him down. "Every-fucking-thing."

CHAPTER EIGHT

MERRI

In a room so filled with testosterone, it was a challenge not to back down as I made eye contact with each of the horsemen. But I had to wait them out, see which one would answer me, and above all, which would give me the truth. Not that I was about to take their word for it. I'd learned my lesson there. And if Malice and Sin hadn't meant for me to use the skills they'd taught me, then maybe they should have thought about that beforehand.

"Well?" I finally demanded when no one said anything after several drawn-out moments.

"We work in specifics, dearest. Where would you like us to start?" Malice drawled, but I could sense the unease lurking in the words.

"Okay. Let's start with what you four chuckle-clowns were discussing when I walked in."

By this point, Grim had settled himself against a serving table set against one wall. He was the picture of male elegance, with his long legs crossed at the ankles and his ungloved hands resting against the wood on either side of his hips. "We want you to resume the dreamwalks."

I huffed out a laugh. "Only because you don't understand the danger."

The chuckle that rumbled from Chaos infuriated me. He hadn't spoken a word, but I heard every one that was implied in that low sound. He thought I was being ridiculous.

"Laugh all you want, but when you realize I've taken you all prisoner with my power, you'll feel differently."

Malice narrowed his eyes, expression serious. "What do you mean by that?"

"Do you know why my kind doesn't dreamwalk anymore?"

"Patriarchy," Sin offered, his voice back to normal though dried tracks of blood remained just beneath his nose.

I rolled my eyes and continued. "Because we've used that as a tool to enslave our victims. With every visit, the noose around their neck grows tighter and the bond stronger. It's forbidden for a reason. The way you want me? It's not because you actually care for me. It's manufactured. It's a trap."

I waited for the explosion of voices. For the outrage. Instead I got bawdy laughter.

"Why the hell are you laughing?" I asked, irritation sparking within me.

"C'mon, kitten. You know I'm immune to you. There's no way you've manufactured anything between us."

"Sin's right. I'm too strong to be ruled by your power," Chaos added.

"We all are," Grim agreed.

I couldn't believe their arrogance. "Oh yeah? Tell that to the guy who passed out. Actually, there were two of you who did that. I distinctly recall Sin appearing mostly dead after our first time together."

Sin held up his hands, palms facing me in supplication. "Okay, okay. We're sorry. We didn't mean to imply that you aren't strong as balls."

"Balls are weak."

Sin rolled his eyes. “Strong as ovaries. Better?”

“Thank you.”

He laughed softly as he continued. “We just meant that we are horsemen.”

“You love to point that out.”

“No, you’re not getting it. We’re horsemen. Not mortals. All those other fools that fell victim to succubi? They were humans. Weak for their mortality. We’re not.”

Could it really be that simple? Lilith had been so sure when she’d warned me. I’d asked her what it would mean if I continued, but then her knowledge of how the bond worked was based on humans. Yes, she was aware I was with the horsemen, but no one had ever attempted such a thing with them before. So anything she said was based on theory and assumption, not fact. What if they were right? The bond wasn’t possible because they were too powerful.

That would be an ideal situation. I could continue my dreamwalks, feed nightly, and ensure my succubus had no reason to hop back into the driver’s seat anytime soon. It sounded pretty on paper, but the truth was, demonbond or not, I would still get more attached to these guys if such visits continued. And I couldn’t allow that to happen unless I knew I could trust them.

“And what about your little competition?” I asked, gut churning as I got to the real reason I’d tracked them down.

“Which competition is that? We always have some wager or another going between us,” Grim asked.

“Oh, I don’t know. How about the one where the four of you are all in a race to impregnate me? Ring any bells?”

As my words landed, I recalled what Sin had taught me and sent out my power to infiltrate their minds. Unlike the last few times I’d tried such a thing, I met no resistance. It was like the one time I’d slipped into Malice’s mind and stumbled upon his memory. And I could only assume that had something to do with how much I’d fed the night before. The more I fed, the stronger my power.

Lucky for them, I wasn't here to snoop around in their innermost thoughts. I only needed the truth from them.

"We aren't competing with each other," Sin said, the clear ring of honesty hanging on every syllable.

"Oh, aren't you?"

He shook his head. "No."

I searched his emotions, reaching out with my power and filtering through all the noise to find the root of his words. Was it truth or deceit? All I was picking up from him was relief and quite a bit of confidence. Although I couldn't help but note that the longer I stared at him without speaking, his confidence wavered, making me think that while he may not be outright lying, there was definitely more to it than what he was telling me.

"Sin, you're keeping something from me."

Closing his eyes, he took a deep breath. That couldn't be good. Sin was unflappable on his worst day.

"What's going on?" I asked, my pulse picking up as the tension in the room rose.

It was Grim who spoke, pulling my attention from the incubus currently sweating bullets under my scrutiny.

"We aren't competing with each other, but we are competing with someone. Sin was telling the truth, but in this case, omission is the same as a lie."

I wasn't sure what I was expecting when I confronted them about this. Wait, yes I was. I thought they'd keep on gaslighting me. So for any of them, but especially Mr. Evasive himself, to cop to the truth had completely caught me off guard.

I held up a hand. "Sorry, let me get this straight. The four of you" —I pointed to each of them respectively—"are working together to get me pregnant before some fifth unknown person can do the job?"

"He's not exactly unknown," Malice muttered, his eyes locked on the cuticles of his left hand.

"Well, he sure as hell is where I'm concerned." Anger was taking control of my focus now, keeping me from using my gift in a productive way. I took a page out of Sin's book and closed my eyes, taking a centering breath.

"How appropriate," Chaos grumbled.

My eyes snapped open. "What was that, tough guy?"

"Hell."

"I'm gonna need you to give me a little more than that. God, it's like pulling teeth to get information from anyone here."

This time Sin chimed in. "It's pretty obvious when you think about the person we're protecting you from, kitten."

I scoffed. "Person? If I recall correctly, you told me it was the, and I quote, *legions of hell.* That's a pretty extensive guest list, pal. So maybe you can narrow it down for me."

"For fuck's sake, it's Lucifer," Malice snapped, his eyes glowing with violet fire as they met mine across the room.

My mouth fell open as his words hung in the air between us. Lucifer wanted me to have his baby?

"Why would he want that? That makes no sense. I thought he just needed me to finish the apocalypse, not procreate with him."

Grim squeezed the bridge of his nose, looking every bit like an annoyed professor. "Procreating with you *would* finish the apocalypse. Just not in the same way it would if we were to do it first."

"You're speaking in circles," I shot back, arms across my chest like they could contain the heart currently racing beneath my ribs.

His eyes slowly lifted, pinning me beneath the weight of his quicksilver stare. "If Lucifer succeeds, he will have the antichrist he needs to seal the deal."

"What's stopping him from knocking up any random woman? Surely it doesn't *have* to be me. There's nothing special about me."

The look on Grim's face was almost piteous, and before he opened his mouth, I knew I'd been dead wrong. "You're his vessel. Made specifically to serve his purpose."

"Made? Like in a test tube?" I shuddered, hating the idea that I was a science project.

"No, Red. Not in a test tube. Your mother knew exactly what she was doing when she conceived you. Your fate has been sealed since before you were born."

I flicked my gaze to Chaos and felt only sadness and truth in his mind. "She . . . You know who she is?"

Sin stepped closer to me, one hand raised as if he was going to touch me, but he stopped himself. "Take a seat, kitten. This is going to be a lot."

Panic tightened my chest as my skin ran hot and then cold, my pulse rushing in my ears. "I'm okay. Just tell me."

"Your mother . . ." Grim started, his voice holding the same gentleness I'd heard when he spoke to his plants. "She's one of us."

"One of you?" I was fucking confused.

"Not literally," Sin rushed to explain.

"A horsewoman. Famine, specifically," Malice drawled, his gaze sliding to Grim and energy radiating annoyance.

"She's one of our female counterparts," Chaos added. "There are four of them, same as us."

My brain didn't know which fact to focus on first, so I couldn't exactly blame myself for the direction it settled on. "Wait, does that make you four like my uncles or something?" I had to put my hand to my mouth because my stomach was actively protesting the idea.

"No. No. Nothing like that. None of us share blood. We are more a brotherhood than anything," Grim said, understanding dawning across his features. "Think of it like you would a team. We work toward the same goal. Share the same type of power."

"And all want to end the world." Sin sauntered over to the free-standing wooden globe near the fireplace and gave it a spin.

I stood there, dumbfounded. This conversation had really taken an unexpected turn.

"Maybe you should sit down," Malice offered.

"I'm fine," I snapped.

I was not fine, but fuck him for pointing it out.

An awkward silence stretched between us while I struggled to process everything. "Is that why Lucifer needs me or my womb or whatever? Because I'm part horseperson and therefore, like, hardwired to end the world or something?"

"No, actually," Chaos said with a sigh. "It's the other part of your bloodline he's interested in."

"Oh God," I whispered, feeling lightheaded. How could there be *another* bomb to drop on me?

"Sabine planned this very meticulously. As soon as she realized she wouldn't get a chance at an apocalypse of her own, she tracked down everything she'd need to ensure she'd have a place at the end of the world. You weren't engineered in a lab, but you might as well have been."

The way Malice spoke, so detached, so formal, made my stomach clench. "Sabine is my mother's name?"

He nodded.

"And she's Famine."

He nodded again.

"Do you know who my father is? Was he in on it?"

The four of them looked at each other in turn, clearly waiting for someone to jump in with the answer to my question.

"No," Sin finally answered when it was clear no one else was going to. "The horsewomen don't tend to clue in the men they use as breeders on their plans."

Malice snorted in derision, and another piece of the puzzle fell into place. Pan's mother was one of these horsewomen.

Tucking that nugget away for a future conversation, I returned my focus to the matter at hand. "So he was an unwitting sperm donor."

"Yes. But one with a very special bloodline that makes you exactly the vessel Lucifer needs. You're built for him," Grim answered.

I scoffed. "How nice for him. Too bad I'm a succubus. I don't know if you've realized this, but we aren't the most fertile."

"About that," Sin said, pulling my attention back his way.

"Nope. This one I'm confident about. Lilith gave me the birds and bees chat when I moved in with her."

"I bet you she didn't mention that dreamwalks increase your fertility, did she? That everything that happens in them is real, and anything . . . deposited stays where it's put?"

I opened my mouth to refute him, but closed it again when snippets of our brief conversation about dreamwalks returned to me. Lilith had sort of mentioned that part of the reason they'd been banned. I'd just assumed, since we were talking about incubi, that it was only the men leaving mortal women pregnant. Not that it worked both ways. And I knew firsthand, given the bruises I'd worn, that what happened in one plane impacted the other.

"Your kind are strongest in the dream realm," Chaos said, interrupting my musing. "All of your abilities are amplified there."

"Well, shit," I whispered. My hand slid to my lower belly. Had they already been successful?

"You're not pregnant, wildflower. Not yet."

"But I need to be?"

Grim nodded, his lips set in a firm line. "If we succeed before Lucifer can, there's a chance we can save the world."

"And if not?"

"If he gets his antichrist, it's game over," Sin offered.

My knees finally gave out, and I sank down onto the ottoman behind me. A little pang had me rubbing at my chest by the time I finally gave voice to my next question. "So your willingness to help me feed, and well, all of this . . . It was never about taking care of me. It was about beating Lucifer?"

"Yes," Grim said.

"Not exactly," Sin countered, glaring at Grim.

Chaos was the next to try to explain. "Taking care of you is a privilege. But, yes, saving the world is the end goal."

Malice sighed. "I don't know why I allow any of you to talk. You're always putting your giant feet in your mouths." Then he looked at me, his expression as severe as ever, but his eyes unusually kind. "Two things can be true, hellcat. We were asked to protect you, and we've done that in every sense of the word. It just so happens that the ways in which we care for you also allow us to accomplish our other task."

Sincerity bled through every word each of them spoke.

Sin locked gazes with me, truth shining in his eyes. "What we're trying to say is, you're so much more than an assignment to us. Help us save the world, kitten, and let us show you how important you are to us."

Ugh, the handsome incubus was really good at making my heart fluttery and warm. Did I want to bear the antichrist for Lucifer? Fuck no. But did I really want a baby with anyone? Glancing around the room at the four handsome men who I'd built a really fucking complicated dynamic with, I realized I wasn't totally against one of them giving me a baby. Perhaps building a post-apocalyptic family wasn't the greatest idea. Maybe we waited until the world settled back down and, you know, the sky wasn't on fire?

"You can ask your questions, wildflower. We'll answer all of them," Grim said, his voice soft.

"Just give her space to process," Malice interjected. "She'll ask her questions when she's ready."

There was something about the combination of those two offers that meant more to me than anything else they'd said so far. The first, the assurance that they weren't going to try to hide anything from me any longer, and the second, that they would sit here with me in silence if I needed, just so I'd know that I wasn't in this alone. It showed how closely they paid attention to me, how in tune they were with my needs. A man who wanted to control me would have barreled right through my hesitation and focused solely on his agenda. That wasn't them. They wanted—no, *needed*—my trust. To be fair, that's probably why they never mentioned this to begin with. They were hoping the situation would resolve itself as a matter of course and it wouldn't be something we had to stress over.

"Question," I said, eyes locking on Grim.

"Ask away."

"Why do you have to get me pregnant? Why not just keep me out of Lucifer's clutches and call it good?"

"If he manages to sire your firstborn, it will be the end of the world as we know it. Period. It doesn't matter if it's now or ten years for now."

"So we could stop all of this for nothing if he somehow found his way to me after and . . ." I trailed off as the weight of that settled in my chest and shoulders.

"You'd never be safe," Chaos affirmed.

I swallowed hard past the lump in my throat. In hiding from the Prince of Darkness for the rest of my life?

"We don't have to do this if you truly don't want a child, Merri. We can protect you from him and hide you as long as we need to, but not without great risk."

"What kind of life would that be?" Sin asked, surprising me with the gravity of his tone.

"And that's assuming we can stay a step ahead of Lucifer. With each Prince he collects, his power grows. We are already outnumbered. It's just a matter of time before the tides turn," Malice said, his eyes locked on mine.

"And we cannot forget the final battle."

"Battle?" I asked, turning to look at Grim. The shadow beneath his feet seemed to be . . . writhing. Tapping back into my power, I sent a little probe his way and was immediately struck by the strength of his agitation. I'd have never sensed it from his facial expressions or body language, but the rippling darkness was definitely a tell. Yet another fact for me to tuck away to examine later.

"If he doesn't get his antichrist, he will still fight to rule the earth."

"An epic battle between heaven and hell. One we will fight to the death," Sin added.

"But you can't die." My voice was sure and strong, but my confidence wavered.

"We are immortal, yes, but in a war between celestial bodies, nothing is certain," Chaos grumbled.

A heavy breath escaped me. My choice was really no choice at all. Let them knock me up and potentially save the world, or bury my head in the sand and let the devil win. I couldn't even picture a scenario where I'd willingly allow him to fuck me. I didn't even know what the dude looked like, but the red horns and tail of it all was enough to put me off the idea. I shuddered, my eyes taking in the men positioned around me. Not a horn or forked tail in sight. Maybe there was a bright side here. I mean, how many people got to fuck some of the hottest beings in existence as a literal part of the resistance?

"Talk about fuck or die," I muttered.

"What a great trope," Sin said, a sly grin on his face.

With a sigh, I sat up a little straighter and looked directly at Chaos. The man had a breeding kink he didn't even try to hide. I wanted to be looking into his eyes when I told him he could try to put a baby in me.

"Okay. Let's do it."

His eyes flashed with molten lust for a moment. All I felt in his mind was a mixture of arousal and concern for me. "Are you sure?"

If I wasn't, his asking would have sealed the deal. Any lingering doubts I had about being able to trust them faded. They could have tried to gaslight me or deny their mission, but they hadn't. Not even a little. Now, more than ever, it felt like the five of us were all on the same page.

"Did I stutter, Chaos? You four want to beat Lucifer to the punch. I want to keep the world spinning. It looks like this is our path to both those things, though again, I can't promise we'll be successful."

"The answer is the dreamwalks, I'm telling you," Sin said.

It was so strange to be sitting here talking about this with them after spending weeks terrified they'd find out what I did and be furious with me. It sort of felt like I was being given a present, but now that I had it in my lap, I didn't really want it anymore. Or maybe

I still did. It was really hard to know what I was feeling right now. The conflict was real.

On one hand, I had no way of knowing for certain that these four men I was in danger of catching very real feelings for actually cared about me. There was no denying that I was a means to an end for all of them, and that if they'd been given a choice, they'd probably all have opted out of this little protective detail.

On the other, I still wasn't fully convinced that the dreamwalks I'd already had with them hadn't managed to manipulate their feelings for me. And was that any better than what they had done? We were all using each other here, one way or another.

So, did I save the world and potentially break my own heart in the process? Or let it burn and lose it all anyway?

Like I said, it was really no choice at all in the end.

"Which one of you wants to go first?"

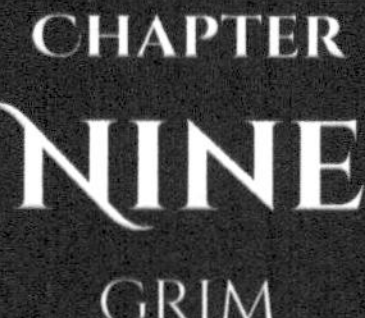

CHAPTER NINE

GRIM

Warm night air enveloped me as I strode through my carefully crafted garden, the scent of rain hanging heavy above me, promising a storm but not yet delivering. The clouds wouldn't dare open until I allowed it, and right now I had other plans. Tonight would hopefully be the first of many, but in case it wasn't, I intended to make every second count. I was too intimately aware of the fickleness of time to ever take it for granted.

I pulled a pocket watch from my suit jacket and checked the time, more to have something to do with my hands than anything else. Just as it snapped closed with a satisfying click, I spotted the boat docking down at the lake. A thrill chased across my skin at the sight of her. Even from a distance, she was breathtaking, her red hair catching the beams of moonlight as they spilled from the parted clouds.

"Fuck," I whispered, every step bringing me closer to the one thing I wanted. My wildflower.

Originally, I'd planned on letting her walk up the stone path to meet me, but I couldn't stand being so far away from her, so instead I half jogged down the path so I could reach her as she climbed out of the boat. She was dressed in a white négligée, the thin layers of gossamer fabric protecting her modesty. Her lips were curled up in a smirk when I greeted her, one gloved hand offered to help her to her feet.

"Someone's in a hurry," she teased.

I'd never hurried for a single soul in my very long existence, but she was right. I wanted to be surrounded by her for as long as possible in this dream. To savor every moment.

"You're a vision."

She looked down her body at the ethereal gown and matching robe I'd conjured for her. "What, this old thing?" Without prompting, she gave me a little twirl, allowing the material to billow out around her ankles. But it was the giggle that accompanied the move, so lighthearted and free, that had my heart seizing in my chest. "I'm honestly shocked dream-you would put dream-me in something with so much fabric."

"Isn't it all part of the process? Slowly unwrapping the most perfect present I've ever received."

She returned my gaze with a flirtatious one of her own. "Why, Grim, I dare say you're trying to seduce me." Then she leaned in and filled my nose with her delectable scent, dropping her voice as she did. "You should know, I'm a sure thing. You don't have to try that hard."

"You deserve slow and deliberate pursuit. I intend to seduce you until you're begging me to take you." My voice was low and controlled, but inside I was already barely able to contain my need.

Merri's eyelashes fluttered as she breathed in deeply. "I think it might be you who will be begging."

"Why not both of us?"

Her smile was warm as she leaned into my side. "I can work with that." Then she let out a murmur of contentment as she took in the garden. "You and your flowers."

"Consider it a gift."

"These are for me?"

"Every variety of night bloomers fills this garden, just for you to enjoy."

She pressed her free hand to her heart. "Of course you wouldn't do anything by half-measure. Other girls get bouquets, but Death gave me a whole-ass garden. I wouldn't have taken you for a romantic, Grimsby. But it suits you."

"I've never had the opportunity to stretch that particular muscle."

She peered up at me, holding my gaze for several heartbeats before replying, "No, I suppose you haven't."

The urge to close the distance between our lips was so strong I nearly choked on it. But a crack of thunder broke the moment. A fat drop of rain landed on her cheek, prompting me to scoop her into my arms as though I were her bridegroom and couldn't wait to carry her over the threshold.

"Oh, well, if you insist," she teased, nuzzling her face against my chest as I strode up the path to the villa. Her warmth radiated through me, even with the fabric of my suit in the way. I wanted more.

By the time we reached the jasmine-laced walls of the villa, the rain was pouring down, drenching us both. With little more than a thought, the fireplace against the back wall of the indoor-outdoor living space blazed to life, along with the hundreds of candles gracing every available surface. We were bathed in a warm glow, the soft light casting romantic shadows around the room as the sound of the rain falling acted as our music.

"You really do think of everything," she said softly, her eyes taking in the room before lifting to mine. "Though that doesn't surprise me. You love to set the scene."

It was obvious she was referencing something specific, but I couldn't quite figure out what she was referring to. There were simply too many options. It wasn't until she intentionally pressed her nose into my chest and inhaled deeply that I got my answer.

"Mmm," she breathed. "I've become addicted to the scent of you ever since you left me that little present in my room."

I stiffened, a slight twinge of guilt worming its way into my mind. "I thought you might be cross about that."

"Why?"

"Because I forced the issue of your resistance to feed. I took matters into my own hands."

She hummed softly to herself and reached up to trace my lips with her fingertip. The sensation of her skin on mine sent tingles skittering down my spine. "I see. My overbearing, dark, and moody daddy."

Fuck me. I hated how much I loved the sound of that on her lips. If only because it was evidence of how much power she held over me. No creature in existence had owned me so thoroughly.

I set her on her feet, loath to let her go, but we wouldn't get anywhere if I didn't move this forward. The rain had washed away any hint of modesty by turning her dressing gown and négligée translucent. Rosy nipples teased me through the fabric, the wet cloth leaving nothing to the imagination. I could see every line of her beautiful form.

She shivered, and my eyes snapped back to her face.

"Are you cold?"

"No," she whispered, even as I maneuvered her to stand in front of the fire. "It was you, the scent of your arousal, I mean." Her eyes fluttered closed, and she breathed deeply. "I'm so hungry. And you taste *so* good."

Gaze locked on hers, I slid my gloves off and dropped them to the floor. "Then allow me to give you what you desire."

With slow, deliberate movements, I brushed the wet strands of hair off her neck and shoulders, repeating the caress with my lips as I exposed the velvety expanse of skin. She was cool beneath the heat of my mouth, and the contrast fascinated me. Every hitch of her breath only served to heighten my own need. My cock ached for attention, but I could wait.

I would.

This moment was about so much more than sex. I wanted her to remember what it felt like to be the object of Death's obsession. Almost as badly as I wanted to memorize the feel of her beneath my hands. There was no inch of her body I wasn't about to explore. This wasn't just about seduction; it was about conquering. Making her mine in every sense of the word.

She reached up to slide her robe off one shoulder, but I stopped her with a nip to her neck.

"No, wildflower. That's my job."

"Then do it faster."

"You'll get what you want, but first, you must be patient."

"I need you."

I pulled back, taking her face between my palms and staring into her bright blue eyes. "Not as much as I need this."

Her breath left her in a soft whoosh. "Oh."

I continued tracing a path along her skin, my thumb skating over her collarbone and up the side of her neck. "You have no idea how long I've yearned to do exactly this."

"Touch me, Grim."

"I intend to."

Unable to resist any longer, I slipped one shoulder of the robe down, then the other, until I'd peeled it off her and it fell to the floor. Then I stepped back until I could sit on the sofa, tugging her with me until she was standing between my spread knees. My palms skated over her hips, up to encircle her waist, over her breasts, and back down as I took in her curves.

"What are you—ah." Her words cut off on a moan as I covered one nipple with my mouth and sucked on her through the fabric between us.

Her fingers threaded through my hair and I had half a mind to stop her, but it felt so bloody good.

"Grim, why are you teasing me like this?"

Releasing her nipple, I rolled my gaze up to meet hers. "Because we only get one first time, wildflower. I want it to last so centuries from now I can recall every detail with vivid clarity."

Emotion clouded her eyes until there was a silvery sheen over the blue. Then she smiled and ran the tips of her fingers through my hair, gently scratching my scalp with her nails and sending tiny shivers down my body. "Okay."

I chuckled. "Was that your way of giving me permission to continue?"

She lifted one shoulder in a shrug. "It was me saying okay."

"To?"

"Anything . . . everything."

"You know exactly what to say to break down my control, don't you? Naughty little succubus."

She reached for my collar, but I stopped her once again, needing the reins so I could have her the way we both wanted. I tore her nightie down her shoulders, stopping when the straps reached her elbows, effectively restraining her. Though if she gave it any effort, she'd be able to free herself easily. This was a game, and she knew the rules.

Leaning forward, I took her nipple in my mouth and sucked hard, drawing out another sexy whimper. My hands had a life of their own, roving over her body and mapping every inch of her I could reach. As much as I wanted this to go slowly so I could commit each touch to memory, I ached to feel her wrapped around me—the real me, not my shadow self.

Before the thought could fully register, I willed away my clothes until I was sat naked before her. Then I grasped her by the backs of her thighs and tugged her down until she straddled my lap.

She collapsed with a breathless laugh, her hands coming to rest on my shoulders. "What happened to slow?"

"Fuck slow. What if we wake before we're finished?"

Her grin was a wicked thing as she leaned in and pressed her forehead to mine. "I think I'm in charge of that. We won't wake until I say so."

"That could be dangerous."

"Well, if it's serious enough, I'm sure it will disrupt my focus and pull us out. But that doesn't have quite the same ring to it, so just go with it."

My lips twitched at her playfulness, but I schooled my face back into its usual somber expression and gave her a nod. "Of course."

I was so focused on her delicious mouth I didn't notice her hand working its way down until she wrapped it around my length. Something between a groan and a shout left me at the contact, and I let my head fall back onto the couch as she stroked from base to tip.

"Fuck, wildflower. You're killing me."

"Me killing Death?"

"Put me inside you. I want to watch you ride me."

She leaned forward so her forehead rested against mine, her breath warm as it teased my lips. "Always so bossy," she whispered, her grip on my shaft tightening as she lined us up.

It was an exquisite sort of agony as she lowered herself down, taking me into her so slowly I held my breath for fear of letting the feel of her send me over the edge before I was ready. The riot of sensations was almost too much for me to process. Her heat. The velvety friction. The tight fit.

Fuck, it was everything. I may not have been a virgin in the literal sense, but anything I'd known before Merri was forgotten. There was no comparison. Joining with her was like experiencing sex for the first time. The way it was truly intended to be.

"Grim."

Her moan of my name had my fingers digging into the soft swell of her hips and urging her to move. She looked away, her eyes downcast, but I was having none of that. I let out a low growl of warning and pulled her forward just a little.

"Take what you want, but look at me while you do it. I've waited this long to have you, and I intend to have all of you."

Her lips parted in a wordless gasp as she obeyed. I found a twin to the wonder I was experiencing in her eyes. This was different for her as well. I'd bet everything I was on it.

I reveled in the sight of her face as she rocked her hips back and forth, the way her brows furrowed with every drag of my cock along that one perfect spot inside her, the effort it took her not to close her eyes. Her pleasure was mine in more ways than one. Not only was I the one responsible for it, but knowing that I was giving it to her amped up my own pleasure tenfold. What she was doing to my body was a carnal symphony in and of itself. But the true eroticism of the moment, the beating heart of my arousal, was giving it back to her.

It was then that I realized my pleasure was secondary to hers. If she wasn't enjoying herself, it wouldn't matter what she was doing to me. I wouldn't be able to find any sort of satisfaction in the act. It would be empty, much like what I'd known before with Hel.

Staring into her eyes now, if I'd had any doubt Merri would be different from my previous experience, it would've been washed away. This wasn't simple fucking. Perhaps it was the dreamwalk intensifying the moment, but right now, with her gaze on mine, our bodies joined, and an explosive climax on the horizon, what we were doing was transcendent. So much more than physical. If pressed to find a name for it, I'd have sworn then and there that Merri and I were quite literally making love. It was an act of creation, so much bigger than the two of us.

And then, of course, I would have punched myself for being such a prat.

But it was still the truth.

"Merri," I whispered, throat tight with everything I was feeling.

"I know, I feel it too."

A frisson of fear touched my heart at the way her voice trembled. She'd done dreamwalks with the others, she'd fucked them. Why would she be reacting this way as well? This wasn't new for her.

Was it because it was me? Was there something about who and what I was that fundamentally impacted this moment for us? Had I gotten it all wrong, and this wasn't some miraculous transcendental act, but the perversion of one?

That seed of doubt clawed at me, trying to take me captive, but Merri wouldn't allow it.

"No," she said, voice firm and cracking like a whip around me. Touching my chin, she pinched just tight enough that my mind emptied of everything but her. "None of that. Stay here with me."

Distantly, I realized she must have picked up on my fear, especially in the seconds it outweighed my arousal. Even as I thought it, the emotion was little more than a distant memory. Something I could recall but no longer give shape or weight to. It was like trying to remember someone's name or face, but all you were left with was a blank spot in your recollection.

"Feel it all with me, Grim. There's only us right now. Nothing else. You and me and our connection."

As though her words flipped a switch in my brain, I did just that. I let it all happen, the sensations between us heightening beyond what I thought possible because I wasn't simply feeling my own euphoria; hers was there too, melding with mine. This was connection, total and complete.

"Come with me, Grim." It wasn't a request so much as a command, even given in that velvety voice of hers. And as with everything when it came to Merri, I realized I was helpless to deny her.

We came, me with an agonized groan as I filled her and secretly hoped I was the one to meet our goal. Not because I wanted to save the world but because I wanted Merri to be mine in some way, even if I knew I wouldn't get to stay.

What better way to eternally preserve this moment between us than with a child? One that could be the physical representation of the connection between us. The connection that felt so real it was almost as if I could see the golden threads of it woven around the two of us, anchoring us to each other.

But no. That was just the firelight playing over our skin.

I chuckled, resting my head against her shoulder as she held me tight.

"Are you seriously laughing right now?" she complained, pulling away and staring at me.

I sighed happily. "You've rendered me stupid."

"Oh?" she asked with a lift of one russet brow.

"I have no words to describe what we just did. Or the effect it's had on me."

She smirked. "Does that mean you enjoyed it?"

"What do you think?" I replied, rocking my hips upward so she could feel my already hard cock as it moved inside her again.

"I wonder if it's always going to be this way between us," she mused.

Her squeals of laughter cut off on a moan as I twisted our bodies until she was pinned beneath me on the sofa.

"Only one way to find out."

OPERATION PFFN SUPER SECRET VIDEO CORRESPONDENCE: #8

Video opens on a haggard-looking Asher outside. The camera is shaky, and Asher moves in and out of frame as he rushes through the forest, bits of ash falling like snow.

<<footsteps running through forest>>

Asher: (breathing hard) Well, folks, shit has officially hit the fan. As you can see, we're running for our fucking lives. I'd apologize for the Blair Witch-style camera work, but all I've got is my phone now.

Remi: (also out of breath) Should've brought that selfie stick I got you for Christmas. But did you listen to me? Noooo. Now look who was right. We're trying to outrun a whole-ass volcano, and you're apologizing for shaky camera work.

Asher: Why are you out of breath? You're a wolf shifter and go running with Ben like every day.

Remi: (normal voice) I didn't want you to feel inadequate with your puny human lungs.

Asher: I'm going to remember you said that later.

Remi: Sounds like my kind of a good time. Hey! Be sure to give them a good look at what's happening. There's so much ash in the sky it looks like it's snowing.

Asher: It sure as shit doesn't feel like snow. It's hot.

<<tree cracking and falling>>

Asher: Jesus, Remi! Watch out!

Remi: Whoa! Spin move! Duck and weave, people! Duck and weave. The sky is falling and taking trees down with it.

Kingston: Alek, grab Eden. She thinks she's fast, but she can't keep up.

Eden: Papa, no! I run! Ahwooo.

Alek: I know, my little Valkyrie. But Daddy Kingston is right. You can run when we're safe from the ash.

<<large wings flapping overhead>>

Thorne: Is that a fucking *dragon?*

Asher: Don't tell me *the* Noah Blackthorne has never seen a dragon before.

Thorne: Fuck off, Asher. I've seen one, just never this close.

Asher: Kai is transporting people who can't run as fast as some of us to the portal site.

Remi: (out of breath) Soooo, that means you, right, babe?

Asher: I told you to knock that off.

Remi moves into view on the screen and gives Asher a kiss on the cheek.

Remi: Sorry, babe.

Asher rolls his eyes and comes to a stop. He shifts the camera so it's more centered on his face.

Asher: In case you can't tell by the state of things, a volcano has erupted not far from us. We're evacuating and en route to a new top-secret hiding place. There's no way to know how much longer comms are going to last. So in case I get cut off before I finish recording, I just wanted to let you know that we have managed to evacuate safely. At least so far. ***heavy breath*** I'm pretty sure you know by now this means the next Prince has arrived. From what Lilith has told us, the hellmouth has grown unstable. Hordes of demons have started to flood the scene and join in on the chaos.

<<heavy footsteps>>
<<crunching leaves>>

Tor: Are you serious? We are quite literally fleeing, and you've stopped to film yourself? What part of the demons chasing us do you not grasp? If something happens to my Dahlia because of your vanity, I will take a page from my father's book and tear your spine from your meat suit.

Remi: *growls* Tor, if you know what's good for you, you'll take several seats. My man is off limits.

Tor: *growls back* You wanna say that again?

Remi: *growls and snarls*

Tor: *growls and snarls back*

<<footsteps drawing closer>>
<<crunching leaves>>
<<clothes rustling>>

Sunday: Okay, that's enough of that, boys. You know Asher is just keeping everyone in the loop. Tor, no need to play Punt the Wolf to prove you're the biggest berserker in the forest.

Alek: Uh, I'm right here. If I wasn't carrying our child in my arms right now, I'd prove it.

Eden: Papa, fishies?

Alek: Later, little one. I promise.

Asher: The church is dead ahead, just over that hill. Keep going. We're nearly there. Then we will move to phase two.

<<crunching leaves>>
<<running footsteps>>

Screen begins bouncing as Asher resumes running.

Remi: (mutters) He wishes he could punt me. I'd take him by the balls and . . .

Asher: We're here. Fuck, it looks so much worse from this vantage point. Aurora Springs is practically vaporized.

Screen flips to a view of a decimated town as Asher pans across the scene. Ben and Caleb stand in front of the abandoned church, both staring up at the facade. Kai, in dragon form, lands, and the people on his back dismount.

Remi: Fuck, I haven't been up here in a long time.

Asher: Are you okay? I didn't even think about how seeing this church again might affect you. It's the highest point in town. Shit, I'm sorry.

Remi: I'm fine. It's Ben I'm worried about. At least he's got a priest on standby, I guess.

Asher: I bet he needs his brother more than an ex-priest. Go check on him. Now that we're somewhere relatively safe, I can do what I need to do for the video.

Camera flips back to Asher's face.

Asher: This might be my last correspondence for Operation PFFN. I'm not sure where we'll end up, but we aren't going to stop fighting. This is a war we can win if we all come together and resist. Demons are going to flood the streets. Nowhere will be completely safe. Arm yourselves. Fight for the world. Be ready to stand with us when the time comes. I may not be ab—

<<footsteps approaching>>
<<crunching of leaves>>

Lilith: There you are. In all of this hullabaloo, I thought we might have lost you, pet.

Asher holds up the phone and gives it a shake.

Asher: Just sending out one last update. In case it's, you know, the *last* update.

Lilith: *hums musingly* Things do look rather dire. The lot of you, trapped outside the very church where all of this began.

Asher: What do you mean?

Nord: There will be time enough for talking once we are safe in Novasgard.

Lilith: Novasgard? ***laughs*** Why ever would we venture there, Nord?

Nord: Where better to flee? While connected to this realm, it is safe from the influence of your apocalypse. And who better to protect you than an Odin-blessed Jarl and his sons?

Lilith: While I appreciate your gallant offer, we cannot run the risk of being out of touch with the goings-on in this realm. Time moves differently in Novasgard. Alek and Tor know better than any of us how dangerous that can be.

Nord: *growls*

Asher: If Novasgard is out, so are Faerie and Ravenndel. Time is wonky there too.

<<dog bark>>

<<footsteps approaching>>

Hades: Asshole is right, the underworld is out too. Janine would have my balls if I tried to get passes secured for all of you this late in the game.

Asher: ***snorts*** I thought you were the head honcho.

Hades: You've clearly never been a leader. A man is only as powerful as the people he surrounds himself with. Janine is a ball buster. It's why I assigned her that position. She keeps things running smoothly so I can deal with shit like this.

Asher: You deal with the end of the world often, big guy?

Hades: More often than you might think.

Asher: ***dark chuckle, then a sigh*** So we have nowhere to go.

Lilith: ***clears throat*** I have a solution that should suffice.

Asher: Great, lay it on me.

Lilith eyes the phone in his hand and gives a slight shake of her head.

Lilith: Best I don't reveal too much, pet. Suffice it to say, the location is secure enough for our purposes and can also feed and house our current numbers.

Asher: Any objections?

Nord: So long as it is defendable and can house my army, I take no issue.

Hades: Seems like it's our only viable option.

Asher nods, face stony.

Asher: Okay. With as many people as we have, we should probably get started. Lilith, how do we get there if we don't know where we're going?

Lilith's lips turn up in a smirk.

Lilith: Leave it to me. I've wrangled worse groups than this.

Lilith walks out of frame, and Asher returns his focus to the camera.

<<footsteps retreating>>
<<crunching of leaves>>

Asher: Now that it's just the two of us, seems like it could be a good time for one final recap. ***blows out a breath*** All right, here we go. As it stands, five of seven Princes have been released. According to Pan's translation of the Book of Lilith, not to mention confirmation from the demon herself, we have two weeks remaining until Lucifer has everything he needs to go into battle. We're an army of thousands, but that means nothing against the power Lucifer will have surrounding him. The Blackthorne vampires and all of their kingdom are with us. Every shifter pack in North America is behind us under the leadership of Kingston Farrell. Nord, the Jarl of Novasgard, has delivered the warriors he promised. And lastly, all of the Shadow Court fae are at our disposal. It's not enough. We were able to make contact with the horsemen, but it's unclear if they're going to stand with us.

Asher's eyes narrow and seem to glow with purple light.

Asher: We *really* hope they do. They are uniquely suited to the task before us and could be the difference between the survival of the human race and utter extinction. Especially since Gabriel is still missing, the vessel hasn't been located—so far as we know anyway—and the world is literally crumbling under our feet. It won't be long now, a couple of weeks at most, before all of this comes to a head.

Asher's gaze shifts away from the camera, his expression unreadable. Then he sighs and shakes his head. When his face returns to the screen, his eyes have returned to normal.

Asher: I gotta say, I didn't think we'd go out like this, ya know? We defeated the big bad, saved the world, and true love proved it was stronger than anything they could throw at us, but here we are again. I can't help but wonder what it's going to take this time. To win, I mean. We barely survived the first attack. Who the hell knows what we're going to have to do to walk away from this one.

<<soft footsteps approaching>>

Rosie: Asher, come on. It's time. We need to go. People will need guidance on the other side of Lilith's portal. They want to hear from you.

Asher pulls Rosie into his side, pressing a tender kiss to the top of her head.

Asher: I know, I know, Rosie. I'm right behind you.

Rosie closes her eyes briefly, enjoying the stolen moment before she pulls away.

Rosie: You better be. I'm not taking a step through that portal without all five of my mates beside me. I refuse to leave a single one of you behind.

Asher gives a decisive nod and returns to the camera. Rosie disappears from view.

<<footsteps retreating>>

Asher: Well, folks. Looks like this is it. I'll see you all on the other side. I hope.

End of transmission.

CHAPTER
TEN
MERRI

BigMan69: Was that live some kind of big finale? Where did you go?

CallMeMommy: Pretty girl, are you ghosting us?

EverySteve: No need to play hard to get. We all watched you fuck that guy, the pussy is out of the bag.

ShyGuy25: Merri, where are you? Please let us know you're okay.

OnMyKnees4U: I'm fucking horny, and I need you to do something about it, baby girl.

Bob1212: I knew it. That rockstar stole her from us.

Magic_Fingie_Dingies: Did you die?

Mayor_Poundtown: You haven't had any lives in almost two weeks. I pay for multiple posts a day and your livestreams. This is bullshit.

ThisLilPiggy: What happened to selfcare Sunday? I thought you were going to test out that new pink polish for us?

CallMeMommy: Has anybody heard from her?

Bob1212: She did a private session with me about a week ago.

Tls4Tony: What gives? Is my money not good enough for you anymore? Do I have to book privates if I want to get off now?

PimpinAintCheezy: Fuck this. I'm out.

JohnBoy27: @Magic_Fingie_Dingies dude, that's not funny. She really could have.

CumGutters11: If you're not posting anymore, I'm taking my big dick somewhere else.

CreamPieLover: RIP Merri. I'll miss your tits the most.

TheRealMan: Can we get a refund if she did?

CallMeMommy: @TheRealMan you're a dick. I hope you suffer from anal leakage, shithead.

TheRealMan: Fuck off. Everyone else here was wondering the same thing.

MakeItClap22: At least give me a picture of your pretty pussy to remember you by. It's not healthy for a guy to let his pipes get backed up.

I finished scrolling through the wall of posts my subscribers had left on my wall with a heavy sigh. Interacting with my site had never felt like a chore, but with the state of the world and my new nightly festivities, I just didn't think I had the bandwidth—or frankly, the need—to continue maintaining it.

Merri's Playground had been born of necessity, not desire. I had no connection to any of my clients . . . well, except for one. My focus drifted back to Cole's comment. I'd distanced myself for a reason, and he was still showing up for me. Still concerned about me.

I flicked my focus to the cell phone sitting face down on my bedside table. It had been days since I'd turned it on, and I was nervous about what might await me when I did.

More comments popped up on my feed, distracting me from my worries about Cole. My subscribers were getting angrier by the second. The old Merri would have jumped right on and given them what they wanted, but the truth was, even if I had the energy to keep this going, I didn't want to. My entire reason for keeping it going this long was so that I could feed without hurting anybody. But now I had a different solution, one that was more satisfying in just about every sense of the word.

And if I was being really honest, something about interacting with strangers this way didn't feel right anymore. Feelings were involved now, for sure between me and Sin, but I'd be willing to bet it was true for the others as well. Regardless of how they felt for me, I couldn't deny I cared for all four of them. That was only going to be more true now that the dreamwalks were back on the table.

Which meant that it was time for me to make a decision.

I clicked on the link that would deactivate my page, eyes widening at the notification telling me how many active subscribers would be refunded. The money wasn't an issue. I had never touched the funds I earned from TwoLips. It simply sat in my account, building with every passing day. This page had been a safety net for me, a place I could always rely on for feeding, a way to survive.

As my cursor hovered over the deactivate button, a wave of panic hit me. What if this was a mistake? Could I really afford to do this? Did I want to put my literal eggs all in the horsemen basket? If they were successful in stopping this apocalypse, they would probably take off and leave me on my own. Well, I guess not totally alone, because if they're successful, then I'd probably be pregnant.

I ran a palm over my lower belly, thinking about what it would be like to be carrying one of their children. They wouldn't just leave. They might not give me their undying devotion, but if Malice is any indicator, they'd want to be there for their child.

You can always start over. You've done it once and know what to do now. There's no reason you can't come back or pick up where you left off if you need to.

That little reminder was all I needed to shove away any lingering doubt. Relief flooded me as soon as I clicked the link and a notification popped up stating my page was no longer available. It was done. Honestly, I felt kind of free.

In a lot of ways, it was the last of the shackles keeping me bound to my old life. The one where I was little more than a prisoner locked up behind *Iniquity's* walls. The one where I was so afraid of my power that I barely interacted with anyone and never got to know what real intimacy could be. Jimmy had been my one moment in time when I'd felt loved, and that ended in tragedy.

For too long, I'd let that overshadow everything else and keep me from truly living. My days could literally be numbered. Technically everyone's were, but now there was an actual apocalypse looming. What better time to finally start living?

Better late than never.

With a gusty sigh, I reached for my phone and booted it up. I might as well delete the app and corresponding messenger from my phone. Oh, and I should probably give Andi a heads-up before she went looking for me and assumed the worst.

As soon as the screen came to life, a flood of notifications popped up, texts from Andi and Cole taking priority. I tackled Andi's messages first.

ANDI:

Girl, where are you? The playground is getting restless.

ANDI:

Helloooooo?

ANDI:

WTF is going on? Did that rockstar fuck you so good you forgot what you do for a living?

ANDI:

Babes, you might be too busy having orgies with your four hotties to remember, but the world is crazy right now. The entire ring of fire just blew, and the Grand Canyon actually CLOSED!!! I don't even know where you are. Next thing we know, the aliens are going to show up and declare our planet uninhabitable.

ANDI:

Can you please just let me know you're okay?

I felt like such an asshole. She was my closest friend, and I'd left her in the dark.

ME:

I'm okay. Safe for now. I shut down my site, though. I can't keep it up any longer.

ANDI:

OMG. Where are you? Are you sure you're safe? I can come get you. I just left my place in the city because tensions were mounting, but things are a lot quieter here. And they seem to be out of range of any of the weird shit going on. At least for now.

ME:

I can't tell you where I am, but I'm fine. I promise.

ANDI:

Are you sure? They say the grid is going to go down any minute because of the eruptions. Do you have supplies? This is so scary.

Was that true? Yikes. I should probably head downstairs and see if the others had heard about the latest catastrophe. With each one, it seemed that the ripple effects were only getting worse. Which tracked when you realized they were accompanied by the release of one of hell's Princes and that they signaled the approach of the end of the world.

ME:

I have everything I need here. These guys are the ultimate doomsday preppers.

ANDI:

I respect your need for privacy, but could you at least give me a general idea of where you're staying? Just like the continent maybe? It wasn't until the eruptions that I realized you could have been in one of the places that was lost and I would have no way to know. And then when you stopped responding . . . girl, I was so scared. It would just be such a relief to know if you are in danger or not.

My chest went tight, my skin itchy with anxiety. I didn't want to put her in more danger. If Lucifer was able to, he'd probably find her and torture the information out of her.

ME:

I'm sorry. I can't. It's too dangerous for you to know anything. We'll get through this, and then when it's over, you and me on a beach sipping a cocktail, okay?

ANDI:

Yeah, okay. Sure. Sounds good.

I could tell that Andi was more than a little hurt that I was still keeping her in the dark. But if she knew what I was trying to protect her from, she'd absolutely understand and forgive me. Maybe one day I would be able to tell her.

ME:

Andi, please don't be mad. There's so much happening I wish I could tell you.

ANDI:

Whatever. Do what you want.

ME:

I'll do my best to check in more until the grid goes down. I promise. Keep yourself safe. You're important to me.

I watched the little text bubbles bouncing, but nothing came through. After a few minutes passed with nothing from her, I realized our conversation was over. I'd fucked up, but I had no idea how else I could've handled that. Hopefully she'd forgive me. If we all survived this.

The next message I needed to tackle was one I'd been anxious to open. I knew I'd hurt him by putting distance between us, but I couldn't make him promises. We weren't together, we couldn't ever be, and my heart was being collected piece by piece by four horsemen.

That said, he was still one of my first and only friends. I'd known Cole almost as long as Andi, and in some respects, the conversations we'd had were much more personal than those I'd had with Andi or the horsemen. Things might be complicated at the moment, but that didn't magically undo years of leaning on each other. He deserved a response from me, at the very least.

Resolved, I clicked on our text thread and pulled up a string of unread messages.

C:

I noticed you've been absent for a few days. Are you okay?

C:

Are you at least far enough away from the blast zone? I'm worried about you.

C:

Merri, please. I know we left things in a weird place but I need to know if you're safe.

Guilt seemed my constant companion these days. It twisted my gut as I read his messages over again.

ME:

I'm okay. Nowhere near the eruptions.

The message changed from *delivered* to *read,* but he didn't reply.

ME:

Cole?

C:

I thought you were dead.

Okay, I probably deserved that.

ME:

My phone has been off. I just found out about the

I struggled to complete my sentence. Andi had only given me a rough sketch of what happened. I didn't have a lot of detail. Which was strange when you stopped to think about the scope of the catastrophe, but also, the entire world was ending, and I was on the lam from Old Scratch himself, so you know, my barometer for fucked up shit was really skewed these days.

After several seconds, I resumed my typing.

ME:

...everything. I was worried about you, too.

There. Now it seemed like I picked up my phone when I realized he might be in danger. Maybe that would earn me a few brownie points.

C:

I'm glad you're okay.

ME:

What about you?

C:

It's bad. I've been keeping my eye on seismic activity after the freak London quake.

That tracked. California was pretty synchronistic with earthquakes. I'd heard people reference how 'the big one' was overdue more than once. And with the way Cole loved his research, it made sense he'd fixate on something like that.

C:

Most of the West Coast is gone. Whole towns obliterated like Pompeii.

Jesus. I knew it had to be bad, but the entire coast? Just wiped away? My brain couldn't even begin to comprehend it.

ME:

But you were spared?

C:

I fled before it happened. I just had a gut feeling and packed my stuff as quickly as I could.

ME:

You actually left your house?

C:

It was between agoraphobia or survival, I chose to survive.

ME:

Where are you now?

C:

I have a lakeside cabin in Illinois. It's the safest place I could think to go.

I blew out a breath I wasn't aware of holding.

ME:

Yay for investment properties, I guess.

ME:

Seriously, though. I'm glad you had somewhere safe to flee to.

C:

It's hard to feel good about it, honestly. A lot of people weren't as lucky.

ME:

That's your survivor's guilt talking. I'm not going to feel bad about being happy you're safe.

C:

You shut down your site.

That was an abrupt subject change. But I supposed he wasn't eager to let me back in after I closed the door on the possibility of *more* between us.

ME:

I had to. For lots of reasons.

C:

I see. Does it have anything to do with that guy?

He meant Sin. And honestly, it did have something to do with Sin, and Grim, and Malice, and Chaos. But how did I tell him that without hurting him?

ME:

He's not the only reason.

C:

I hope you're happy, Merri. I really do.

ME:

Stay safe, Cole. 🩶

I hated that we were leaving this conversation just as tense and distant as our last one, but I wouldn't lie to him outright. He didn't deserve that, and neither did the four men I was with. Heaving a sigh, I placed my phone back on the bedside table. I had plenty on my agenda, and none of it could be taken care of by falling into a doom spiral.

Just as I finished pulling my hair into a ponytail and was about to head downstairs, my phone buzzed.

Heart in my throat, I grabbed it and stared down at the message from Cole.

C:

Find me if you need me. I'm still here for you, Merri.

C would like to share his location with you.

CHAPTER ELEVEN

SIN

"You know, if the sky wasn't still on fire, I'd say we were in one of those Gothic romances. Grim could reprise his role as Heathcliff," I said as I dropped the heavy curtain and stepped away from the rain-splattered window panes. "You were the original inspiration for that broody bastard, weren't you?" I cut a glance at said broody bastard, but he ignored me, instead turning the page of the ancient book he was reading.

It was storming again. Or, more accurately, still. The rain started yesterday and hadn't let up since. If anything, it was only getting worse. The thunder was so close now, it wasn't just the windows rattling, it was the whole damn house. I usually enjoyed a good thunderstorm, but not this time, and not when it continued for days.

"This storm is only going to get worse. The heat from above is giving it more power," Chaos said, his brow furrowed in concern. "We might need to board up the windows before they shatter."

"I'll chat with Christian," Malice murmured before taking a sip of his tea.

"Chat with Christian about what?" Merri asked, striding into the room like a goddess stepping down from Mount Olympus. Oh my God. What has she done to me? I'm a seducer, not a simp.

It wasn't just me, though. It was all four of us. Grim's eyes locked onto her as he set his book down, and he made a show of putting his leather gloves on. Chaos was a bit more subtle, but only just, as his position shifted so that he was always facing her as she wandered further into the room. And then there was Malice, who nearly missed the table when he placed his teacup too close to the edge because he was watching her every step.

We were so fucked.

A couple weeks ago, I would have tried to blame it on the waves of power rolling off her. Merri's time with Grim had obviously gone well. She was so radiant this morning she all but glowed.

"I take it last night went well," Malice said, his thoughts mirroring my own.

"Is that a note of jealousy I'm detecting?" Grim asked, though his attention was still wholly locked on Merri.

"It's an entire book." Was he talking to me? No. Did I still answer for myself? Yes.

Merri took a seat next to Grim, placing her palm on his thigh like he couldn't kill her with a touch. "Hi," she whispered.

"Hi."

"Oh, come off it, you two. Stop putting on a show." Malice was well and truly annoyed now.

Merri grinned at him. "So you are jealous."

"I'm not going to dignify that with a response."

"You'll get your turn. But not before me." Chaos's deep timbre rolled through the room, not unlike the thunder overhead.

"Or me," I added, not to be forgotten.

"Drawing straws was an absolutely asinine idea," Malice muttered, angrily picking up his tea and rage-drinking it. I didn't know it was possible to rage drink tea, but here we were, rage pinky and all.

"Careful," I teased. "You might break your precious china if you grip it any tighter."

Before I could poke the bear any harder, Christian rushed into the room, hair mussed, eyes wild. "Messieurs, mademoiselle, you must see this."

He waved his phone around, clearly indicating that was what he wanted us to look at.

"I'm not sure now is the appropriate time to perv on your—"

Christian cut me off, his eyes wild. "Non. This is serious. There's been another disaster."

"Of course there has," Malice drawled, allowing his now-empty cup to fall harmlessly to the rug.

"Look," Christian insisted, holding out his phone.

The five of us gathered around the small device and waited as he pressed Play on the video in question.

The screen showed nothing but chaos and destruction in the middle of a city that looked like it used to be Paris. Then a man's face appeared, coated in dust, his once-coiffed hair now a flattened mess of multicolored curls.

"*Oh, mon dieu, mes amis.* It's Jean-Marie Antoinette here with another impossible-to-believe update. The tea is so hot it's lava, and I'm not sure we will make it out this time."

The camera flipped back to the carnage around our flamboyant host, showcasing people running through the streets, broken shop windows and looters blatantly stealing from stores, tail lights as far as the eye could see.

"The world has gone mad since the Grand Canyon collapsed. The ripple effects of the major earthquake that closed the once-historic canyon set off not just the ring of fire, but what now seems to be every known and unknown volcano on the planet. The ocean is quite literally boiling in some places. Were the crazies who stand on street corners screaming about the end of the world right? Already news sources are warning about tsunamis heading our way. Along with acid rain, ash storms, and aftershocks so strong they would count as major earthquakes in their own right. You know I love my skincare, but an acid rain peel is not on my to-do list. Not to mention that all the interference is said to impact the power grid. It may only be a matter of time before the world as we know it ceases to exist."

Merri gasped next to me and put her hand in mine. I simply squeezed it tight, telling her silently that I had her.

"I'm not sure how long I will be able to continue broadcasting, *mes amis*. But I'll do my best for you." Jean-Marie stared meaningfully into the camera and then, with a weak smile, said, "Until we meet again, remember, I may be only half French, but I'm aaallll cake."

Christian pulled his phone back and looked at us all in turn. "It's so much worse out there than I thought."

"Me too," Merri whispered. "I'd assumed it was bad, but seeing it . . . I mean, that was just Paris. Imagine what the states affected by the eruptions look like. So many homes . . . so many lives, gone. Just like that."

On instinct, I pulled her closer. For all her strength, Merri was soft at heart. That was something I wasn't used to. My brothers were anything but soft.

"Are we in danger here?" Merri asked, twisting her face up to look at mine.

"We are as safe as we can be here. I've done everything possible to make this a fortress," Malice said, but there was tension in his tone.

"We're always in danger. The worst mistake we could make is to assume we aren't. We can't forget about the enemy's plan." Chaos glanced at the drawn curtains, then back to us.

"We don't actually know his plan, though, right?" Merri asked. "I mean, other than the broad strokes."

"Exactly my point. We know he wants you. Which means he's doing everything he can to find you," Chaos answered. "No matter how well we plan our defense, we don't know what he's going to do."

She huffed. "Make plans and God laughs. Is that what you're getting at?"

"Perhaps not God this ti—" Grim began, but before he could finish, the power cut off, leaving us in the dark, save the tepid daylight that crept under the closed curtains.

Merri jolted, then laughed at herself. "I was warned three times this morning that the power could drop at any moment, and I still jumped."

Christian made a disgruntled sound, calling my attention to where he had settled in a chair behind our group. "What?"

"I have no service. Nothing."

Malice pulled his phone from his pocket and examined it for a moment, his expression hardening. "Me as well."

"Do you think the whole grid went down?" Grim asked.

Chaos nodded. "It was only a matter of time."

"I cannot do anything about the phones, but we have an automatic generator." Christian frowned as he said the words. "It should have come on by now. I will go check and see what happened. Perhaps a branch fell on it or something." He got to his feet, calling over his shoulder as he made his way toward the door. "I'll be right back."

I snickered. "Someone's never watched *Scream*."

"What was that?" Merri asked.

"First rule of . . . nevermind," I murmured. Jokes were never as good when you had to explain them.

"Whilst he's gone," Malice said as he tapped his phone until the screen lit up. He held it out to us just like Christian had when we'd watched the video of Paris. "Hades sent this to me this morning. Luckily I had the foresight to download it. Apparently we've been missing quite the rise of the resistance, of which we are an integral part."

"Well, that's hardly news, is it?" Merri said, rubbing her arms. "I'd be more surprised if you'd told me we got to sit this one out."

"Feeling the strain of being the chosen one, kitten?" I teased, voice low and only for her.

She cut me a glare. "I told you, she dies in the end. Twice."

Malice heaved a sigh, pulling our focus back to the matter at hand. "They've amassed quite an army."

"It won't be enough," Chaos interjected.

"No, but we aren't alone in this anymore. Our goal is still the same, but when we fight, we fight with allies."

"We've never needed allies before." Chaos's voice was a low murmur. He was right. We'd only ever had one goal. Bring about the apocalypse.

"We've also never had to take a side before," Grim pointed out. "We were always supposed to remain neutral."

"Our counterparts set this into motion when they chose Lucifer." Malice was pacing now, as though he was working to figure out a puzzle.

"So this is about balance?" Merri asked. "They chose a side, and as a result, you ended up on the other?"

"No," I said, a little surprised by the vehemence of my reply.

"Then why? What made you choose?"

The tension in the room thickened, the air heavy like just before a storm. My first thought was, *You*, but before I could say what was in my heart, Grim spoke.

"Lilith. She changed it all when she charged us with taking you."

It wasn't necessarily a lie, but I knew Grim well enough to know that he was minimizing the situation. This might have started off as us repaying a favor, but I would bet everything I was that it stopped being solely about that weeks ago. Being around Merri, being *with* Merri, had changed things.

No. It had changed *us*.

We used to be cold and uncaring. Focused only on our needs, our goals, our purpose. But I saw the cracks in all of our facades start to widen and grow. Soon, I'd be more human than horseman. Because of her.

Oh, Grim wasn't going to like that one bit.

"Show us the video," Grim ordered. "If Hades sent it, we need to see it."

"Okay, but I'll warn you now, this is long. These guys like to ramble."

As soon as he pressed play, I felt Merri stiffen at my side.

A bedraggled man appeared on screen, ash raining down around him as he ran through the forest. *"Well, folks, shit has officially hit the fan."*

She only grew more tense as he continued speaking. "What's wrong?" I whispered.

"I recognize him."

"The guy on the screen?"

She nodded.

"From where? Blackwood?"

"No," Merri whispered, her freckles a stark contrast to her pale skin. "In my dream."

"Shh," Malice chastised. "Pay attention."

I gave Merri a long-suffering look that made her smile as we settled in to watch the rest of the video play out. As Malice had warned, it was long and filled with some familiar and not-so-familiar faces. I was sure all of us had a similar reaction when Lilith appeared on the screen. If she was there, that meant we truly needed to be paying attention.

"I know some of them," Merri whispered. "And Auntie Lilith is there. I'm so glad she's safe."

"Keep watching, hellcat. There's more." Malice's words were gentler than we typically got from him.

"It's not enough. We were able to make contact with the horsemen, but it's unclear if they're going to stand with us.

"We really *hope that they do. They are uniquely suited to the task before us and could be the difference between the survival of the human race and utter extinction. Especially since Gabriel is still missing, the vessel hasn't been located—so far as we know anyway—and the world is literally*

crumbling under our feet. It won't be long now, a couple of weeks at most, before all of this comes to a head."

Malice stopped the video before tucking his phone away. "That's the most important part. The rest we don't need to bother with."

"Gabriel is missing," Chaos muttered. "That can't be good."

"Why not? Who is he?" Merri asked.

"The Messenger of God." Grim broke off from the group, walking to the window and opening the curtain. The storm had turned the sky dark as night now, even in the middle of the day. "Someone is trying to weaken heaven's army."

"Lucifer," Chaos answered. "It's got to be him."

"That's my guess as well," Malice said.

Chaos let out a derisive snort. "A couple of fae warriors and a bunch of supernaturals? I can't believe they are the army that's supposed to defeat him. There's no chance they'll make it out of a war with hell alive."

"Isn't that what we're for?" I asked.

Chaos shook his head. "The four of us are powerful, but no match for the entirety of hell's legion. No. If we're meant to win, we'll need heaven's ranks on our side. Which brings me back to Gabriel. Without him in play, I bet the celestial realm has no clue what's happening."

"You don't think they know what's happening?" Merri asked. "Surely heaven pays attention."

The bark of laughter that escaped Malice made Merri jump. "They're a bunch of snobs. Think of them like the first-class passengers on the Titanic. They knew they'd be fine, so they did as little as needed to ensure they survived and fuck the rest of the peasants below deck."

Merri grimaced. "Oh."

I scrubbed a hand over my face, letting out a breath I'd been holding. "Gabriel is forced to interact with the humans, which means he's the most empathetic to their cause. Without him around to act as a go-between, there's no one to plead their case. Heaven will be fine no matter what happens. It's the earthly plane that will suffer."

Malice glanced at the door and sighed. "Speaking of suffering. Where the bloody hell is Christian, and why has the generator not come on?"

"See? I told him not to say he'd be right back. Kiss of death."

"Not helpful, Sinclair," Malice growled. "I'll go find him. We will need light, at the very least. I'll—"

"Don't say it!"

Malice flashed a rare smirk as he left the room. "Be right back."

Well, now I had to go with him. "Fuck. Come on, guys."

CHAPTER TWELVE

MALICE

"Guys, I have a question," Sin said as we made our way toward the back of the château.

"Of course you do. What else is new?" Chaos muttered.

"Curiosity is a good thing. Don't try to make me hide my light under a bushel."

"Go on, Sinclair. Ask your question," I said.

Merri was sandwiched between me and Sin, her perfume more noticeable than usual. Perhaps it was because she was so close to me, or perhaps she spritzed more on than normal, but either way, her scent was delectable and, unfortunately, distracting.

"That obviously wasn't the first video. Are there more? And if there are, how many? What do you think we missed?"

"That was three questions," I pointed out, biting back a smile when Merri snorted a laugh.

"Fine. I have three questions. They're still pertinent."

Merri twisted her head his way and pressed a kiss to his arm. "Very pertinent," she said, her voice soft enough I don't think it traveled beyond the three of us.

"The video was clearly a call to arms. We can assume that any others that preceded the one Hades sent conveyed a similar message." Chaos's answer was delivered so matter of factly it left little room for argument.

"It's so weird to hear you call him Hades," Merri said.

"Why wouldn't we call him Hades? That's his name."

"Should we call him Lord of the Underworld?" Sin added. "Henceforth and forevermore, I shall be called the Horseman Famine. Emphasis on the 'The'."

Merri smacked Sin on the arm. "Shut up, smartass. I meant because when we were at Blackwood together, his name was Cain. We had group therapy together a few times."

I snorted. "I cannot picture Hades in therapy, let alone group therapy."

"I can," Sin said. "It's hilarious. I bet he loved talking about his feelings."

Merri made a soft, dissenting sound. "More like he was allergic to them."

"Who among us," I muttered.

"No wonder you two are buddies."

Bristling, I stood a little straighter as Grim opened the door to the back garden for us. "I am not *buddies* with anyone."

"Ouch," Sin said, clutching his heart as we stepped over the threshold and into the storm. "O true apothecary. Thy drugs are quick."

"Really? Shakespeare?" Grim said, his annoyance bleeding through the words.

Merri snickered. "It was hard to find the movie star beneath all the grunge of rockstar, but I see it now."

"A rose by any other name . . ." Sin intoned, adopting a foppish stance, the wind and rain only making him appear more ridiculous.

"Okay, Romeo. You know that's a tragedy and not a romance, right?"

"I write sins, not tragedies," he said with a wink.

"Wow," I said in disbelief, stopping dead in my tracks. "I can't believe you just did that."

"How does anything that comes out of his mouth surprise you after all these years?" Chaos asked after a loud clap of thunder.

"I keep thinking he's hit the bottom of the barrel, and then he manages to outdo himself."

Sin smiled so hard his dimples flashed, and I'd have sworn there was a twinkle on his front tooth. He could not look more pleased by my assessment. Which was completely in character for the self-obsessed playboy.

"There's nowhere for me to go but up."

"Oh my God," Merri gasped.

"I know. He's insuffera—" I stopped in my tracks, following Merri's gaze to where Christian was slumped over against a tree, clearly unconscious.

"Is he dead?" Merri asked, eyes darting to Grim.

"No," he said firmly, his shadow seeming to triple in size behind him. "He's . . . not entirely connected to this plane at the moment, though. His soul is weak. Close to death."

"What happened to him?" She attempted to rush to his side, but I snatched her wrist and tugged her until she crashed against my chest, her drenched hair slapping me as the long ponytail fell down her back.

"No. Don't touch him. Not until we know it's safe. This could be a well-laid trap."

"Wouldn't the wards have warned us?"

"Quiet," Chaos snapped. His expression was fierce as he surveyed the scene, taking a few steps one way, inspecting some crushed leaves, standing and repeating his investigation a few feet in the opposite direction. He paused beside the smoking generator, pointing to an area that had clear scorch marks. "I think either he or it was struck by lightning."

"He's lucky to be alive." Grim joined Chaos at the generator, sniffing the air near the marks. "It smells like ozone. The marks are still warm. I believe you're correct, Chaos."

Another clap of thunder boomed, lightning striking nearby and raising the hairs on the nape of my neck.

"We need to get him and Merri inside. It's not safe out here," Sin said.

Chaos stalked across to my fallen groundskeeper and made to pick him up, but Merri stopped him with a cry of protest.

"Careful! You can't just throw him over your shoulder. He was electrocuted. He's all but human and Grim said it himself, Christian is near death. Be gentle."

Grumbling, Chaos gently readjusted Christian's position, laying him on the wet ground before jerking his chin at Sinclair. "Help me. You get his feet, I'll get his shoulders."

Sin was clearly about to debate the issue.

"It has to be you. I'm going to look over the generator, and it can't be Grim."

"Unless you want me to accidentally help him along," Grim offered. He never had forgiven Christian for assuming he was Merri's father.

"Take Merri inside with you?" I asked Grim. "I won't be a minute. She can't stay out here and risk a lightning strike."

"Come on, wildflower," Grim said, offering her his elbow.

Merri gave the rest of us a worried look before acquiescing.

"We'll go prepare a room for him," Grim added, which seemed to bolster her willingness to leave the rest of us behind.

"Put him in the teal room. It's already made up." It took everything I had to look away from Merri as I approached the generator. We'd survive without it, but things would be infinitely more comfortable if I could get it up and running.

All I had to do was switch it on, and the house illuminated. That means Christian had been struck almost instantly when he got out here. How long had he been out there waiting for us to find him?

I winced, feeling uncharacteristically guilty. I wasn't used to being responsible for the well-being of others. It was sort of the diametrical opposite of my existence, actually. The realization immediately comforted me. I could hardly be blamed for any shortcomings or mistakes I made. It was all new to me. Besides, this was clearly an act of God. Well, perhaps not God directly, but the elements. And that wasn't something that could be easily planned for.

"All set?" I asked, checking on Chaos and Sin's progress.

They had Christian hoisted between them, his limp form and waxy pallor telling a very compelling story. He very well may not survive this injury.

"Follow me. The closest path to the teal room is up the servant's staircase."

Merri and Grim were ready for us, the bedding pulled down and the pillows carefully arranged. There was also a spare bathrobe laid out on the bottom of the four-poster. That level of thoughtfulness had Merri written all over it. Grim would never care for such details. Not unless it was for her benefit.

"Merri, turn around. We need to get him out of his wet clothes," I said.

"Allow me," Grim offered, sending his shadows out to cloak Sin and Chaos as they stripped Christian and reclothed him in the robe.

In moments, Christian was settled in the bed, his clammy, pale skin reminiscent of many a plague I'd caused.

"Will he be okay?" Merri whispered, wringing her hands at the side of the bed. I could tell that she wanted to do something so she could feel like she was helping aid his recovery.

"Only time will tell," I answered. "With an injury such as this, a comfortable place to sleep is all we can provide. He's got to do the rest on his own. None of us can heal him, and there isn't a functional hospital anywhere near."

She stood over him, watching as he drew labored breaths.

"I hate that I can't do anything for him."

"We found him. Getting him inside and in bed is the best thing we can do."

Merri shivered, her teeth chattering even though it wasn't cold in the room. Fear that she was going into shock twisted inside me.

"Get yourself changed and into something warm, hellcat."

"I'll make us all something to drink and get a fire going in the morning room," Chaos offered.

She nodded, walking numbly out of the bedroom and toward her own.

Once we were alone, Chaos asked the question I was sure each of us contemplated. "Foul play?"

Grim shook his head. "Not as far as I can ascertain. Seems to be a legitimate accident."

Chaos frowned at the news.

"And that upsets you why, exactly?" Sin asked.

"Because it feels convenient and too much like a coincidence."

"It's just Christian," Sin said.

"And it could have just as easily been Merri," Chaos snapped.

That shut Sin up, and the four of us wandered wordlessly back down to the morning room.

Merri joined us a few minutes later, her hair still wet but now braided over her shoulder, body covered in a soft robe, feet covered in fluffy slippers.

"I checked on him. He's still sleeping, but his breathing is better."

"Good," I said, and it was true. Christian had become quite an asset here. I didn't want to lose him.

"Here, Red. Come sit and have a drink." Chaos gestured to the spot beside him on the sofa.

Merri padded over, her expression distant as she flopped gracelessly into the seat Chaos had indicated. "What a morning," she groaned, accepting the glass he handed her. Before taking a sip, she let out a humorless laugh and shook her head. "I thought the biggest thing I'd do today was shut down my site. But the apocalypse wanted to one-up me, I guess. So it basically took out the western half of the US and then decided that wasn't enough chaos—"

War cleared his throat.

"Sorry," she murmured, offering him a smile as she continued with her rant. "I already had a weird déjà vu moment with the guy on that video being in my dream a few nights ago, but then Christian almost dying? I don't know how much more I can handle in a day. It's not even lunchtime."

"Wait, hang on a second," Sin said. "I'm glad you brought that up. You said you saw Asher in your dream, that you recognized him. You knew some of the others he's with, but you've never seen him before?"

She took a swallow of her drink, grimaced, and then shook her head. "Never. I thought he was just a weird figment of my imagination. I've made up plenty of people to hang out with while sleeping."

Chaos's free hand balled into a fist. "Another coincidence. Have I told you lately that I don't believe in coincidences?"

"Why not?" Merri asked, grimacing again as she took another sip of her drink.

"Coincidences take a lot of planning."

"He's part of the resistance. There's no way the connection isn't part of something bigger."

"According to Hades, we're connected to him and everyone with him," Grim reminded us.

"So you're saying fate put him in my dream?" Merri asked.

Chaos shrugged. "Stranger things have happened. Who's to say you wouldn't find yourself in one of the key player's dreams? Dreamwalking is rapidly becoming your forte."

"It wasn't that kind of dream," she insisted.

"Even so. Maybe that's how we're supposed to find them. Especially now that the grid is down. We can't exactly call Hades up and ask where they are. Maybe your dreams are what will lead us to them? Or them to us?"

She heaved a sigh. "How am I supposed to feed, find our allies, and get knocked up all in a night's work?"

"Start taking naps?" Sin offered.

Merri gave him a droll look. "Maybe I should just ask Malice to put me in a coma, and then I can work around the clock."

"I mean . . ."

Merri narrowed her eyes at Sin, effectively cutting him off.

Grim stood, his shadows spreading, betraying his frustration. "We cannot worry about finding them, not right now. We have a very specific task we need to focus on. If fate is at work, then we'll be brought together when the time is right. Whether we want it or not."

"So until then," Merri started.

Grim met and held Merri's stare, a bolt of lust bursting through the room and obliterating any lingering tension. "Until then, we stay the course."

"And by stay the course, you mean . . ."

Grim's lips twitched in what had to be his version of a playful smile. "I mean, we fuck our succubus."

CHAPTER THIRTEEN

MERRI

I told myself there was nothing wrong with walking past Christian's door on my way downstairs. As far as I knew, he'd yet to come to after his freak accident yesterday. Malice had checked on him multiple times in the night, and Grim assured me he'd be able to sense if his death was imminent. All of that should have kept the niggling worm of guilt from poking at my mind, but it didn't. There was nothing I could do to help. I knew that. It didn't change the fact Christian was the closest thing to a friend I had here, horsemen excluded.

Besides, Christian had gone out of his way to check on me. Repaying the favor was the least I could do.

Something told me that standing outside his sickroom with my ear pressed against the door didn't exactly fit the bill. But that's exactly what I was doing all the same. I wasn't sure what I was listening for. Snores? Signs of life? A muffled thump changed everything, spurring me into action.

"Christian?" I called, opening the door and rushing inside the room.

The man was on his hands and knees, breaths coming in labored drags as he attempted to get to his feet.

"Sorry to disturb, mademoiselle," he rasped, clearly still in pain. "I was just trying to get outside."

I took in his bathrobe and bare feet with a lift of my brows. "Dressed like that?"

He gave me a sheepish smile as I helped him back to his bed. "The storm has stopped. I thought I might make a potion to help with the healing. You need me at my best. This is not my best."

I shook my head as I tucked him under the blankets. "Christian, do you realize how close to death you came yesterday?"

"No. I don't remember anything beyond going to the generator. Then a flash of light and after that . . . nothing." He plucked at the front of his robe. "Clearly things did not end well."

"How are you feeling?" I asked, placing the back of my hand on his forehead to check for a fever before realizing that was absolutely unhelpful and letting my arm fall back to my side.

"Everything hurts at the same time. My head is . . . how do you say? Foggy."

"You were struck by lightning. The internet isn't working anymore for me to confirm, but I'm pretty sure those symptoms all line up."

His brows lifted in surprise. "That explains why everything smells a bit like burnt hair. It's me. *I* smell of burnt hair."

I couldn't resist the urge to tousle the chestnut waves still in place on top of his head. "Don't worry. It's all where it's supposed to be."

"And you would know that how?" he asked with a flirty wink. It was immediately followed by a wheezing cough as he tried to make himself comfortable.

"That's enough flirting from you. Are you hungry? Thirsty? Do you need anything?"

His expression grew serious, lips pressing into a grim line. "I need to be back to my old self. I can't do anything useful while I'm stuck in here."

"You mentioned a potion. Is that something I could grab for you?"

Christian sighed and gave a very slow shake of his head. "Non. It's not the kind of thing one can make in big batches. It has to be used while it is fresh."

"So it's supplies you need?"

Looking like he'd just run a marathon, Christian gave a weak nod. Sweat was dotting his brow, and he'd already lost what little color he'd had. Just talking was taking everything out of him.

"If you make me a list, maybe I can collect them for you?" I offered, feeling the need to do anything I could to help him.

"Are you sure?"

"Of course I am. Do I have to leave the property? That is the only thing that would stop me. The guys won't want me to do that."

"No, but the most important ingredient is near the château's lake. It's a rare flower typically only found in Japan." My skeptical stare had him offering a weak chuckle. "I have cultivated it here so it blooms throughout all seasons with the help of magic. It's called diphylleia grayi, the skeleton flower. You'll know it when you see the nearly translucent petals, turned clear because of their reaction to the constant mist that coats the lake's surface. There's nothing like it."

I immediately thought of Grim and his greenhouse, wondering if I might be able to pluck one of these super-rare flowers and bring it back for him to enjoy.

"Okay, sounds easy enough. How many do you need?"

"Five should be more than enough. I will need the stem as well as the blooms, so when you pluck them, make sure to grab them as close to the root as possible."

I nodded, nothing about the task seeming overly complicated. "And the other ingredients?"

"Worry about the flower first. The potion is useless without it. By the time you get back, I'll have a list of the rest, which can all be collected from the garden by my cottage."

"All right. I'll go look now. Don't try to get out of bed while I'm gone, please. The last thing you need is an injury on top of everything else you have going on."

"I am lucky to have someone like you looking after me, Merri. Merci."

A few minutes later, I was headed for the front door, basket in one hand, clippers in the other. After a quick glance outside, I snagged Chaos's hoodie, which he'd hung by the door. The sky wasn't clear like it had been before the eruption, and the wind was strong enough that I could see the tops of trees bending under the force of the gusts, but at least we weren't dealing with torrential rain and dangerous thunderstorms anymore. That didn't mean I would be warm enough in just my long-sleeved shirt and jeans. Chaos wouldn't mind.

Or if he did, I'd just distract him until he forgot why he was mad.

I smirked, already making plans for just such an occasion. Knowing Chaos's temper, they'd come in handy sooner or later. And thinking through distractions for him doubled as a distraction for me. I didn't mind a nature walk or even a mild hike, but trudging through mud didn't qualify as either of those things. It was unpleasant, to say the least. Every step made a sucking sound as I moved through the grounds on a path that would take me to the lake.

The storm had done a number on so much, but I hadn't accounted for everything around me to resemble a swamp rather than the beautiful, well-maintained grounds we'd been greeted by.

"I have to be almost there by now," I muttered to myself, not accustomed to this new-to-me area of the property. I'd done some walks in the last few weeks, obviously, but never one this far away from the house. Mostly because the weather hadn't permitted it. Not that I considered this much more welcoming, but I guess mud was preferable to snow if one had to traipse around. My little Keds were ruined, though.

Damn.

I really liked these shoes.

The earthy scent of standing water tickled my nose. It wasn't unpleasant, just different. I picked up my pace, hopeful my quest wouldn't last much longer so I could get Christian what he needed.

The lake was eerily beautiful as it came into view below me. I hadn't realized the château was situated at a higher elevation, but the evidence was here, clear as day. Just as Christian had described, mist hovered over the water, barely kissing the surface. The groundskeeper had mentioned that the petals turn translucent when touched by water, so the flowers had to be near its edge. Which meant I needed to get down this hill.

It wasn't a massive one by any stretch, but it was steep. And as I'd mentioned, it was incredibly muddy, which made my descent a bit more tricky than it should have been. Every step I took was done with care because the waterlogged earth under my feet kept shifting and threatening to send me ass over teakettle. I loved The Princess Bride as much as the next girl, but I wasn't eager to act out Buttercup's tumble down the hill today. Especially since I wasn't chasing after my sweet Westley.

Unfortunately, the land had other plans. Between one awkward step and the next, a huge chunk of mud gave way beneath my feet. Likely due to the pressure of the steps I'd taken from higher up, which had created enough instability to unsettle the entire section I was climbing down.

"Oh fuck!" I cried, fingers clawing into the dirt in vain as I attempted to stop myself. But there was nothing to grab onto. The mud and I were practically one as we slid the rest of the way down the hill, gaining momentum as we did. "Fuck, fuck, fuck," I half chanted, half screamed as I went unexpectedly airborne and then crashed through the mist and into the nearly freezing lake.

Mud and rocks followed behind me, pushing me down, down, down, impossibly deep into the frigid water. I'd had no idea the water would be so deep or that I would be going for an impromptu swim. I hadn't had a chance to take a deep breath before being submerged, and thanks to my fall, I was so disoriented I couldn't tell which way was up.

I opened my eyes in the murky water and released the little air I had in my lungs, praying I'd be able to see which way the bubble went so I could kick to the surface. Luckily, the water allowed just enough visibility, and I found my way up, swimming as hard as I could even though Chaos's hoodie and my jeans dragged me down with their weight.

I was panicking, my lungs burning with the lack of air. I didn't even allow myself to contemplate the odds of catching hypothermia the longer I stayed in the water. My only thought was up. I needed to keep moving up.

My head broke the surface just before I took an involuntary gasp, one that would have sealed my fate if I'd been a second slower. Coughing and spluttering, the taste of dirt in my mouth, I dragged in much-needed oxygen as I swam to the water's edge. My limbs were shaking, and it was too hard to keep myself upright, so I flopped down beside the water while struggling to catch my breath.

I had no way to track how much time passed while I lay there. I didn't try moving again until my lungs stopped feeling as though they were filled with fire, and my limbs were no longer twitching from the exertion.

"Good . . . job . . . Merri. Way to . . . fucking go." I rolled to my side and got to my hands and knees.

I was still shivering from the cold but thought I could manage to get to my feet. I certainly couldn't just lie here forever. My basket and clippers were long gone, but that was the least of my worries. Though, I didn't fully appreciate how true that statement was right away.

It wasn't until I was standing, body turned in the direction of what I thought was the hill I'd just slid down, that I knew I was in big trouble. I say thought because nothing looked the same. No hill. No evidence of any kind of mudslide, no château in the distance.

"What the hell?" I whispered.

I spun back around and tried to orient myself because I couldn't tell where I was at all. Not a familiar landmark to be found. But I could see the seaside village beyond our little haven. And what I found as I gazed across the inlet separating our island from the rest of the archipelago was horrifying. Huge plumes of black smoke curled up from decimated buildings, flames glowed in the distance, and the beach was littered with dark shapes that I didn't want to examine too closely because I was already pretty sure I knew what they were.

My stomach churned. Was this the reality of the world around us? My men and I had been living our lives in a literal bubble of safety on this island, and I'd been so wrapped up in my own shit I hadn't taken the time to really look at what was happening.

My pulse kicked into overdrive, and once again, it was hard to catch my breath. I was on the brink of a full-blown panic attack, but it was a bit like watching a train in the distance. Knowing it was coming directly for you but unable to get out of its way. My mind was reeling, oscillating between what I was witnessing and the fact that I had no idea where I was or how I was supposed to get back. If I could calm down, maybe I could string some coherent thoughts together, but I was too afraid.

Glancing at the lake once more, I steeled myself to re-enter the water. The only way I could know for sure if I was stuck in this reality was to try and go back the way I came. I dragged in a bracing breath, or the closest thing I could manage, and took a step. Instead of my foot meeting water, my face slammed into what I first thought must be an invisible wall. But as I bounced backward, powerful hands grabbed my arms and hauled me into a chest I knew very well. I looked up and found furious hazel eyes staring down at me.

"What the fuck do you think you're doing, Red?"

CHAPTER

FOURTEEN

CHAOS

"Motherfucker!"

Malice's shout triggered every primal instinct I had, sending me bolting for the door in nothing but a towel. I didn't even notice that I'd summoned a sword until I barreled down the hall and made it to his door.

"What is it? What's wrong?" I bellowed as I stormed inside his room without so much as knocking.

Sin and Grim weren't far behind me. Grim's shadows bled outward along the floor, darkening most of the room and betraying his agitation.

"Someone or something triggered the wards." Malice was leaning over his desk, eyes scanning the multiple computer screens.

"Where's Merri?" Grim demanded. His expression would have been terrifying if I didn't know mine was the same.

"She's not in her room?" I growled.

Sin shook his head. "I was just there. She's not."

"Fuck," Grim snarled.

Apparently I was too furious for words, but that didn't keep me from expressing myself. A tremor sent the books on Malice's shelves crashing to the floor.

"Knock it off," Malice snapped, his eyes finding mine. "We have no way to know if this was done by an enemy or something as innocuous as a tree falling after the storm."

"Always assume it's an enemy. That's the only way to stay alive." Even still, I put away my sword.

"Well then, what are we waiting for? We need to find Merri and fuck up whoever breached our wards." Sin turned on his heel but stopped, looking over his shoulder at me. "You might want to put some pants on first."

I had fought wars wearing less, but he was probably right. I bared my teeth by way of answer and shoved past him on my way back to my room. It took precious seconds for me to yank on a pair of joggers and shove my feet into shoes, but I still managed to catch up to them as we all gathered at the front door. Reaching for my hoodie, I frowned to find it missing, but a stray red hair on the bench beneath the row of hooks told me everything I needed to know.

Knowing Merri had snagged it quelled a small piece of the storm raging within me. But it didn't come close to ending it. She was most definitely outside. I had no doubt now. Which meant that she could be in danger.

"Merri is out there too. We need to split up and each take one of the four quadrants of the property. Find her first. She is the priority. The rest we can deal with after she is safe."

"Agreed. We scour the property, locate Merri, then kill whoever came through. Malice, I assume you don't need to be told that Christian will have to answer for this?" Grim said, his voice low and measured.

"Once we know what happened, I'll see if that's necessary." Malice was tense, the muscles in his jaw flexing at the stress of what Grim insinuated. Christian fucked up.

"Let's get going. Every minute we waste talking is a minute Merri is at risk." Sin borrowed my earlier move as he shoved past the other two horsemen, determination radiating off him as he headed outside. He opted to go south, and I went west. I was already sprinting, so there was no way for me to know which route the other two opted for. Nor did I care. All that mattered was getting to Merri before anyone or anything else.

As soon as I left the main grounds, I caught sight of footprints in the muddy path that were too small to be anyone other than Merri's. The others were too far away now, but that was fine. I'd find her, they'd find the intruder. Everyone wins.

The tracks she'd left were clear, and they didn't waver. It wasn't the usual path she selected for a walk, and given the unwelcoming conditions of the terrain, the fact that she hadn't opted for an easier route told me she'd come this way for a reason.

"What the hell were you up to, Red?"

As I went deeper into the rough, my stomach sank. The soil was unstable, shifting alarmingly under my feet, and with a glance down toward the lake, it was obvious the earth had given way recently. The water was cloudy, and a mess of rocks, dirt, and trees lay on the shoreline.

"No," I whispered as my eyes locked on the dirty white shoe floating at the water's edge. Merri's dirty white shoe.

If she had fallen into the water, none of us would know. She could be hurt—or worse. I rushed down the hillside, moving with the loose dirt and letting it help me along. I hadn't even reached the water before Merri slammed into my chest, her soaking wet body making a loud smacking noise.

My relief at finding her hale and whole was immediately overshadowed by anger, and I pulled her hard against me.

"What the fuck do you think you're doing, Red?"

"Me? Oh, you know, just nearly drowning in a lake deeper than I've ever seen in my life. No big deal." Her voice was high-pitched and on the verge of hysterical. "Malice should really have a sign made. People could get hurt."

I gave her a little shake. "Why the hell did you cross the ward?"

She blinked at me in confusion. "What? I just told you I fell into the lake and nearly drowned." She tugged on the waterlogged hoodie she wore for emphasis. "You were supposed to keep me warm, not kill me."

"I would never kill you. What are you talking about?"

Pulling the hoodie over her head, she balled it up and tossed it at me. "Not you. This damn thing. It tried to drown me. Why do you have to be such a giant?"

I frowned down at the same hoodie I'd searched for earlier before letting it fall to the muddy banks. "Merri, answer my fucking question. Why did you cross the ward?"

As I repeated myself, I assessed our surroundings. I should have been able to see her even though she'd stepped through the magical barrier. In fact, everything on this side of the ward should have been visible before I crossed. Looking at the state of things, we hadn't been seeing the truth at all.

"I didn't mean to. The mudslide tossed me into the lake, and when I surfaced, I was . . . here."

I frowned, glancing back over my shoulder in the direction Merri had indicated. The lack of familiar landmarks wasn't a surprise to me; that was the ward at work. It hid the truth of the island from anyone on the outside. But it was only supposed to do that in one direction. Those inside the ward should be able to see the reality of what was on the other side. Like a two-way mirror.

"I was starting to worry I'd gone through a portal or something and that I was going to have to get in the lake again to make it back to you." She shivered, and on instinct, I wrapped her tighter in my arms.

"No. There is no portal."

"I knew the world was ending, but it's worse than I thought." She laughed bitterly. "I don't know what I expected. Why would you guys want to keep the truth from me?"

My frown deepened. "It was never about keeping the truth from you. It was about keeping you safe."

She let out a derisive snort. "Oh, trust me. One look at this, and I wouldn't try to go anywhere. You should have shown this to me weeks ago. I'd have become a voluntary shut-in."

"It wasn't supposed to be hidden from you or any of us. Something is wrong."

I needed to get her back to the safety of the warded property. Merri most likely was the trigger for Malice's alarm. Not an intruder. That eased some of my mind, but frustration and anger were still there, pushing at me.

"Come on," I growled. "We need to get back."

She yanked out of my hold. "No. Not yet. I need to get something."

"Absolutely fucking not. You're shivering and wet. You need to come with me."

The glare she shot me was straight out of Grim's handbook. "I did not come all this way and nearly die not to get Christian his stupid flowers."

"Are you fucking kidding me? You crossed the ward to pick *flowers*? Do you know how risky that is?"

"First of all, we've already established that I did not mean to cross the wards. Second, fuck all the way off. I am trying to *save* him. You might be okay with people dying, but I'm not. Not when I can do something about it. Did I go for a walk to pick flowers for a potion that could help my friend? Yes, I fucking did. And I'm not returning to the house empty-handed. So either you help me or stay out of my way."

So help me, I was going to take her over my knee in a moment. "Look around, Merri. Do you see anything that remotely resembles flowers over here? All I see are dead things. Even the grass on this side of the ward is brown."

Her eyes narrowed and she clenched her jaw. I was half expecting her to stamp her foot for good measure. Instead she just muttered, "Fine," and took two steps into the lake.

"What the fuck do you think you're doing?" I shouted, grabbing her by the back of the neck and hauling her out.

She windmilled her arms and kicked out with her feet, sputtering, "Let me go, you big oaf."

"You're going the wrong fucking way."

I didn't give her the option to argue with me. In one smooth motion, I scooped her up and began striding in the right direction.

"Put me down!" she screeched.

"Not fucking happening."

"Chaos, I swear to all that is holy, I'm going to give you the worst tittie twister of your fucking life. Put. Me. Down."

As far as threats went, it wasn't particularly effective. Mostly because I had no clue what that was, but I didn't doubt she meant every word. I knew better than to tell her that.

Thankfully, as the world around us returned to the idyllic setting we'd been fed by the spell, some small piece of me relaxed. They couldn't get her here. She was as safe as she could be. So I set her on her feet.

She glared at me, looking more than a little like a half-drowned rat. Even so, she was still the most beautiful thing I'd ever seen. Her eyes were shining like gemstones, and her skin was flawless. The urge to pick her back up and never let her go was so strong my hand shook with the need to do just that.

Her gaze lit on something behind me, and she pushed me out of the way, saying, "Bazinga!"

With one bare foot and the other still clad in a soaked shoe, she unevenly stomped through the muck before dropping to her knees in front of the strangest blossoms I'd ever seen. Merri plucked almost a handful out by their stems, sending dirt and roots flying. When she shifted her weight to grab another bunch, her knee gave out and she stumbled.

I shot forward, grabbing her around the hips to steady her before she could face-plant into the bush.

"You need to feed," I grumbled, taking the blossoms from her despite her protests.

"I'm fine."

"You're not. You missed our dreamwalk last night and just nearly drowned. You need to fuel yourself."

"Give me back my flowers."

I grabbed the shoe that was floating nearby and dumped out the water before tucking the flowers inside for safekeeping. "There. Nothing will happen to them now."

"It's not much of a vase," she muttered.

"You need to work on your thank yous."

She opened her mouth to retort but snapped it closed. "You're right. Sorry. Thanks."

"I have a much better way for you to show your gratitude."

I knew I had her when she smirked. "Oh, really? I'm sure you do."

I just held her stare with my own.

She rolled her eyes. "Oh my God, you are so stubborn. Fine." Her words were dismissive, but her eyes were hot with interest. She leaned forward, tilting her chin up so her lips were on offer as she trailed the tips of her nails down my torso. I was grateful I'd skipped the shirt earlier so there was nothing between me and the heat of her body as she pressed it against me.

I couldn't deny her a kiss. Not now, not ever. That ship had sailed. "You infuriate me, Red."

"Ditto."

My mouth crashed down on hers as I cupped the back of her head and held her to me. I felt giddy with lust, though there was no way to know if it was all mine or influenced by her succubus power. Not that I cared either way.

Merri might have denied her hunger, but I could feel it tugging at me. She wasn't starved, but my woman needed me. She slid her hand further down my stomach, reaching for my waistband.

I snagged her wrist, stopping her before she could claim her prize. "Not here."

Breathing heavily, she flicked her eyes open, pupils blown wide, lust heavy between us. "Wh—" she started, but stopped herself before looking down at her wet clothes and dirt-covered legs. "You're right. I'm a mess."

I caught her by the chin and dragged her face back up to mine. "Not what I meant. A little dirt will never keep me from wanting you."

Her eyelashes fluttered as she let out a breathless giggle. "Okay, then."

"This will be more effective in a dreamwalk. Come, lie down with me. Then you can take exactly what you want."

"I prefer it when you take what you want."

Pride swelled in my chest. "Noted."

I led her over to a nearby copse of trees. They created a sense of seclusion, even if we were still technically out in the open. Was it fair of me to steal some time with Merri while the others were still out looking for her? Probably not. Was I going to do it anyway because it's what she needed? Hell yes.

Settling us on the soft moss-covered ground under an ancient tree, I tucked her into my side and had to fight the urge to kiss the top of her head. She needed passion, not tenderness, right now. We both did.

"I'm not sure how to do this. I've never intentionally dropped into a dream with someone who wasn't already sleeping."

I shrugged, hardly an expert myself. "Well, you're not technically asleep when you enter someone else's dream, right?"

"No, I guess not."

"So how do you usually find the person whose dream you're trying to join?"

"I just sort of think about them."

"Maybe try that?"

"But you're not asleep."

"Is that a prerequisite?"

"Maybe?"

I gave her a little squeeze. "Just try it, Red."

She took a deep breath and nodded before closing her eyes. In the time it took her to exhale, I was unconscious.

THE FIRST THING I noticed was the warm breeze caressing my body. And I mean *all* of my body.

I opened my eyes with a laugh. "Couldn't wait to get me naked, could you, Red?"

She hummed softly and nuzzled closer to me. I didn't know how she could possibly get any closer, though. She was nestled against me, her face resting on my chest, body pressed to mine, leg thrown over me.

"I love the way your skin feels on mine," I murmured.

"Things you might hear from a lover or a serial killer for two hundred, Alex."

"I'm not sure about serial killer. More of a mass murderer, if anything."

Merri let out a shocked laugh as she scrambled to get away from me. "That's it, I'm out of here."

"Like hell you are," I said, grabbing her by the hips and tugging her back. Then I proceeded to tickle her sides until she squealed, her hands attempting to pry mine off her.

"I yield! I yield!" she shrieked.

I stopped with a smile, taking in her flushed cheeks and wild hair.

"What the hell was that for?"

"I didn't feel like chasing you right now. We can try that another time."

Her flush deepened as she picked up on my meaning, but instead of taking the bait, she asked, "So you went with tickle fight?"

"Seems to have worked."

"You know what we don't do with girlfriends? We don't tickle them."

I grabbed her and moved her until she was straddling me, her red hair a tumble of scarlet in the sunlight.

For a moment, she was all mine, her attention only on me, but then she glanced around at the dream world she'd conjured for us. "Apparently we're exhibitionists. Outside in the middle of a meadow, naked as the day we were born. Anyone could come upon us, Chaos."

The thought of someone watching me claim what was mine sent arousal careening through me. I'd fuck my woman anywhere and any time. I didn't care who saw.

Sliding my palm across her lower belly and then up until I cupped one breast, I watched her watch me. She wasn't looking at my hand; she was focused on my eyes, my expression.

"What?" I asked, curious about what had caught her attention.

"Nothing."

"Tell me," I demanded, wiggling my fingers in mock threat.

She tilted her head, sending waves of hair cascading over her shoulder. "Uh oh, someone pulled out the big guns."

I snickered.

"I was just thinking that for as much as I can feel your arousal, seeing it is almost more powerful."

"I can show you how much I want you any time you like. In dreams or real life."

A pinch of her nipple had her gasping and grinding against my pelvis. My cock was hard and ready for her, but this position wouldn't work without some adjustments. All she had to do was lean forward and give me access.

I shifted my hips to give her a little nudge. "I need you to move so I can put a baby in you."

Her soft intake of breath and the way her eyes widened had me leaking precum in anticipation of the feel of her cunt wrapped around me. "How do you want me?"

"Lean forward and kiss me, Red. I'll take care of the rest."

She made a soft humming sound as she leaned down, her hair a curtain around our faces. It created an immediate sense of privacy. Like even out here in the middle of a field, we were the only two people in existence.

"Hey, Chaos?"

"Hmm?"

"You ever had sex at the circus?"

"What?" I asked, so fucking confused by the topic shift.

"It's fucking in tents."

I laughed but pulled her closer. "Stop making jokes and kiss me, woman."

As our lips met, I lifted my hips, lining up with her already wet opening. I wouldn't admit it to her, but I needed this as much as she did, just in a different way. Mine was a hunger based on craving, though I'd argue it was every bit as crucial to my survival as hers.

I drank in the sound of her gasp as I slid home in one smooth thrust.

"Fuck, your pussy squeezes me so tight," I groaned. "Fucking made for me."

"Look at you, knowing just how to sweet talk a girl."

"There's plenty more where that came from, but I wouldn't call it sweet talk."

She rolled her hips, and I groaned in response. "What would you call it?"

"Dirty."

"Show me."

I grabbed her by the nape and kissed her as she moved over my length again and again, biting her lower lip until she whimpered. Then, after finally letting her up for air, I looked into her lust-filled eyes and said, "Ride me like you want to milk every drop of cum from me until there's no way you won't be pregnant when we're done."

Her reaction was instant. Her pussy walls clamped down hard, as if begging me to do exactly that.

Palming her ass, I took control of her movements. I might be on the bottom, but I was still in charge.

She sat up, tossing her head back and giving me the most perfect view of her full tits as she writhed and rolled. Every time I brushed up against one special spot inside her, she flooded my cock with more wetness.

"Look at you, taking me so well. I'm going to pump you so full of me we'll have to put a plug in to keep my cum from dripping down your thighs."

She answered with a soft whimper.

"You like that? You want my baby, don't you?"

"Mmm-hmm."

"You're so close for me, aren't you?"

Her brows were furrowed in concentration as she let me fuck her like this. I loved watching the pleasure on her face, the way she bit her lip and fondled her breasts as though searching for something to do with her hands.

"I can't," she moaned raggedly.

"Yes you can."

Her eyes were so bright they practically glowed as they found mine. "No, not before you."

"Too bad. Because I want you to come first. I'll be right there with you, I promise."

Sweat glistened on both of us, making us glow in the golden light of the sun. My skin buzzed with frenetic energy, the sensation only growing the longer she looked into my eyes.

"Come for me, Merri. Come for me so I can fill you up."

Once again, her inner walls flexed around me, telling me how much she loved my words.

"The other three never stood a chance. You know that right? This cunt is mine. Just like any child you bear."

"God, yes."

"Good answer," I growled, grabbing her tight before I rolled us so she was under me, at my mercy.

From this position, I could drive in deep, make sure she got every fucking drop I could give her. I placed her ankles on my shoulders and thrust into her, over and over, the sound of our bodies slapping together only adding to the intensity between us. I wanted her so badly, but not just her body. I wanted that look in her eyes, the way she said my name, the gentle touches and shy smiles.

"Tell me you're mine, Merri."

"I . . . I'm yours," she panted, nails raking down my back as if trying to pull me even closer to her.

It must have been a trick of the light, but I would have sworn the glow from the sun grew stronger, encapsulating the two of us completely. Even the parts of her shaded by my form were glowing.

"I'm so close," she moaned.

"That's it, Red. Come for me."

She did. She came with a broken cry of my name—*my* fucking name—and pulled me right over the edge with her. My vision went white as pleasure raced along my spine, and I spilled inside her, long pulses that had me shaking and groaning as I rode them out.

"Take it. Fucking take everything I have, Merri. It's all for you."

She clung to me, her body still pulsing around me as we came down from our high. As I watched her return to herself, that glow faded, and for the first time, I wondered if we'd just made magic and it wasn't a trick of the light. We were in a dream, after all. Surely anything was possible.

"Hello? Earth to Chaos. You in there, buddy?" Sin's voice broke through the warm buzzing afterglow I wanted to exist in.

The unexpected interruption, especially in this moment, was enough to pull me straight out of the dream. I sat up, finding Sin standing over my and Merri's bodies with a wry grin.

"I see you found her. Thanks so much for letting us know before your . . . what is this exactly? A victory nap?"

"Merri needed to feed," I snapped, feeling a little bit of guilt. Not enough to make me regret my actions, though. If given the chance, I'd have done it again without question.

"Wonderful. A sex nap. Even better. I didn't know those were allowed." Sin held out a hand to Merri. "Come on, kitten. Everyone is worried. Let's show them you're okay, and then maybe we can take a sex nap."

As Sin began leading her down the trail toward the château, she stopped and looked back, her eyes wide. "My flowers."

I held up her ruined shoe, filled with the delicate blossoms, and winked. "Way ahead of you."

CHAPTER
FIFTEEN
LUCIFER

"Well, isn't this cozy? Boy, girl, girl, boy . . ." I waited to see if any of them would get my excellent *White Christmas* reference, but alas, uncultured swine, the lot of them.

Gluttony, Pride, Lust, Greed, and Envy all sat around the boardroom table, three of the four horsewomen scattered between them. Apparently, the sisters weren't so close these days.

"Where's Famine?" I asked, realizing I hadn't seen head or pointed tail of her since her little disappearing act.

"How are we supposed to know?" Death asked, her pert little nose wrinkling as if she'd smelled something rotten. "She abandoned us all after my success."

"And here I always took Pestilence as the jealous one," I mused, not bothering to hide my laugh when she sneered at me.

"I am not jealous," she snapped.

"Keep telling yourself that, darling," War crooned.

Slamming my palms on the table, I let my frustration get the better of me and sent a wave of power surging. The lights flared so brightly I wondered if they'd burst, but they didn't. Still, it shut them all up.

"Are you quite finished?" I asked, my voice dripping with saccharine sweetness.

No one responded.

"I'll take that as a yes." Rising from my chair, I stood over them all, fingers steepled in front of me. "Gluttony, why don't you introduce yourself since you're the newest member of our tribunal?"

I stared at the Prince in question, almost envious of his beauty. I said almost, because he'll never quite reach my level of insurmountable glory. But then, who could?

Gluttony raised a dark brow. "Everyone already knows who I am."

I blinked at him, my ire surging at the disrespect. I'd just given him an order, and he willfully ignored it. That was not how this was supposed to go.

"Indulge me," I gritted out, noting the start of a twitch in my eye.

Do not kill your Princes.

Do not kill your Princes.

Well, at least not before success is guaranteed.

Gluttony stood and cast his dark gaze around the room, his eyes lingering a beat longer on Greed than the others. Those two had always had a thing, though whether it was a pseudo-rivalry or something else, I couldn't be sure. If they could ever set aside their egos long enough, they'd make quite the mess together.

"I am Gluttony," he said, and I stood there crestfallen. Where was the gravitas? The pomp? The circumstance? What an utter disappointment.

"Just . . . sit down," I said with a gusty sigh. Pride began a slow clap as I was speaking, and I whipped my head to the side to glare. "No."

"Sorry, boss," he muttered. Despite the deference of his voice, his eyes tightened in anger and the tips of his ears were bright red. He didn't appreciate being called out in front of his brethren.

Greed snickered but pulled herself together.

Lust glanced around the room, quietly drawing the attention of the rest of us, as was their habit. Androgynous and ever-changing, Lust was whatever the person looking at them wanted them to be. A perfect fit each and every time. The fluidity of their gift made Lust one of the most powerful Princes.

"When are we going to get to the point, Dark Lord? I had hoped to hurry this along. We caught a whiff of your intended. Just a blip, really, but she was there. I'd like to speak with my Knights and begin pinpointing the origin of her lust."

"Now that's what I like to see. Look at that initiative. Why can't the rest of you be more like Lust?"

As suspected, that went over about as well as a bologna sandwich at a vegan food festival. But nothing motivates this lot quite as well as a bit of not-so-friendly competition.

"I don't see why Lust is getting all the praise. My Knights have been scouring the whole of Europe looking for your vessel."

I shot Envy a narrow-eyed glare. "Your name certainly fits. I'm really quite disappointed you aren't actually green."

Envy bared his teeth, which were a little too pointy for comfort. Add in a forked tongue, and he'd have made an excellent snake. I should know.

See what I did there? Aren't I just the most clever boy at the ball? One might even call me a fox.

"Tracking her is the most important, of course, but we can't stop with simply finding her," Greed mused.

"What do you mean by that?" Gluttony asked.

I sighed and rolled my eyes. "She means, you absolute imbecile, that there are more adversaries on the horizon. I must claim my bride and procreate, but time is of the essence. There are those out in the world who seek to block her from view, and we must stop them."

"Which is where I come in," Pride interjected, ever the eager puppy. "My Knights are hot on the heels of the Siren coven. All four of them."

My skin prickled with rage at the mention of the coven who imprisoned me over a quarter of a century ago. Unfairly, might I add.

Death cleared her throat.

"Have something to add?"

"Well, since you asked," she said, giving me a blindingly bright smile. Annoying as her incessantly cheerful personality was, I didn't hate her. She was instrumental in releasing me from my cage, after all. "I think your focus on collecting adversaries is narrow-minded. What you really need are allies." She paused for dramatic effect, her lips curling into a self-indulgent smirk. "Especially unwilling ones."

"You know how I hate it when you speak in riddles," I snapped.

"No riddles, my lord. The four of us created the most powerful allies you could possibly need. One who is instrumental in bringing about the antichrist. Do you really think we would allow them to truly defeat us without a backup plan for exactly this scenario?"

If she didn't get to the point soon, I was going to have her chained on the wall like I had Famine. Raising one eyebrow, I gestured for her to go on.

"No matter how they might feel about us, they're linked to us forever," War pointed out.

"Unfortunately," Pestilence sneered, none too happy with her sons. Though, who would be after such a betrayal?

Death waved a hand. "We don't care about feelings. All we need is their power. It was ours first, and it will always be ours. We just have to collect it." She tossed me a wink. "Worked beautifully the last time."

"How are you going to do that? Do you even know where they are?" Pride asked haughtily.

War snapped her gaze to him. "Of course you would ask such a stupid question. A mother always knows. They think we are gone. They have no reason to hide from us. And now that the second generation is growing, we will have even more power to siphon."

"Do we really want a new batch of watered-down demons running amok?" Pestilence asked.

It took everything in me not to say "amok, amok, amok" out loud.

"I thought you'd be pleased to be a grandmother," Death teased.

"Those little brats she is carrying aren't related to me. Pan and Asher haven't yet contributed anything more than disappointment to our cause."

I hummed quietly to myself as the idea percolated. I hadn't considered the power of the horsewomen's bloodlines.

"All the more reason to seduce them to our cause," Death said.

Lust's smile had the temperature in the room ratcheting up. "Excellent choice of words."

Death beamed. "So glad you approve."

"They just risked everything to defeat the three of you. Why would they join you now? It makes no logical sense," Envy drawled.

If War's expression were a dagger, he'd be dead. "Because they'd do anything to protect their precious children. We know exactly where to hit them to get exactly what we want."

"I'm starting to suspect whomever first referred to love as a battlefield was intimately familiar with you."

No one laughed at my incredibly well-timed reference. Plebeians. All of them.

Death gave a little shrug. "Anyway, like I was saying. Willing or not, allies are what we need. Especially ones with the ability to increase our own strength exponentially. We find them. Capture them."

"Kill them?" Pride offered.

"No, you absolute tit. Have you been paying attention at all?" Pestilence snapped, then added below her breath, "How the hell did this one make the roster?"

"He's pretty," I replied, which only enraged her further.

"No, dear Pride. We are not going to kill them. Not when we can drain them, their mates, and their children."

"And then we kill them?" Pride asked, sitting a little straighter.

"Why bother? They're a renewable energy source. And with that much magic at our disposal, we will ensure our"—Death shifted her gaze to lock onto mine—"*your* success."

With her words, the tension in the room shifted. Suddenly everyone was much more alert and interested. One might go so far as to say they were excited. Glancing at each member of my war council, I took notice of the agreement in their expressions. Not a single protest. This was good. Perhaps working with a team was better than I thought.

I locked eyes with Death, excitement burning in my veins at this new possibility. "Bring them to me."

CHAPTER SIXTEEN

MERRI

The first thing I heard when the dream materialized around me wasn't the crashing of waves or the birds in the trees on this tropical beach. It was . . . a Tarzan call?

"Ah-ah-ahhhhhh!"

"What in the world?"

I didn't know if I was more surprised or amused, but when it came to Sin, I was usually a bit of both.

The sound echoed in the distance again, causing me to abandon the sandy shore and go in search of the man. He was the reason I'd come here in the first place, after all.

"Sin?" I called, pushing past the thick flora and fauna as I wandered deeper into the jungle.

"Looking for me?"

I glanced around, not seeing him anywhere. "Are we playing hide and seek?"

"Up here!"

I lifted my gaze just in time to see him swinging from a thick vine and landing on a tree branch. Even from this vantage point, I could see the sweat glistening on his muscles, his skin bronzed by the sun.

That loincloth also left very little to the imagination. Hell, I knew what he was packing under there, and I still had a reaction to seeing him clad in so little.

I could tell he was pleased with himself, so I did my best to swallow a laugh as I asked, "What is all this?"

"Me Sin." He thumped a fist on his chest and then pointed to me. "You Merri."

I tilted my head, taking in his cascade of golden hair and bright smile. "I dunno, man. You look more like George of the Jungle to me."

"So . . . you think I'm hot." His smirk was a deadly weapon aimed right at me.

"That goes without saying."

In a graceful series of movements, he jumped down from the tree and landed directly in front of me. "I thought we could do a little role-play. I'll be the man raised by apes. You can be the brilliant, bookish explorer. You teach me everything you know. And by everything, I mean . . ." He leaned in and waggled his eyebrows.

"Is that so?"

"Well, you enjoyed it so much the last time, I figured why not next level the shit out of it?" He shrugged. "But if you aren't into it, we can go a different route. Chaos mentioned you were into the idea of playing chase. Do you want me to put on that *Scream* mask? I could try to catch you as you run. Except I won't kill you, and the only thing I'll impale you with is my dick."

As he was speaking, the jungle around us shifted. Instead of bright greens and dappled sunlight, I was now surrounded by a forest shaded in moonlight. The mask in question was now draped over his face, along with an all-black ensemble that camouflaged him too well.

"What do you say, kitten? Wanna run?" His voice was a deep growl in my ear.

My heart flipped in my chest, and I let out a breathy laugh as I placed my hand on his chest. "Tempting, but maybe something less terrifying?"

"Okay, okay. Challenge accepted." He pulled the mask off his face and dropped a kiss on my lips. "No psycho killer. We could be two astronauts stuck in space. The only thing keeping us going is the fiery passion between us. Forced proximity is so hot right now."

Before the setting could change to a very un-sexy anti-gravity space station, I shook my head.

"Also scary. I've seen Alien. No, thank you." I couldn't keep the laughter from my voice.

He tapped his lower lip, his eyes going hazy as his mind worked. "Okay, so what I'm hearing is you want less fantasy/sci-fi and more contemporary romance. I could bring back OriginalSin and introduce you to your cowboy era?"

My nipples hardened at the mention of Emmett and that accent he used when he was pretending not to be the Sin I knew and adored.

"I'll take that as a hell yes, darlin'," he drawled, the forest melting and being replaced by a sprawling ranch with the warm sun setting behind majestic mountains.

This time he was clad in low-slung Wranglers, with a shiny belt buckle and a cowboy hat dipped low over his eyes. I'd be a lying liar who lied if I said my ovaries didn't have a whole implosion over the picture he painted. Hussies.

But it still wasn't what I was craving.

I moved closer until our bodies all but touched and gave him a sweet kiss. "Let's just be Sin and Merri."

"How very domestic. I like it." He took off his hat, and it disappeared before his palms cupped my ass. "Kiss me, baby."

He didn't have to tell me twice. Closing my eyes, I gave in to him and let myself fall into the magic of kissing Sin. The man lived up to his name. Every sense came to life when his lips were on mine. He practically turned kissing into an Olympic sport. Tens across the board.

As his tongue danced with mine, my stupid heart gave a twitterpated flutter, and I sank further into the sensation of being his. I didn't break the kiss until he sat me down on a cold, hard surface. Apparently I wasn't wearing anything under this little silk nightie I'd manifested. Good job past me.

My eyes fluttered open to find the two of us in an unfamiliar kitchen. Something was bubbling away on the stovetop behind Sin, and there were a couple of candles scattered around that smelled delicious. Everything about the setting was sweet and cozy. Definitely much more my style.

Don't get me wrong, the out-there fantasies were fun. But I'd denied myself these simple intimacies for my entire life. These were the experiences I was most interested in collecting.

"What's cooking?" I murmured, nuzzling his neck and peppering light kisses up to his jaw.

"Don't know. Don't care. The only thing I want to eat is you."

My whole body tightened at the promise in those words.

"I mean . . . I won't stop you."

He grinned, his hands warm on my thighs as they slid up higher, pushing the little nightie up as they did. "What my girl wants, she gets." Eyes darkening with lust, he whispered, "Lie back for me, kitten. Spread those legs and let's start with dessert."

I leaned back on my elbows so that I could support myself and watch him work. As he dropped to his knees, I widened my legs as far as they would go to make space for his broad shoulders. He closed his eyes as he leaned forward and ran his nose along my seam.

"Mmm, fucking delicious."

"You really think so?" I asked, a blush heating my cheeks.

"I don't get to do this for you enough. If I could, I'd settle myself between your thighs and make you come over and over on my tongue until your legs tremble and you beg me to stop. Every." Lick. "Fucking." Kiss. "Day."

Then he sucked my clit into his mouth, and we both stopped talking.

I was reduced to little more than moans as I dug my fingers into his hair and held on to him for dear life. The things he could do with his mouth were, well, sinful. I was so on board with what he was doing to my body that I didn't even feel the need to beg for forgiveness. I was a total convert.

He wanted to do this every day? Sign me the fuck up. He needed to feed too. I could take care of him. Honestly, I should. He did the same for me.

"Fuck, Sin," I moaned, whimpering when he slid two fingers inside me and curled them upward, pressing right fucking there.

"I know, baby. You're being so good for me. Taking everything I'm giving you with such pretty whimpers." He pulled back just far enough that he could look up at me, his lips shiny with my arousal. "But I'm a glutton, and I won't be satisfied until I have all of you."

"Don't make me come yet. If I come, you will too, and you have to be inside me if you're going to get me pregnant." Was that my voice that sounded so high-pitched and frantic? Yes. Yes, it was.

"Christ," he muttered, pressing his forehead to my inner thigh. "I never thought the idea of knocking someone up would make me so hard, but those words from your lips have me leaking."

I reached down and grabbed his arms, tugging so I could get him to stand. I needed to see exactly what I was doing to him. "Show me."

Rising, he stood there on display, his clothes completely gone, dick standing proudly at attention, the tip glistening with precum, a drop falling to the floor as I watched.

"You're wasting it," I whispered. "Everything you can give me belongs inside."

His cock twitched, hands grabbing my thighs hard enough I'd have bruises. Twin pulses of arousal punched through the room, blanketing us in each other's pheromones and sending our need for each other through the roof.

"Stop teasing me, Sin. Fuck me and breed me already."

His expression was feral as he leaned in to steal another kiss. "You could not be more perfect," he breathed.

Impatient, I snaked a hand between us and grabbed his length, giving it one long stroke that made him groan before notching him at my slick entrance. “Please.”

“As much as I love hearing you beg, you never need to. I’m pretty sure I was born to take care of you, Merri.”

He drove home, bottoming out in a deep thrust that had us both making unintelligible sounds of pleasure.

“Yes. More.” I was nearly incoherent as I clawed at his back and wrapped my legs around his hips.

It didn’t seem to matter how often I fed these days. When it came to my four horsemen, I was always a needy bitch. And they loved to cater to my needs.

I really loved that for me.

“Fuck, kitten. Your cunt is squeezing me so tight.”

“Yes.”

“You want to make me come in your pretty pussy?”

“God, yes.”

“You want my baby.”

The way those words caused my belly to clench made him gasp, and I was pretty sure his knees buckled there for a second.

“I’ll take that as a yes.”

As much as his breeding talk was doing for my impending orgasm, it was suddenly super important that he know that wasn’t all this was. Yes, we needed to save the world. And yes, he needed to impregnate me for that to happen. But even without that, I wanted more of this. More of him.

Cupping his cheek in my hand, I made sure he was looking at me when I bared a tiny sliver of my soul. “I . . .” I stopped myself as words I wasn’t ready for danced on the tip of my tongue. No, that wasn’t something I would say. Not now. Possibly not ever again.

“What, baby?”

“I want it all with you, Sin.”

The look that crossed his face was a mixture of peace and euphoria as my words hit and his orgasm followed. He groaned my name, his hips losing their rhythm as he came deep inside me. His pleasure took me along for the ride, setting off my own climax, but this time it was different. There was something new that floated in the hazy aftermath of our shared release. It was hard to pinpoint it, but there was no denying the *rightness* of this moment. I was sated. I was content. I was . . . whole.

Like for once in my life, I was exactly where I was supposed to be. And *with* exactly who I was supposed to be. I didn't have the words to describe it other than that. But I knew Sin was feeling it too. I could see my wonder reflected in his warm gaze.

He tucked a stray lock of my hair behind my ear before sighing happily. "It's never been like this with anyone before. Every time we're together, this feeling just gets stronger."

I couldn't deny he was right. Exciting as it was, I'd spent so much of my life trying to keep myself from losing someone I cared about. That niggle of fear I tried to bury worked its way to the surface.

"I know. I feel it too," I finally said.

He kissed me again. When I opened my eyes, I was in my bed —alone.

Well, not completely alone.

It took a couple of tries to get my eyes to focus in the darkness. It was morning, but only just as the light from the rising sun barely made a dent in the shadows. Even so, I could make out a familiar masculine shape. A place where the shadows were so dark they were impenetrable. As I got to my feet, the form vanished, and the light in the corner where he'd been standing guard changed. He was gone, but I knew now. Daddy Death had been keeping watch.

The question was . . . why?

CHAPTER SEVENTEEN

MALICE

I couldn't get Merri off my mind. Not since I finally broke and fucked her like a man possessed. I've been at least half-hard all day, every day. Nothing eased the ache. Not plotting world domination. Not working on the security of the estate. Not running until my muscles throbbed and my brain was mostly quiet. Not even cold fucking showers.

I was so tired of cold showers.

Sweat coated my skin, soaking through my shirt and causing a chill to pass through me as I finished yet another punishing workout. My shirt fell to the tile floor of my en suite bathroom with a disgusting plop. I needed to wash the day off my body, and hopefully the water would take some of this infernal yearning down the drain with it.

I did not *yearn*.

Liar.

That crooning voice inside my head could fuck all the way off. A man was allowed to have his delusions. It's called coping.

With a frustrated groan, I turned the cold water all the way up, ignoring the second knob completely. There was only one way to deal with a mess like this. And by mess, I meant my feelings—shudder—for Merri. I had to purify myself. Trial by fire, but in this case, the purifying flames were actually icy rivulets.

Everything in my body protested the thought. It wanted nothing to do with standing in a frigid downpour. No matter what people claimed about the healing benefits. But it did serve to kill my erections—at least momentarily.

Seriously, was there anything worse than a cold shower? I don't know what the Vikings were smoking when they decided cold plunges were the wave of the future. Pretty sure it was a practical joke, but everyone was too ashamed to admit how much they hated it, so voilà, history was rewritten, and it was instead considered rejuvenating, and into the icy depths the rest of them went forevermore.

Can you feel my eye roll? Seriously, I think one of my eyes is stuck. Utter shite, the lot of it.

Taking a few steady breaths in preparation, I steeled myself for the shock of the cold, then stepped under the spray.

"Bloody hell, this is a load of complete bollocks," I gritted out as the water needled my chest and trickled down to my crotch.

Closing my eyes, I attempted to let the temperature do its worst, but instead I was greeted with vivid memories of Merri taking me into her body. Why couldn't I simply free myself of the sickness of wanting her? That's what this was. A virus that infected me and was ravaging my body, working its way to my heart. If it reached that vital organ, I didn't know what would happen.

I turned my back to the showerhead and braced both palms on the wall, hanging my head as I tried to will her from my thoughts. It didn't work. I don't know why I thought it would when nothing else did.

There was no purging myself of this . . . *infestation.*

"Damn you," I growled, though whether the words were for Merri or the reappearance of this incessant fucking erection, I wasn't sure.

Reaching between my legs, I palmed the swollen length and

squeezed the base. What was I hoping for? Not the bolt of pleasure that raced up my spine. Nor the echo of Merri's hitched breath when I filled her that first time.

I allowed my hand to shuttle along my cock, the soft scrape of my palm a sorry imitation of Merri's warmth. But it didn't seem to matter. All I wanted was more.

Me. The man who went centuries without sexual touch of any kind had been reduced to a wank in the shower, like some common dudebro. But perhaps the only way to purge myself of this affliction was to release the pent-up lust she caused.

"Physician, heal thyself," I muttered, eyes squeezed shut as I envisioned Merri splayed out on my bed.

One palm still pressed to the tile, I worked my cock with abandon, giving myself over to the fantasy of the woman who'd stolen my self-control so effortlessly. It wouldn't take long for me to reach my peak, not with how desperately I wanted her. No one had to know.

"Fuck," I rasped, my balls tightening with my impending release. "Yes, Merri."

Precum pulsed from my tip, and I was very nearly there, so ready to come my jaw ached from the clenching of my teeth and the tension in my neck and shoulders. Just before the blissful climax took me to a brief oblivion, a phantom hook twisted inside my chest, effectively killing everything, including my erection. Balls throbbing, I released my now flaccid cock and stood straight, alarm replacing my desire.

There was no way I could mistake the feeling for anything else. Especially not after experiencing it only a couple days prior.

The wards had been breached.

A-fucking-gain.

I cut off the water and grabbed a towel, drying myself as I moved into my room. If that little succubus stumbled her way through the wards again, I'd have her over my knee for punishment. The sensation continued, though, over and over, that twisting warning going off like someone was ringing a bell. Multiple warnings. Multiple breaches. Something was very wrong.

"Shit. Fuck." I was only partially dry, which made pulling on my pants far more complicated than it should have been. Every second that slipped by felt like an eternity.

Christian burst into my room, healed but not quite back to peak strength. His face was pale, dark circles beneath his worried eyes. "Monsieur Laurent, there's been a—"

"I know!" I snapped, cutting him off so I could ask him the only thing that truly mattered. "Where's Merri?"

"I am not sure. I have not seen her since she visited me this morning to check on me."

Storming out of the room, I shouted down the staircase, "Chaos! Grimsby! Sinclair! Where is our succubus?"

Merri's head poked out of her room. "What are you shouting about?"

Sweet merciful God.

I closed my eyes as relief nearly sent me to my knees. I rushed toward her, taking her into my arms and holding her tight. Not a second later, her finger dug into my belly, forcing me to pull back.

"This is nice and all, but what the hell is going on? You're acting like I died."

Gathering my composure, I cleared my throat. "Something triggered the wards again."

"Well, it wasn't me this time."

"Obviously." The relief that she was here, that I could touch her and know she was safe, was palpable.

Thundering footsteps called my attention to the staircase where Sin and Chaos were rushing to us. Grim manifested in a haze of shadows next to Merri as they reached us.

"What happened?" he asked, expression deadly.

"Merri, are you hurt?" Chaos all but shouted.

"Do I look hurt?" she sassed.

"You look perfect to me," Sin offered with a smirk.

Knowing exactly where that was headed if I didn't cut him off at the pass, I interjected, "The wards were breached. Multiple times, I think," I added, absently rubbing at my chest where the phantom hook continued to twist.

My brothers and I shared a look, all of us thinking the same thing. Had he finally found us?

"Merri, you stay with Christian. Do not leave your room until one of us comes for you," I snapped.

Her eyes narrowed. "No."

Insolence looked good on her, but she didn't need to know that.

"Merri," Chaos growled while Grim sighed and pinched the bridge of his nose.

"You're not leaving me behind."

"Absolutely not," I insisted. "If it's Lucifer, we're not just going to hand you to him like some kind of prized mare. You'll stay here, where it's safe."

Merri popped her hands on her hips, staring at me like I was too stupid for words. "Oh yeah? And what happens when he just shows up here to abscond with me like some sort of Hades and Persephone reenactment come to life? What then, Mr. Horsemen? While the four of you are off who knows where unable to do a damn thing about it?"

"She has a point," Sin conceded.

Chaos heaved a frustrated sigh. "As much as I hate to agree with him, she will be safer with the four of us to protect her." He cut a glance at Christian, who was leaning against the wall as though winded from simply standing. "What can he possibly do to keep her from harm? A strong breeze will knock him over."

Grim didn't say a word, and I knew he was silently considering every possible avenue. He, perhaps even more than the rest of us, would rather eat nails than put Merri in harm's way. It would go against his every instinct to willingly thrust her headlong into danger. The only way he'd agree to her coming with us was if he truly believed it to be the best option.

"Fuck," I grunted as another twist in my chest set me further on edge. "There are more. We need to find them and put a stop to this." For good measure, I turned to Christian and added, "And once we've secured the premises, you and I are going to have a little chat about how the hell this happened."

Grim's steely gaze met mine. "Fine. She comes with us, but she is never to be unprotected. Two of us at her front. Two at her back. Understood?"

The three of us nodded our agreement while Merri huffed and rolled her eyes.

"Like you could really keep me here against my will."

Grim's shadow swelled until a bigger-than-life-sized version loomed over her on the wall. "If you think we couldn't, then you still have no fucking idea who we are, wildflower."

"You heard him, guys," Sin said, rubbing his hands together in anticipatory glee.

"Saddle up. It's time for the four horsemen to ride." When the only response was a series of groans from the rest of us, he looked around. "What? Was it something I said?"

CHAPTER EIGHTEEN

GRIM

"Are you fucking kidding me?" Chaos grumbled as soon as we caught sight of the gate.

Well, what remained of the now broken gate.

"Uh, buddy, I think we've got bigger problems," Sin said, giving Chaos's arm a light slap while pointing to the group of twenty-plus humans that had yet to notice our approach.

"That isn't possible." The disbelief in Malice's voice only added to my unease. It most definitely shouldn't have been possible, but here we were with a small army of unwanted adversaries armed with weapons, rage, and desperation coming for us.

"Do you think they know who we are?" Merri asked.

"Definitely not," I said, categorically dismissing the notion. No one was that fucking stupid. "They're scavengers in search of supplies. They have no idea their decision to come here is the last one they'll ever make."

I snagged Merri's sweatshirt-covered arm and pulled her back until she was behind me. "Hey!"

"Not another word, wildflower. They might only be humans, but they're still dangerous. You aren't immortal."

She huffed in frustration but didn't refute my claim. I'd be lying if I said I wasn't surprised. Me saying something true had never seemed to stop her from disagreeing before. She liked to argue for argument's sake when it came to me.

We had minutes at best before the horde noticed us. "Divide and conquer?" I asked, glancing at Chaos.

"My favorite game," he replied, his voice edged with violence.

"I would have thought you preferred Hide the Salami," Sin muttered under his breath.

"He *is* really good at that one."

We all looked at Merri and she shrugged.

"It's a gift." Chaos returned his attention to the approaching humans. "Don't let them get off any shots. We can't risk Merri taking a stray bullet."

"Consider it handled," Sin said, the reminder that Merri could still be hurt sobering him up in a way not even the impending fight could. There was very little Sinclair took seriously, but Merri had worked her way to the top of his short list.

Chaos bolted toward the crowd, his presence causing the five men in the front to shout in surprise. He made quick work of them, cutting them down with his sword in moments.

I spared Merri a glance, annoyance creeping in when I caught her look of awe. For someone else.

She thought that was impressive? She hadn't seen anything.

Stepping away from the group, I stalked toward the invaders with deadly intent burning through me. Slowly, I removed first one glove, then the other, and when I reached the first man who stared up at me with terror on his face, all I had to do was brush a fingertip over his cheek. The light left his eyes instantly, his soul claimed by me in the space between breaths.

See? So much more impressive than needing a weapon.

I *was* a weapon.

Between Chaos and I, these fools would be dealt with in seconds.

A sharp whistle cut through the air, preceding the sound of hammering footfall.

Fuck. I jinxed it.

Had Sin been the one to make the mistake, he'd already be wiping the blood from his chin.

"Merri, stay fucking put. Do you hear me?" Malice bellowed as he raced into the fray. "There are too many of them. They can't come through."

I swiped my palm over another's forehead, dropping him like a fly meeting a swatter. Malice touched the man next to me, and had I not known the power of pestilence, I would have thought him ineffective. But in mere heartbeats, the man he'd touched began twitching involuntarily, his eyes rolling, mouth frothing as he coughed bloody spittle into the face of the fighter next to him.

And so the infection spread. One by one, those taken by Malice's gift turned upon one another, only adding to the madness. Or at least they did until they succumbed to the inevitable.

I continued working my way through the throng beside my brothers, sparing a single glance for Sin, who had just taken a man by the throat and brought his face a hairsbreadth away from his own. With a wicked smirk, Sin inhaled, pulling the poor bastard's soul out of his body through his mouth. The man's body shriveled up, as though all the moisture had been sucked from him in one fell swoop. When he fell to the ground, he was little more than a mummy.

We continued on in this fashion until I was certain we'd be finished in less than a handful of minutes. But, alas, I hadn't counted on the fifth member of our hunting party.

Not content with sitting the fight out, Merri worked magic of her own.

"What the hell do you think you're doing?" I shouted back at her.

"Helping!"

She had a group of men mesmerized, staring at her as she

projected lust magic onto them. "Get on your knees for me," she purred.

They fell to the gravel road, still staring up at her.

"How dare you look at me. Take out your eyes. Put them on the road for me as an offering."

My stomach twisted as the men she had in her snare used their fingers to claw out their own eyes, screaming as they did it.

"Holy shit," Sin breathed. "Is it just me, or is that the fucking hottest thing you've ever seen?"

For perhaps the first time in his existence, Sin wasn't wrong. I was definitely hard when I hadn't been mere seconds prior.

"She's like an avenging godde—" Sin's words cut off in a wet gurgle at the crack of a gunshot. Blood spilled from his mouth, his eyes wide as his throat exploded in a mess of gore and tissue and thicker things.

"Sin!" Merri screamed.

He fell to the ground, gurgling and twitching as he struggled to heal. He would survive, but it wasn't an injury he could immediately recover from.

Chaos let out a primal roar, mowing down the men in front of him. But once again, it was Merri who stole the show.

In a move straight out of a horseman's handbook, she took several steps forward, palm out, eyes narrowed in rage and swirling with power. I watched in a mix of terror and fascination as her eyes turned milky white and two tiny black horns appeared at her hairline.

She was the spitting image of her mother.

Then, as Malice, Chaos, and I stood by, Merri sucked the souls out of every remaining human on our property. They crumpled into heaps, eyes staring vacantly, pure horror etched onto their deathly visages while she positively glowed from the power. Hands held out at her sides, she lifted her face to the sky, and her hair swirled around her as her feet lifted from the ground an inch.

I swallowed past the lump in my throat as I watched the woman I had pledged to protect fully come into her power. She turned those milky eyes on me, and her feet returned to solid ground.

All I could manage was a heartfelt, "Fuck."

CHAPTER

NINETEEN

CHAOS

"Merri?" I said, my voice a tight rasp as I watched the horns retreat and her eyes return to normal.

She turned her attention away from Grim and trained her gaze on me in painfully slow motion. "W-why are you looking at me like that?"

"Like what?" I asked.

"Like you don't recognize me."

"I've never seen you do anything like what you just did, Red. Forgive me for being taken aback."

My focus flicked to the bodies littering the ground before us. The power she just displayed would have terrified a weaker man. In my case, a healthy dose of caution was definitely warranted.

"They're dead," Malice confirmed, voice low. "All of them."

"She sucked out their souls. I watched it." Grim's voice held both awe and pride as he walked into the mass of death, stepping over the fallen humans and inspecting them as he went.

"I didn't. Did I?" Merri's frantic question had me closing the distance between us. I needed her to know she wasn't in trouble for exercising her power. She stopped them. She defended herself and us. That was more than we could have hoped for. It was what we'd been training her to do all this time.

Taking her face between my palms, I whispered, "You were incredible."

"But . . . but . . . I killed them."

"It was them or you, Red. You saw what they did to Sin. You would have been their next target."

"Oh my God. Sin!" She tried to twist her head out of my hold, but I tightened my grip.

"No need to look. He'll be fine, and you don't need that image in your memory."

"But—"

"No," I repeated firmly.

I'd been trying to assuage her panic, but I could see it in her eyes as they darted from body to body. "I killed them. Oh my God. I killed them all. I'm the monster Lilith always said I was."

"What are you going on about?" Malice asked. "You were amazing. That"—he pointed at the pile of corpses at our feet—"was a thing of beauty. Do not for a second regret what just happened."

Her wide eyes swung to him. "How can you say that? They're innocent humans."

"They were trying to kill us," he retorted, disbelief lacing every word.

"They were desperate. They're starving and dying in the streets. The world is ending, and they don't understand, and I . . . I just killed them all without a second thought."

"You are the daughter of a horsewoman, and you were threatened and trying to protect those you cared about. That is the beginning and the end of the conversation," Grim stated.

"But—"

"No," I said, agreeing wholeheartedly with Grimsby. "You did what you were born to do, Red. There's nothing to feel sorry about."

"I wasn't born to do this. Succubi feed for survival, not to kill. I've never killed on purpose. Not once."

I was still holding her face, so I dropped my hands to her shoulders so I could give her a little shake and interrupt her spiral. "That wasn't a succubus power, Red. That was all Famine."

"Excuse me?"

"What you just did? That was from your mother. Sin can do the same thing. We've seen him do it. It's called soul stealing."

"If I did it, they'd call it reaping," Grim offered.

"Not helping," Malice muttered. The assertion mirrored my own, telling me that Malice was as laser focused on Merri and her state of mind as I was.

"Why aren't you more upset with me? Lilith hid me away after I killed Jimmy. She wouldn't let me be near her clientele after I accidentally fed on them all. She wasn't proud of what I could do. She was scared."

Grim shifted until he was in my line of sight, allowing us to exchange a look.

"Pretty sure that had nothing to do with power and everything to do with control," I mused. "In both those cases, your use of power was unintentional."

"So was this," she shouted, flinging out her arm.

"Was it, though?" Malice asked.

Merri flinched. "Of course it was."

"No, wildflower. You knew exactly what you wanted to do. The only reason you're upset right now is because you're not familiar with that part of yourself. There's a difference between instinct and losing control. Losing control would have been not stopping until every human who walks the earth was laying at your feet."

"Trust him on that one. He would know," I said.

Beside me, Malice nodded. "As would I."

Tears swam in her eyes, and as one crystalline drop fell, I caught it with the pad of my thumb. "You were so very brave, little succubus."

A wet cough came from Sin as he lay on the ground, slowly healing. Merri's shoulders tensed, and she jerked in an attempt to go to him.

"Sin," she whispered, but I stopped her.

"He's fine, Red. Don't look at him right now. He's too vain to let you see him like this." As I glanced over to the bloody mess that was the horseman Famine, he gave me a thumbs up. I let out a soft huff of laughter. "I promise he's okay. He'll be good as new in no time."

I could see the disbelief in her eyes, but she'd been through this with us before. We couldn't die.

Cupping the back of her head, I pulled her into me and pressed my lips to the top of her head. "We will always come back to you."

"I hope so."

Malice cleared his throat. "As touching as this is, we need to get back to the château, and I suppose we'll have to figure out how to dispose of these bodies. It won't be long before the stench is unbearable."

"That's rich, coming from you," Grim said. "You specialize in rot and decay."

"Doesn't mean I want to roll around in it. I'll leave that to you."

I rolled my eyes, still holding Merri close. "Maybe we should worry about how the hell they got through the wards in the first place."

"Isn't it obvious?" Malice countered.

"No?"

"Desperation."

"How can desperation supersede magic?" Grim asked. "They shouldn't have even been able to see the place."

"But desperate people with nowhere to go will push through discomfort in search of safety. To them, it looked like nothing more than uninhabited land. Even if their hackles were raised by the wards, they might still continue on in the hope they'd find salvation. Humans are nothing if not stubborn."

"What's the point of wards, then?" Grim grumbled.

"Well, they were never going to be a physical barrier for humans. Just a repellent."

"Maybe it should have been," Grim said.

"They weren't the ones we were worried about," I reminded him.

"If the humans found us, does that mean Lucifer can?" Merri asked, her voice small and tight.

I pulled her in closer and squeezed her. I didn't have an answer for her, and neither did the others.

She looked up at me, something flashing across her face before she asked, "Was this because of Christian being injured? Did that somehow weaken the wards?"

"No," Malice answered. "The magic doesn't work like that. Wards weaken over time, but he just replenished them, so they should be as strong as ever."

"Maybe someone spotted Merri when she fell through the wards and decided to come investigate," I said.

"The shore was visible from my vantage point after I surfaced in the lake." Merri pulled away from me and blurted, "Oh God, did I cause this?"

"It certainly didn't fucking help." Malice could be a real asshole most days. Today wasn't an exception.

"So our cover is blown. Do we need to run?"

"No," Grim said. "We stay, shore up the wards once Christian is at full strength, and we stay the course."

"Grim's right. We have to hold our ground and focus on beating Lucifer at his own game." At Sin's words, Merri turned and rushed to where he was standing, bloody, a little unsteady, but healed.

"Sin! Are you okay? Do you hurt anywhere?" She ran her hands over his face and across his throat as though searching for wounds.

"If I say it hurts, will you kiss it better?"

She wrinkled her nose as she inspected the gore-specked front of him. "If you really need me to . . ."

He laughed and pulled her in for a hug. "Nah. I already have everything I need."

The implication was clear and none of us, including Merri, missed it.

"For someone who just nearly had their head blown off, you look quite chipper," Malice said.

Sin beamed, his arms never leaving Merri. "Of course I fucking do. My girl loves me."

All of us except Grim visibly startled.

"I do?" she asked.

"Babe, everyone knows that razing your lover's enemies to the ground is the number one sign of true love. I might be a horseman, but I was an actor first. I'm practically an expert in love stories."

His logic was flawed, as romantic as it was. I had never loved anyone, but I've razed entire armies simply for the sake of bloodlust.

"I . . . Holy shit, you might be right," Merri said, stopping my thoughts in their tracks.

With a grin, Sinclair booped her on the nose and said, "I know."

I shot Malice a look, wondering what he thought about this new development as a cold sweat broke out across my skin. Was he like me? Feeling a very unwelcome mix of panic and jealousy? Panic because how did this happen, but jealousy because if she loved him, where did that leave me? I mean us. No. I didn't care about the others right now. They could fight their own battles. She said it herself. Loving someone meant the center of your world changed. So if she truly loved Sin, how could there be any part of her world left for anyone else?

"As touching as this moment is," Grim interrupted, attention locked on the corpses beside us, "we've got bigger problems."

Thankful for the reprieve from dealing with a plethora of unwanted feelings, my gaze followed his to the bodies . . . and the demons that were climbing out of them.

CHAPTER TWENTY

SIN

"Fucking hell, can we never catch a break?" I muttered, swiftly coming down from the high of what Merri did for me. And what it meant.

"What do you think this is, a bloody vacation?" Malice snapped, eyes darting between the growing demon horde.

"It was supposed to be a sex-cation. Like a babymoon, except we haven't made the baby yet."

One by one, the demons shuffled to their feet, all different shapes and sizes, but they were all lust demons. Their forms varied, along with the specificity of their powers. A handful of them gathered together closer to Merri than I'd like. They were reminiscent of satyrs with horns and goat legs, their power rooted in distraction via sex seemingly harmless, but in truth, it was often deadly. Another group had more humanoid figures, their bodies shaped like the most beautiful, well-formed statues that could lock you in a loop of ecstasy with a single kiss that would only end with your death. And then there were the most dangerous of them, the shapeshifter. These creatures fed on desire and could transform into whatever their target most craved. The perfect lure.

People assumed lust was always sexual, but it wasn't. Ever heard of a lust for power? What about a bloodlust? At the end of the day, it was about desire. A longing to fill the void within. The highest tier of lust demon, the shapeshifter, was able to tap into *whatever* it was that you most desired. Be that a need for fame—hello darkness, my old friend—money, sex, family . . . You get the idea. There was nothing more addictive than finally obtaining something you thought you'd never have.

Merri's gasp pulled my focus from the demons currently approaching. She was feet from me, too far for my liking, and a satyr had his goat-like eyes locked on her, his almost comically large member standing at attention as he sized her up.

"Get away from her!" I snarled, intending to rush over and tackle the asshole. Unfortunately, the Mystique wannabe closest to me had other plans.

The cool brush of fingers gliding down the back of my neck had my muscles locking in place. But it was the sensual croon in my ear that had my vision shifting. "She's right here, Sinclair."

As she spoke, a new scene took place, superimposing itself over the mouth of the property. Had I been anyone else, I wouldn't have been able to sense the trap. But I was also a creature of lust, so I recognized it for what it was.

The surroundings were perfect. Everything I could want was laid out before me. Merri, wearing one of my band's T-shirts—the Apocalyptic Unicorns logo had never looked so good—and nothing else, her hair tumbling over her shoulders, a smile on her face that was only for me.

"I love you, Sin," she murmured as she reached for me. "Come back to bed."

God, I wanted her.

When I didn't immediately move, she pouted. "What are you waiting for? Don't make me start without you."

Unfortunately, just because I knew it was fake didn't mean I was fully immune to it. I might still be able to make out my brothers also frozen in place with shapeshifters of their own latched onto them like a bunch of fucking leeches, but the vision of Merri pulling her shirt up and over her head had me paralyzed.

I was a slave to my desire for her.

Helpless.

Weak.

Prey.

No.

That wasn't *my* voice. Those weren't *my* words. They were hers. The creature trying to unmake me.

Merri's palm traced down my front, stopping at my belt as she looked up my body. "Please, Sin. I need you."

It almost got me. The gentle begging, the big-eyed stare. But then I heard the real Merri scream. My hand shot out in front of me, gripping the creature by the throat and shattering the illusion.

"Oh, you're good," I snarled. "Good, but not good enough."

Lifting the creature with one hand, I stared into the pitch-black eyes and tapped into my own power. Demons may not have souls in the way humans did, but they were still animated by something *other*. Spirit, or whatever you wanted to call it. And that was enough for me to lock onto. Inhaling deeply, I sucked every ounce of life force from the shapeshifter, taking without care for what I'd leave behind.

She dropped at my feet like a sack of bones, which frankly suited me just fine. I preferred her this way. Namely dead.

I spared my brothers a quick glance, clocking that they were still locked in whatever fantasy their demons had created. It would be easier to deal with these fuckers with their assistance, but they'd be fine. Merri needed me.

"Get your fucking hands off my succubus!" I shouted, advancing on the three satyrs who had Merri in their clutches. They were taking her kicking and screaming, her power worthless against them. With as much of it as she'd just used avenging my honor—fucking swoon—and without the rage fueling her instinctual use of it, she was little more than a baby calf attempting to walk. Not that I'd tell her so. I wasn't a complete moron.

One of the three peeled away from the others, coming at me with a lascivious smirk.

"Cute," I taunted, beckoning him closer with a finger.

He raced toward me, head lowering like he was about to ram into me.

"Ba-aa-aa-aa-aad satyr," I mocked as I grabbed him by a horn and tugged down hard, bringing up my knee at the same time and slamming it into his throat. The jarring force of the impact was enough that I was able to snap the horn from his head. Before he could do more than let out a garbled scream, I swung my arm around and impaled the fucker with it.

He dropped dead at my feet.

What? You didn't think I knew how to wreck a bitch?

Ye of little faith.

You don't become a Horseman of the motherfucking Apocalypse without picking up a few skills.

"Merri!" I shouted when one of the satyrs tossed her over his shoulder.

She reached between the goat-man's legs and grabbed his balls with a vicious grip, causing him to scream in agony. He dropped her, falling to the ground and holding himself as he worked through the pain. Merri's palm was bloody, and I'm not gonna lie, a twinge of sympathy pain for the demon's ruined balls hit me.

"Good job, kitten," I called to her before turning my attention to the last guy.

He stared me down, indecision racing across his face.

"Come get some," I crooned, my smile pure threat. It had been a while since I'd been able to show off like this, and knowing my girl was watching and I was kicking some serious ass was sort of turning me on.

Maybe when we were done here, she'd let me take her up against a tree and play out our own Bacchanalian fantasy.

"Get her out of here, Sin!" Chaos shouted, his body covered in black blood and ichor from the shapeshifter he'd defeated. Malice and Grim were still in the thrall of their attackers, but it looked as though Grim was already coming out of it.

Rushing to my girl, I snatched her up in the cradle of my arms and, as I turned back toward the estate, transported us both to the relative safety of the house. It was a huge power suck to do so, but I'd just topped off and Merri needed a quick escape.

She wobbled on her feet as we appeared back in the château's main foyer. "Since when can you do that?" she asked, leaning into me.

"Forever."

"So why do you guys waste time walking places?"

"That's basically like asking why we don't use a bazooka instead of a fork when we eat. Different tools for different occasions. Plus, it uses a lot of power, and up until recently, we were pretty drained."

"Fair enough," she said with a dry chuckle before her face creased into worried lines. "What were those things?"

"We'll have to save the explanations for later, kitten. I gotta go back and make sure none of those assholes get away. Stay with Christian, all right?"

Christian appeared at the top of the staircase as though I'd summoned him. "Come with me, mademoiselle. I will keep you safe."

"Don't let anything happen to her, Chris. She's the only priority, you got me?"

"Of course."

Grabbing Merri by the nape, I tugged her into me and kissed her hard, not caring that I was mostly coated in dried blood.

"You," I said through a weirdly tight throat. "Don't do anything stupid. We're going to kill these fuckers and regroup. Stay here and let us do our jobs."

Her only response was a swift nod.

"Oh, and kitten?"

"Yeah?"

"I love you too. In case you hadn't figured that out yet."

She opened her mouth to reply, but I vanished and rematerialized in the middle of the carnage with my brothers before she had the chance. As suspected, Malice was still lost in the thick of it with his demon while Chaos and Grim dealt with the remaining monsters. There weren't nearly as many of them as there had been of the humans, but the demons required a bit more effort for us to dispatch. Grim couldn't simply touch them and kill them. They didn't have the requisite souls for his type of magic. But he was just as strong as the rest of us, and he could rip a demon's heart from its chest with a well-placed blow.

Realizing that those two had things in hand, I turned my attention instead to Malice, thinking he might need some help getting free. Cracking my neck and shaking out my arms, I stepped into place behind him and set my hand on his shoulder to establish a connection. The physical contact wasn't necessary for me to slip into his mind, but it certainly made things easier. And right now, every second counted.

But, Sin. Why wouldn't you just kill the demon? You ask. Good question. I would love to tell you. These demons altered consciousness. They sucked their prey into a dreamlike state, much like Merri and I could. This was almost like sleepwalking or a night terror. Everyone knows you don't wake someone up in the middle of that without risking serious damage. The last thing Malice needed was more trauma.

Slipping into someone else's mind was second nature to me, but it was still jarring every time. If only because you never knew what you would find waiting for you on the other side. And this wasn't a normal situation; I was quite literally sliding into a demon's lair. It just so happened to also be Malice-coded.

If I was being honest, I was pretty curious to find out what Malice's deepest, darkest desire would be. Gotta say, though, as open-minded as I was, I was in no way prepared to come face-to-face with Malice standing off with a seven-foot tall purple demon.

"Can you ever forgive me for my absence, Pan?" Malice was asking, a pathetic plea in his voice. "I want to be a father to you. I always wanted to."

Oh shiiiiit. I really shouldn't be seeing this.

"You're not capable of being a father. Why else would my mother bar you from my presence? She knew what a waste of space you were. You'll never be part of my life, no matter how you beg."

Yikes. No wonder Malice was struggling to break free. This had to be a nightmare scenario for him.

"Hey buddy, it's time to go," I called, propelling myself forward until I was right beside Malice. I'd heard the word tormented before, obviously, but I'd never seen it in action. Not like this. A couple more barbed comments from Pan and Malice would be in the fetal position.

"Pan . . . p-please. Just listen to me," he whispered.

"I. Despise. You. And I always will."

One hand on Mal's shoulder, I gripped him hard enough to cause pain and said, "This isn't your son. Open your eyes, Mal. This is trickery."

A shudder ran down Pestilence's body, but his gaze was still locked on the manifestation of his lost child. "Pan, please," he whimpered.

Whimpered.

Fuck my life. He was going to murder me when he realized what I'd seen. He barely forgave Merri, and he *liked* her.

"Okay, listen, I didn't want to do this, but I've got no other choice." It wasn't the wisest decision to interfere, but Malice wasn't getting on top of the creature's power. He'd forgive me. Eventually.

I reached past Mal and grabbed the demon's shoulder, sending my magic into it in an attempt to break the connection between them. If I could get the glamour to drop, Mal would snap out of it.

It was harder than I wanted it to be. Not only were these demons powerful in general, but this one had been allowed to latch onto Malice without challenge, which only strengthened its hold. The longer the fantasy played out, the tighter the bond became until it was the equivalent of mental superglue. We were somewhere in the setting cement stage of things. In other words, difficult but not yet impossible to undo.

It went a long way that my desire to overpower the demon's mind was stronger than the demon's desire to hold on to Mal. They weren't here for us. We were an obstacle keeping them from their goal—Merri. I guess you could say they were just following orders while we were fighting for our lives. Willpower went a long fucking way in evening the score.

Being a horseman didn't hurt either. The demons were badasses, but so were we.

The clash of wills went on until I sensed the first crack. If it were a physical thing, I'd say the demon's knees buckled. I pounced, seizing the opportunity and pouring more of my influence into the opening until I was the only one in control. In a rush of shifting energy, the veil lifted, and Pan disappeared, revealing the truth. He'd never been there at all.

A guttural snarl escaped from somewhere deep inside Malice as the change registered. I released him, backing out of his mind and letting him take control so he could get his vengeance.

It was a thing of terrible beauty, watching Malice rage.

With a movement so fast I almost couldn't register what I was seeing, Mal's hands penetrated the creature's sternum, splitting the bones with a sickening crack.

"Open wide," he growled. "Show me that demented heart."

The demon sputtered and screamed but couldn't move as Malice spread open its chest and exposed the beating black organ. He was a doctor performing surgery. If the doctor was a vengeful god and the surgery was extermination. Maybe he was more of a mortician.

With a cruel smile, Malice tapped a single finger against the creature's heart. The organ visibly stuttered, like a runner losing its rhythm and stumbling before reaching the finish line. Before I could blink, the organ started to bubble and melt. The effect was immediate, and frankly, terrifying. That would have been enough to get the job done, but Malice was nothing if not thorough. His infection spread, moving from the heart to the rest of the vital organs, and it didn't stop until the once alien-like beauty was a pool of bubbling black liquid.

"Well . . . that should do it," I said, hands in my pockets as I rocked back on my heels.

Malice's eyes slid to mine, and for a moment, I thought he might punch me. Instead, he placed his goo-covered hand on my shoulder and said, "Thank you."

To my credit, I didn't flinch. This shirt was a goner, anyway.

"Yeah, man. No problem."

It went without saying I wasn't about to mention what I'd seen. It would go in the vault. If I had one. Which I didn't. But, you know, bro code.

Chaos and Grim joined us, both of them spattered with blood and other things. The demons were nothing more than stains on the earth.

"Fuck yeah, we are such a badass team," I said.

"Always were," Grim said. "Where is she?"

"Safe with Christian. She even promised me she wouldn't leave."

Grim let out a disbelieving chuckle. "And you took her at her word?"

"For once, she seemed to be on board. Probably because she saw what we were up against and realized she would be more of a hindrance," I said.

We exchanged loaded looks, all of us thinking back to Merri's insane takedown of the humans. I'd seen Sabine take down plenty of mortals, had done the same myself even, but never more than one at a time. Merri was something else, powerful in a way none of us fully understood.

"What the fuck just happened?" Chaos asked.

"Well . . ." I started. "As you know, those were lust demons. And we fought them and just won."

Chaos glared at me. "But *how*?"

I opened my mouth, and he stopped me with a dirty palm over the bottom half of my face. "Not you. You," he clarified, pointing to Malice.

Malice looked from the gate and then back toward the house, shaking his head. "Demons should never have been able to pass the barrier."

"So how did they, then?" Grim asked, echoing the original question.

A breeze set the tree limbs rustling, and Malice frowned. "Not here. Let's get back. We need to talk to Christian."

I, for one couldn't wait to get back to Merri. Everything had changed after this fight. I was pretty confident that it wasn't just in relation to me. Everything had changed . . . for all of us.

CHAPTER TWENTY-ONE

MALICE

My mind was an absolute shitshow, to borrow one of Sin's favorite expressions. I hadn't known I was susceptible to a lust demon, but then, they'd never had reason to set their sights on me before. I'd had no defense. None. All my bluff and bluster about Merri needing to work on her mental barriers, and here I was, the weakest link in our chain.

Shameful. I'd never live it down.

"Christian!" I bellowed, forcing myself to push down the distracting emotions trying to control me. "Christian!"

My groundskeeper, resident mage, and most trusted human employee was in for a reckoning. He appeared with Merri at his side at the top of the stairs, looking better than he had but still a bit peaked.

He raised his hands in a placating gesture, already sensing what was coming. "Merri filled me in. I have no explanation, monsieur. It should not have been possible."

Merri appeared behind him, freshly showered and barefoot. "Do you think the humans were a way for them to trick the wards?" she asked as she raced down the stairs and toward us.

I don't know what possessed me, but as soon as she was within reach, I grabbed her and pulled her into my arms. Her sweet scent soothed something inside me, and I couldn't help but take a few deep inhalations of her shampoo.

She accepted the embrace willingly, returning it with a strong one of her own. Then she surprised me by not only staying put but snuggling closer.

"Hi," she murmured.

"Hello, hellcat."

A pointed cough had both of us turning in Chaos's direction, Sin and Grim standing just behind him.

"To answer your question," he said, "it shouldn't work that way."

"But it did," she pointed out.

"It did," he confirmed, arms crossed as he sat back against a sideboard.

Christian scrubbed a hand down his face. "I suppose they could have used some sort of cloaking spell, their possession of the humans in partnership with the spell fully masking the demonic presence, but . . ." He shrugged helplessly. "I've never encountered anything like it. I don't think there's any way to know for sure."

"This cannot happen, Christian. Merri's safety is of the utmost importance. I expect you to rectify this situation."

Merri pulled away from me and looked into my eyes. "How can he? As far as I know, wards don't work like a force field for human bodies. If the demons are using them as Trojan horses, I don't know what we can do."

"I would need an entire coven behind me for something of that caliber."

"Do you have one?"

Christian shook his head. "My family has been on our own for a long time. Our allegiance is to our goddess and this land. Covens have too many rules that conflict with the vows we've already taken."

"Is there someone you trust enough to partner with?" she asked, eyes flicking up to me before returning to him, telling me that the question was for both of us.

Christian let out a heavy sigh. "None that I have connections with. This isn't the sort of favor you spring on someone. It comes with strings. And potential alliances that are in direct conflict with our own interests."

"Politics," Chaos spat.

"*Exactement.*"

A thought wormed its way to the surface, and I looked to Grim. "There may be someone we could ask."

He frowned, not quite following me. Surprisingly, though perhaps by now it shouldn't have been, Merri did.

"What about that guy that sent the video? Asher?"

Grim's gaze went to Merri, then to Chaos, before landing on me at the warrior's nod. "Contact Hades. See what he knows."

"We don't have a way to reach him while the phones are down," I pointed out.

"I might have a way," Christian offered. "But it will take me awhile to gather what I need."

"Do it."

He nodded and rushed off.

"And in the meantime?" Sin asked. "Are we supposed to just sit around and wait for the next attack?"

"Doesn't seem like we have much of a choice," Chaos said. "At least now we know what to expect. And the wards still give us a heads-up, so it's something. Even if it's not much."

That was for me, and I didn't dignify it with a response.

Instead I turned to Merri. "We can't forget the task at hand, even with the enemies we just faced. That's what they want. We've stopped them once again, at least for the time being. Now that the immediate threat has been dealt with, we continue on with our quest to end this apocalypse before Lucifer can claim his throne."

"So . . . fucking?" Sin asked with an amused grin.

"Fucking," I agreed. My eyes never left Merri's, which is why I caught the flare of arousal the instant it sparked.

"Come on then," she said, taking my hand. "It's your turn."

FALLING asleep on purpose was a unique experience. There was no slow, steady descent where you can't quite connect the dots between sleep and consciousness. It was more akin to plunging into a cold pool. Immediate, overwhelming, and more than a little disorientating.

I didn't mind it, though, not when Merri was joining me and I was going to get my chance to show her exactly what being mine meant. This dreamwalk gave me so much Merri couldn't comprehend. The freedom to let go of everything else swirling in my head and focus on her, on us. I also needed to erase the lingering pain of the nightmare that demon had trapped me in, and I couldn't think of a better way than losing myself in Merri.

Or maybe what I was truly trying to do was find myself. Seeing my son—fictional as he'd been—had unmoored me, and I was in desperate need of a safe haven.

"What has you frowning like that, Mal?" Merri's voice pulled me from the threat of despair.

"My thoughts are getting the better of me."

"The demon?" she guessed, expression free from judgment.

I nodded, a muscle twitching in my clenched jaw.

"Come here," she murmured, cupping my cheek with her hand and feathering her lips over mine.

I closed my eyes and just let myself feel her, the tension melting away as quickly as the two of us melted into the kiss. Why couldn't I be this man for her all the time? The one who could give himself over to her without fear of being destroyed again?

Merri let out a soft hum of contentment as she pulled back. My eyes were slow to open, as if keeping them closed might extend the moment we'd just shared. When they finally opened, I found the space around us transformed. I hadn't paid much attention to it when I'd arrived, but I thought it had just been my room from the château. Now it was something far more sumptuous, the bed covered in a thick black comforter and the room filled with candlelight.

I arched a brow and gave her an inquisitive look. "Very romantic, hellcat."

She shrugged, reaching up and brushing her fingers through my hair. "I thought we deserved it. Our first time wasn't what I'd have chosen for us."

Hearing her echo my thoughts from a few days ago made me smile. "Me neither."

"So you like it?"

I grasped her arse and reeled her back into my body. "More than," I admitted, my free hand weaving into her long hair and pulling her face back to mine.

Her little gasp of delight washed over me, settling directly between my legs.

I'd been more than a little bitter that I'd drawn the short straw when it came time to divvy out the dreamwalk assignments. I assumed that being last meant that Merri might forget about what was blossoming between us. But I should have known better. Merri never made any of us feel less than. Whoever she was with was the only person she was thinking about, the only one who mattered. And that was more than enough for me.

Oh hell, I was more of a romantic than I'd ever admitted to myself. But perhaps that wasn't such a bad thing. Perhaps keeping myself closed off from everyone and everything had only hurt me in the end.

Scooping Merri up, I twisted until I could walk us to the bed. "You're brilliant, Merri. In so many ways."

Placing her in the center of the lush bedclothes, I took her in. The delicate black lace covering her was so sheer it was almost obscene, and the fall of her scarlet locks spilled down her shoulders. She was everything I never thought I could have.

I placed a knee on the bed, intending to crawl over her, but she stopped me with a hand to the chest. "This is more to me than just trying to get pregnant and feeding. I need you to know that. It started out as a means to an end, but I'm . . . attached to all four of you."

Any lingering denial fled. Here, if nowhere else, I could be honest. With her and myself.

"For me too. I'm not like the others, Merri. I don't do casual. I don't know how. There's no half-measure. It's all or nothing for me."

Fisting the fabric of my shirt, she pulled me toward her. "All, Malice. Give me all of you."

Warmth spread through my chest, and my lips twitched up in a smile. "I'm pretty sure I warned you about asking me for that."

She matched my smile, her eyes twinkling in the soft golden light. "Malice, you and I both know I am more than a match for you. Do your worst." Then she winked. "And by worst, I mean very, very best."

Kissing her long and slow, I ran my hands down her body until I reached her thighs and the hem of the piss-poor excuse for a nightie. Pain blossomed on my bottom lip as her teeth caught it and she bit down, not hard enough to draw blood, but soundly enough to elicit an erotic groan.

I chuckled. "Naughty, naughty, hellcat."

She purred up at me while simultaneously raking her nails down my back. "Just living up to your name for me."

"Fuck," I said in a harsh whisper.

"That is the idea."

Running my fingers up, up, up until I found her slick, bare pussy, I teased her until she was writhing and begging me to let her come.

"Watch me while I fill you up," I ordered, freeing myself from my clothes and taking my cock in hand.

Her eyes found mine, the bright blue full of want, and it was all directed at me.

My gaze locked with hers, I pressed into her tight opening, memorizing the way her mouth parted on a sigh and the way color spread across her chest and cheeks. The feel of her hot, wet cunt squeezing my cock was even better than I remembered. Last time we'd been frantic with need, but tonight time wasn't an issue. I watched her expression change with every inch I fed into her, little hitches of breath betraying her pleasure. Fuck, she was perfect.

"You feel so good," she breathed.

"Likewise."

"Kiss me," she begged, reaching up for me.

I dropped a fist on either side of her head so our faces were separated by inches. "As you wish."

Then I drove all the way inside her, sinking to the hilt. Our tongues danced as we moved together, trading sighs and moans with each languid thrust. Our pleasure built together, but I never increased my tempo. I wanted to keep us right here on the edge for as long as possible.

Merri never complained, but it wasn't long before her thighs were trembling and she was clutching at both me and the sheets. I needed to be closer to her, to hold her tight and make sure she knew how much this moment meant. Wrapping my arms around her, I closed the distance between us and buried my face in her neck, kissing and biting the soft place where her neck met her shoulder.

"Merri, fuck. I'm close. I'm so fucking close."

"Me too. God, it feels like you've been edging me for hours."

I laughed, but it was little more than a harsh bark. "I wanted to make up for the last time."

She turned until she could meet my gaze again. "Malice, you have nothing to make up for, you . . . You are, and have always been, exactly what I need. You're mine."

The words absolutely decimated what little control I had left.

I came with a last roll of my hips, pressing deep and holding there until I could no longer tell where I ended and she began.

She fed on me; I knew it was happening, but this new connection and honesty between us made that all the more meaningful. I gave her what she needed and together, we created something beautiful. All I wanted was for us to continue on this path forever.

Pulling out of her, I rolled onto my back and brought her with me until she was resting on my chest. I ran my fingertips along her spine and pressed a kiss to her forehead.

"I just want to hold you for a while, if you don't mind."

She hummed happily. "Hold me as long as you want. Never let go."

Emotion clogged my throat, and it took me longer than usual before I could form a response.

"Careful, hellcat. You might get what you want."

CHAPTER TWENTY-TWO

MERRI

Who knew the horseman Pestilence would giggle in his sleep? I sure didn't, but here we were, napping on my bed after an amazing dreamwalk together, and the man giggled loud enough it woke me.

Out of all the horsemen, Malice and Grim were both restrained, but it was Malice who always felt the most closed off. I'd managed to learn things about Grim through his love of plants and the conflict he felt about his power, but Malice was locked up tighter than a cock cage—or maybe a chastity belt. So this rare moment of unfiltered vulnerability from him was the equivalent of waving a hot fudge sundae under my nose. It was absolutely irresistible.

His chest rose and fell in that deep, rhythmic way you only achieved through sleep, and I wanted nothing more than to stay here with my body against his, listening for more of those uninhibited laughs his dream was causing. Glancing up at his face, I had to fight a sigh at his handsome features. Chiseled cheekbones, an aristocratic nose, insanely long eyelashes that went blond at the tips, full kissable lips with just the tiniest indentation in the middle of the bottom one, which somehow only made it seem more lush—hence the reason I bit the fuck out of it during our dream. He even had the slightest dusting of freckles across the bridge of his nose that made him seem almost boyish in his sleep. Even with the sexy golden stubble covering his jaw.

He might be the lord of Pestilence, but he was pretty as all hell.

"I feel you staring at me, hellcat," he murmured, eyes still closed.

"Is that a crime?"

One amethyst eye opened, then closed again. "No. I suppose not. Unless you're plotting against me."

"Mmmm . . . not at the moment." I trailed my fingertip across his defined chest, circling one nipple and watching as it tightened. "I'll let you know if that changes."

"I'm waiting with bated breath."

At first I thought he might scoot away from me, leave, and go take care of whatever it was Pestilence did, but he simply tightened his hold on me and pulled me closer.

I didn't anticipate the wave of relief the cuddle sent through me. I guess part of me had been worried that the intimacy we'd shared in the dream wouldn't translate to the real world. Not because he hadn't meant it, but because Malice didn't usually allow himself to express his feelings.

"You're not doing a very good job of hiding your thoughts, Merri. I can feel your relief."

"I wasn't trying to hide anything from you. This is nice, you and me in bed. I just didn't expect you to be a cuddles-after-sex kind of guy."

A low, rumbling chuckle vibrated through his chest as he ran his knuckles down my side. "Honestly, I didn't think I was either. In my limited experience, cuddling wasn't on the menu."

This felt like an opening to ask about his last relationship, but I didn't want to ruin the moment with something that clearly still weighed on him. Before I could decide whether to risk it, Malice let out another laugh and an amused, "Fuck."

"What's so funny?"

"Sin."

I pushed myself up on my elbow so I could look down at him. "You're lying here with me thinking about *Sin*?" I asked in mock outrage.

"He's going to be so jealous I'm the one getting all the romantic snuggle time. Especially after what you admitted."

It didn't feel right talking about my feelings for Sin while lying in Malice's bed, at least not before Sin and I talked about it, so I just let out a soft hum and snuggled back into Mal's side.

"That's between me and him. I owe him that privacy."

"I owe him as well. After what he did for me, he deserves my respect."

"What did he do?"

Malice heaved a sigh, his fingers tightening their grip on me for a second before he relaxed. "I couldn't get free of the demon's snare. He rescued me."

I could sense his frustration with himself, so I booped him on the nose. "You're a very handsome damsel."

"Quite."

Tension had his jaw set and brows pulled tight. I wasn't going to let him shut down, not now that we'd made such progress.

"What did the demon show you?"

"One of my greatest desires and most terrible fears, all wrapped in one package."

Malice didn't have to say anything else. I knew exactly what he was referring to. Somehow we'd already found our way back to the topic I was most curious about. Instinct warned me that I might never get another chance to ask him about his son.

"She showed you Pan," I stated, keeping my voice even and free of any kind of judgment.

His knuckles continued to drag back and forth along my body, a soothing gesture for both of us, I suspected. "Yes. She knew he would be the key to my undoing."

"Have you ever . . ." I bit down on my lip, second-guessing

myself. The last thing I wanted was for Malice to think I was prying and shut me out again. It certainly hadn't ended well for me the last time I'd treaded where he hadn't wanted me.

"Tried to find him?" he guessed.

I nodded.

"Countless times."

"No luck?"

"I've seen him. Watched him grow."

"But you haven't met him?"

"No. Not once. I couldn't risk his life for my own selfish desires."

I hated this for him. So much. All Malice wanted was to know his son, but if he took any opportunity to speak to him face-to-face, Pan would be killed.

"I can't imagine how hard that is for you. I'm so sorry, Mal."

He let out a derisive snort. "It's probably for the best. The last thing he needs is another shit parent interfering with his life. I mean, I'm a horseman. What do I know about rearing a child?"

I sat up and adjusted my body until I was facing him. "What does anyone know about it? No one goes into parenthood with the knowledge of how to not fuck up their kid."

"Isn't that the entire point?"

"Yep. And even the best parents still mess up. No one is perfect."

Malice made a soft, non-committal sound, his eyes not quite meeting mine.

"I mean it, Mal. You would make an excellent father. Not because you'd be perfect at it, but because you would be you."

His eyes snapped to mine, hope and disbelief at war in the amethyst depths. "You're just being kind."

"I'm not. Look at what you've done for me. You're an amazing teacher. Patient when you want to be. Think of all the things you could have taught your son. And you're actually pretty selfless. Whenever I've needed you most, you've set aside your own interests to take care of me. Not just once, but many times. And I know without a single doubt that you would do it again without a second thought. You're devoted, Malice. Loyal. Caring."

He stopped me with a finger on my lips. "Enough," he said in a rough voice.

Taking his hand, I held it tightly before looking him directly in the eyes and saying, "You are a good man, Malice. One of the best men I've ever known. You deserve to be happy."

He held my gaze, and I watched his throat bob a couple of times before he managed, "I have had little opportunity to know happiness, Merri. But you . . . you make me happy."

Well, shit.

My eyes burned with the threat of tears, and I had to blink a few times to clear them. "Ditto."

Malice snorted a laugh. "Look at us making declarations." He rolled his eyes as he let out a long-suffering sigh. "I will have you know, Meredith Deveraux, that I make it a point to avoid feelings."

"Oh yeah?"

He nodded, his lips twisting into a wry grin. "It would seem that when it comes to you, I break all of my rules."

That made my heart flutter, along with other parts of me. "Good. You need to loosen up."

"Think I'm a stodgy old horseman, do you?"

"Yep."

He surprised me by grabbing me around the waist and pulling me astride him. "I'll show you."

And that's exactly what he did all morning long.

CHAPTER TWENTY-THREE

CHAOS

My fist connected with the heavy sandbag I'd suspended from a beam in the converted carriage house. Plumes of dust exploded from the back and sides as the seams threatened to split. I'd already destroyed three others, their carcasses sitting abandoned on the now sand-covered floor. Malice wouldn't be thrilled with the mess, but what he didn't know wouldn't hurt him.

A growl ripped from my throat as I let loose another punch that sent the bag flying across the room.

Make that four carcasses.

The whole point of coming down here early was to get Malice off my mind. Namely, who he was with and what they were doing.

Grabbing a fresh bag, I hung it up and got back in place.

There's no reason to be jealous. It was his turn. She wasn't choosing him over you.

But what if that's exactly what happened?

My chest gave a sharp pang, stopping me mid-swing. I'd never known jealousy like this before. The only time in my existence I'd been in competition with anyone, it had been battle related. And that was easily remedied. Didn't have the skills to get the attention I wanted? Train harder. So long as I was willing to put in the work, it would eventually pay off.

But Merri wasn't a commanding officer. She was a woman. If she made up her mind that Malice . . . or Sin . . . was who she wanted, there was nothing I could do to sway her. I was at a complete loss, my need for control spinning me into a frenzy I couldn't rein in.

I was so far up my own ass, I didn't hear the approaching footsteps.

"Wow, did they insult your mother or something?" Merri asked, inspecting the mess I'd made of the space.

Landing a powerful blow to the center of the sandbag, I heaved a sigh as it split.

That was five.

"You're late. As usual," I snapped, turning to face her.

"Ooookay, then. Someone woke up on the wrong side of the bed."

It hurt to look at her. She was fresh as a fucking daisy, clearly bursting with power, and its effect on her nearly sent me to my knees. Was it too much to hope for one of her gentle touches? Everyone else seemed to get one.

Another growl escaped me as I scrubbed a hand down my face. I swear to God, I was ready to crawl across this mess of a floor just to kiss the top of her damn shoe.

I fucking hated this. I was *not* this person. I was a proud Spartan warrior who faced legions without fear. I was the horseman War who could decimate armies with the sweep of my sword. Who knew Merri would be my kryptonite?

Ever since Sin made his declaration yesterday, I hadn't been able to stop thinking about it. She fucking loved him. How did I stand a chance with her now? I'd lost her just when I realized how much I wanted her.

I was my very own Greek tragedy.

"Helloooo, earth to Chaos. An apocalyptic one, but you know, still earth." Her smile was so charming, goddamn blue birds might as well flutter around her head like a crown. I half expected music to play with every step she took, or sunshine to burst out of her perfect ass.

"We should start with sparring. You're out of practice." Adjusting my stance, I readied the makeshift pad we used for her safety, pulling the modified straps over my forearm and holding it in front of my torso. "Remember the rotation I taught you?"

Merri nodded, tightening her ponytail as she repeated it back to me, "Right, left, right, left hook, and front kick. Then switch."

I smacked the pad and braced. "Let's go then. We're wasting time."

Her jabs were powerful enough they'd do damage to a human, but nowhere near so strong as to drop a demon. I worried, as I always did, that if she found herself up against a supernatural creature without us around to help, she'd be a sitting duck. She needed us with her, and even if she chose Sin or Malice over me, I'd always be there for her. I'd protect her for the rest of her days while one of them claimed her nights.

Fuck.

Just the thought of not getting to have her in my arms again after her choice was made sent agony ripping through me. I was so caught up in the thought, I didn't realize my grip had relaxed and the shield positioning had slipped. Merri was still focused on herself, like I'd taught her, so it wasn't until the exploding pain in both my cock and balls that either of us understood what happened.

I crashed to my knees with a garbled, "Motherfucker."

"Ohmigod! I'm so sorry. Are you okay?"

Nausea rolled my stomach as the shield fell and I clutched my throbbing crotch. Everything hurt and I was dying.

"No," I wheezed, tears blurring my eyes.

"Chaos, I . . . shit. I didn't know you dropped your shield. I was just focused on the—"

"Stop. Talking." Every word was a chore, but I needed her to stop apologizing for my mistake. She was kneeling next to me at this point, but being upright was more than I could bear, so I curled in on myself and rolled to the side.

"Can I get you something?" she whispered, as if her volume was the issue. "An ice pack, maybe?"

"Just leave me here to die."

She plopped down on her ass next to me. "Well, that's a little dramatic, don't you think?"

"No."

Merri laughed. "Aw, come on. I'm sure that isn't the first time you've gotten clocked in the nuts."

"It's not any less terrible with repetition, Red. It's always bad. The worst."

She ran her fingers through my hair, brushing a lock away from my face. "What can I do?"

"Nothing. I just have to wait it out."

"Are you sure? I could kiss him better. You know, since I was so mean to him."

There was a definite twitch of interest, but it only sent another wave of agony through me. "For the love of God, please stop. I can't—"

Picking up on my distress, she smothered her laugh. "I really am sorry. I feel terrible. I should have realized you were distracted and pulled the kick." She bit her lip and studied me, her hand sort of hovering over my head. "Do you want to talk about it?"

"My mangled dick?"

She stuck her tongue out at me as I gingerly got to my feet. "Whatever is on your mind?"

"I'm fine." Holding a hand out, I helped her up before I began walking with slow steps to the end of the room. The best way to get over this kind of injury was to walk it off. Even if it hurt like a sonofabitch.

"You're clearly not. You'll barely look at me."

I gave her a look filled with meaning. "Looking at you hurts."

A wounded expression crossed her face before her eyes dropped to the hand at my crotch and her eyes widened. "*Oh.* Gotcha. Guess I should have gone for the baggy sweats and loose shirt combo instead of this lycra number."

"Wouldn't make a difference. You could be wearing a flour sack and I'd still want you."

Her cheeks went pink, gaze now trained on the floor. How could this beautiful, powerful creature still be shy around any of us? She certainly wasn't shy around Sin.

"Do you really love him?" I found myself blurting like an absolute idiot.

Her head snapped up. "What?"

Ignoring the dulling pain between my legs, it was nothing compared to what was happening in my chest anyway, I closed the distance between us. "Do. You. Love. Him?"

Confusion sent her brows veeing low over her eyes. "*That's* what this is about?"

"Yes. Because I don't understand any of it. If you were going to choose him all along, why give me hope? Why teach me what love looks like and show me I am capable of it if you had no intention of choosing me?"

"What are you—"

"No. I'm not done. Until you, I'd never had any interest in love. It wasn't something I considered possible. Or even important. I was loyal to nothing but my cause. But then you tumbled into my life and told me about it. Showed me what loving someone could mean. Gave me hope for a life I never imagined. Now it's the only thing I want for myself. So I need you to choose me, Merri. If you are going to love anyone, love *me*. Don't abandon what we have for Sin. Let me prove to you we should be together."

My heart felt like it was ready to burst out of my chest by the time the words finished falling from my lips.

"Are you done now?" Merri asked, head tilted to the side and expression strangely hard to read.

I ran a hand over the back of my neck. "Um, yeah."

She moved until she was standing directly in front of me, her hands cupping either side of my face and tugging me down until we were mostly eye level. "Silly warrior. I already have chosen you. I chose all of you when I agreed to stay here and save the world with you."

Shock ran over my skin like someone had touched me with a live wire. "But . . . Sin."

"Yes. I love him."

"I see," I rasped, understanding now that she'd never love me the way she did him, but she would still choose us all. I didn't like it, but if that was all I could have, I'd take it.

"I love Sin. But, Chaos," she whispered. "Look at me, please?"

I couldn't deny her, even though my heart ached at the look in her eyes.

There was so much sincerity ringing in her voice when she added, "I love *you* too."

I couldn't believe what I was hearing. Generally speaking, I considered myself a fairly intelligent being, but love and all the emotions that came with it were as foreign to me as another planet. Which was why the best I could manage was a strangled "How?"

"What do you mean, how?"

"You said that when you love someone, they become the center of your world. So how can you love more than one person? That's too many centers. By definition, they'd be in conflict with one another."

Her lips quirked in a slight smile, but she schooled her expression. "My axis can be whatever I want it to be. Love isn't finite. There is always room for more of it."

"So I have to share your heart." It was a statement because I knew the truth of it.

"Yes."

"But only with the other three." I shared everything else with the horsemen, so in a way, it made perfect sense we'd all be in this together. Not just to spite Lucifer, but because we'd chosen each other.

Her lips twitched again. "Well, maybe another one or two."

"What?" That flame of jealousy sparked again.

"You are trying to get me pregnant, aren't you? I'll have to make room in my heart if you're successful."

Oh.

An embarrassed flush crept up my cheeks. I couldn't believe I was jealous of my future child. The gods were laughing at me for my hubris.

"Of course," I muttered, sliding my palm down until it rested over her lower belly. "Do you think we were successful?"

Glancing down her body, she took a long breath before looking at me again. "It's too soon to know. I'm sure Daddy Death will tell us as soon as he can."

"I guess in the meantime, we just keep trying, then."

She smirked. "Why am I not surprised that's your suggestion?"

"Because I'm a man who appreciates a good strategy?"

"Uh-huh."

Merri playfully walked her fingers down my chest, not stopping until she reached my waistband.

"What are you doing, little succubus?"

"Seducing you?"

Humming in approval, I leaned down, even though my cock still ached. I'd push through. I'd fought battles with broken bones and nearly cleaved in two. I could deal with a bruise.

Hooking a finger under her chin, I tipped her head up. "Say it again."

It only took her a second to catch my meaning. Throwing her arms around my neck, she pressed her body close to mine. "I love you, Chaos."

Warmth filled my chest, expanding until I was enveloped in its glow. There was no stopping the smile that stretched across my face.

"I love you too, Red."

She giggled. "You know, you could have just started with that."

Huffing out my own laugh, I said, "Words are hard."

"I know. We got there in the end."

Brushing my lips over hers, I whispered, "Yeah. We did."

Yoga was calming.

Yoga was fucking hard.

It should have pulled my focus from the heavy things weighing on me. But with each measured breath, each pose, each pull of my muscles, I didn't find the meditative ease I was searching for. Nope. I was assaulted by racing thoughts. Pregnancy. Apocalypse. Lucifer. Demons. Freaking lightning strikes and cute weirdos in my dreams. I'd been so busy racing from one crisis to the next that I hadn't had time to dwell on any of them.

Until now, apparently.

I guess the rare moment of solitude was the perfect time for it all to come crashing down and send me on one hell of a panic spiral. Which, frankly, I just did not have the time for. Because the world was still ending, no matter what I thought about it. And I'd much rather deal with it head-on than metaphorically curled up in the fetal position.

"Focus, Meredith," I chastised myself as I stood tall in mountain pose before swan-diving into a terrible forward fold.

Every pang of discomfort pulled my focus and let more thoughts in.

Lilith's continued silence. Asher and the resistance he was apparently leading. Whether the horsemen had been successful. Whether another demon attack was incoming. If Andi and Cole were still alive.

"Fuck it," I grumbled before settling myself on the plush carpet and getting into a cross-legged position. If yoga wasn't working, maybe some meditation would.

Shoving all the intrusive thoughts out of my mind, I focused instead on counting my breaths. I pictured each inhale filling the now empty space in my mind, cleansing and purifying, while each exhale would send the thoughts further away. It wasn't a perfect metaphor, but it was working better than yoga.

The quiet room afforded me tranquility, my breaths now soft and slow rather than loud and purposeful. In their place, I heard the wind in the trees outside, the leaves rustling, and the gentle crunch of gravel under someone's feet.

"There you are, love. I've been missing you." A voice I hadn't heard for the better part of a week floated through my head.

"Luc?" I whispered, unable to open my eyes to see if he was really there.

A tickle at my ear preceded his crooned response. "I love the sound of my name on your lips."

I tried to turn my head, but I couldn't get my body to respond. I knew I wasn't asleep. I could feel myself sitting in the middle of my room, my tailbone a little sore from the lack of padding beneath it and my legs and arms heavy in their resting position, but I couldn't move.

"Why can't I see you? Am I dreaming?"

"Just a little daydream. About me, as it should be. You must've missed me too. Me and all the fun we have together." Fingers brushed my throat and trailed down until they traced my collarbone. "It's been ages since our last chat. What have you been up to?"

"Oh, you know, just trying to survive the end of the world. No big deal."

"With your four guardians keeping you sequestered like a princess in a tower, I'm sure that hasn't been so hard."

Memories of the demon attack whipped through my mind. "You'd be surprised."

"Your mind is buzzing with stressful energy, darling."

"What can I say? It's a stressful time."

Warm breath, followed by soft lips on my neck, made me shiver. Damn, my fantasies were good.

"You know how to decompress, don't you? Release some of that oxytocin your body craves."

An orgasm would be pretty nice right now. Sometimes a girl just needed to take care of herself.

What happened to the meditation, Merri?

As soon as the thought registered, it dissipated, sort of like ink in water.

"I guess I could be persuaded," I murmured as strong fingers worked at the knots in my neck and shoulders. Everything felt so real, I'd have sworn Luc was in the room with me. But that was impossible. He was a creation of my imagination. A beautiful one.

"Let me have you, love. I'll make you feel so good you'll forget all your troubles." Teeth sank into my earlobe, the bright pain making me yelp in surprise, but a flood of arousal followed.

"Mmm, Luc." It was all I could do to get the soft moan out.

I expected another kiss or caress, but instead a hard shove tipped me backwards. My eyes snapped open as I caught myself before I fell. Luc was gone, my daydream rudely interrupted, and a very familiar shadow man loomed over me.

"Grim! What the hell was that for?"

Grim

I sat in the morning room with my chair facing the large windows, but I wasn't watching the world outside. I was focused on what my shadow saw: Merri meditating in her room, her eyes closed, hair piled on her head in a messy bun, shoulders tense even though she was attempting to harness inner peace.

I'd taken to watching over her whenever she was alone, telling myself it was for her own good, but that wasn't entirely true. She had become something I craved. I knew my obsession with her was bordering on unhealthy, if it wasn't fully there already. But I couldn't find it in myself to care. Merri was mine. Mine to watch over. Mine to protect. Mine to . . . well.

A change in her breathing alerted me that all was not as serene as it appeared, though it wasn't until she started talking to herself that I realized something was very wrong. The odd phrase here and there could be explained away, but she was holding an entire one-sided conversation.

"It's a stressful time . . . I guess I could be persuaded . . . Mmm, Luc."

That last one got my back up. *Luc?*

Tensing in my chair, I sent my shadow out from the corner where he'd been lurking and used him to jolt her out of whatever trance she was caught in. I held on to the connection with him, ensuring I'd miss nothing while summoning the power I'd need to teleport to her room.

Merri fell backward from the power of the shove but caught herself before she could make contact with the ground. Her eyes snapped open, a cross look on her face as she registered my shadow form. "Grim! What the hell was that for?"

She hadn't even finished speaking before I materialized in front of my shadow, our twin visions momentarily superimposing before solidifying into one. Glowering down at her, I snarled, "Who the fuck is Luc?"

Merri blinked up at me, her nose wrinkling in confusion. "Huh?"

"You heard me. Now answer the fucking question."

She got to her feet, cheeks flushed with embarrassment. "No."

"What was that?" The way my palm itched to redden her arse for her defiance had me gritting out the words.

"I don't want to tell you about my personal fantasies."

The room dimmed as shadows burst out of me, the dark growl of my voice betraying exactly what I thought about her fantasizing about other men. "There are only four men you should be fantasizing about, wildflower. Luc isn't one of them. Tell me."

If she was impressed by my little display of power, she didn't show it. Instead, she shrugged before sitting on her bed. "He's just someone I dream about."

A harsh laugh escaped me. "You dream about someone named

Luc and didn't think that was relevant information to share with the men protecting you?"

"He's not real. He's my subconscious."

"You cannot possibly be that stupid."

She reeled back as if I'd slapped her. "Excuse me?"

"What do you think Luc is short for, Merri?"

"Lucas?"

"Try again."

"Lucian?"

I pinched the bridge of my nose. "No, Merri. Lucifer. Luc is short for *Lucifer*. You know, the creature scouring the earth for you. The one man who cannot find you, but will stop at nothing until he does. The one who wants to use you and your body to end the fucking world."

There was not a doubt in my mind that I had the right of it. Chaos had taught me long ago true coincidence was rare to the point of nonexistence. The chances of Merri having innocent, totally unrelated to our current situation dreams about a man named Luc? Impossible.

She paled, mouth dropping open. "I . . . but . . . how could he find me in my dreams? He's not an incubus."

"I don't know, but I also have no doubt he's figured out a way. How long have you been dreaming of him?" Every word was like a punch to the gut. We'd failed her, and we hadn't even known it.

"A few days after you took me."

Blinding rage nearly swallowed me whole as a new, terrifying thought gripped me. "Has he fucked you in your dreams?"

"Wh-what? No! No, of course not."

I glared at her, silently willing her to tell me the truth if she was trying to hide it from me.

"The only fucking that's been happening is with you four. I swear."

It took several moments before I could relax enough to release the breath I'd been holding. All this time, he'd been right under our noses, and we'd had no idea. But then, he was Lucifer, a master of all things deceit and trickery. We should have realized he'd find a way. We should have . . . I blew out a breath and hung my head. It didn't matter what we should have done; the facts wouldn't change. Lucifer had gotten to her.

"I don't see why you're so upset. It was just a daydream—"

My gaze snapped back to hers. "Just a daydream? Come on, Merri. You know better than that. Even if it was something as innocuous as a dream, you know exactly how real and dangerous those can be. But setting all that aside, what happened here wasn't *just* anything. You were in a trance, Merri."

"No," she said, shaking her head. "My mind had just wandered while I was meditating . . ."

"You were talking and completely unaware of your surroundings. He had you completely in his thrall."

She opened her mouth to deny it but couldn't.

"What happens next time if one of us isn't there to pull you out? Or worse, if he tricks you into giving him the very thing he needs."

"He won't."

"You moaned his name." I hated how hurt I sounded, but I couldn't disguise the way that made me feel.

Guilt flashed across her face, and I knew my suspicions were correct. He'd been trying to seduce her. More than that, he'd been well on his way to succeeding.

She shrugged helplessly. "He told me it would relax me. I thought I was alone. You stopped him from getting anywhere close, though." Silence stretched between us for a beat before she tentatively asked, "Are we going to talk about why you keep spying on me?"

The last thing happening right now was me admitting to my obsession. Especially when it was the thing that just saved her.

"It's a good thing I was, wasn't it?"

She looked down at her knees, hands clasped between them.

I hated to see my courageous and defiant wildflower's spirit so wilted, but not as much as I hated the thought that we'd left her in harm's way. "These dreams with him cannot continue."

Big blue eyes locked onto mine. "I don't know how to keep him out."

Neither did I. But there was one horseman who specialized in exactly that, and he'd clearly been neglecting his curriculum.

"Come with me."

"Where are we going?"

"To talk to Malice."

CHAPTER

TWENTY-FIVE

MALICE

The rustle of the paper as I turned a page of my favorite issue of *The Lancet* filled my room. I'd read this one so many times I had the text memorized, but if I didn't give my mind something to focus on aside from all the ways Merri had infiltrated my heart, I'd go mad. My head spun with worries about how this could go epically wrong, fears that she'd see the light and leave me after only just getting me to trust again, and even worse, hope for the possibility of actual happiness.

Me? Happy? Without a plague in sight? What was the world coming to?

Oh, right, it was ending.

That tracked.

My door swung open with enough force to hit the wall, and I was sure the handle left a dent in the ancient plaster.

"Oi, careful with—"

"Are you fucking serious?" Grim asked, interrupting me as I geared up to scold him. "Lucifer is mucking about in Merri's mind, and you're in here having a nice lie down and *reading*?"

My journal fell forgotten from my fingers. "What do you mean

Lucifer is mucking about in Merri's mind?" My eyes snapped to the redhead in question, peeking guiltily around Grim's side. "Did you forget everything I've taught you?"

"She didn't even know it was him. He's been playing in her dreams for weeks."

Merri's guilt vanished and was replaced by irritation as she crossed her arms under her ample chest. "She is right here and would appreciate not being talked over."

Grim twisted his body to the side and waved an arm as if gesturing for her to go on ahead.

I couldn't help but raise a brow as the bastard invited her to enter *my* bedroom. Not that I'd have stopped her, but it wasn't exactly his place, was it? It wasn't just my room; it was my bloody château. Where did he get off playing Lord of the Manor?

"Grim is right. I didn't know it was happening. I thought he was just a dream lover my brain made up to help me cope with loneliness."

The way my whole body clenched at the word lover had to have been obvious. There was no disguising the reaction. I saw the same echoed in Grim's countenance, though it was much more subtle. We were past the point of not caring who she wanted, fictional or otherwise.

Merri definitely clocked my response, but if I was expecting some sort of remorse on her part, I was hugely disappointed. She flung her hands up, voice raising to nearly a shout, "It was a *dream,* Malice. You cannot possibly be mad at me for a dream!"

"I sure as hell can when it's one of *your* dreams."

"What does that mean? I don't go around policing your dreams. What gives you the right to have opinions about mine?"

"The difference, hellcat, is that you are a succubus, and the dream realm is your fucking playground. You get a choice in what happens in your dreams, and you chose to flirt with another man."

"Not just a man," Grim interjected. "The devil himself."

"Oh, bite me," Merri muttered.

"Careful, wildflower."

"Or what? You'll do exactly that? Doubtful. That's big talk for someone who can't even touch me."

"He can't, but I can. And I'll do a whole lot more than bite you."

The pulse of arousal that hit the room was wholly out of place for the simmering rage and fear Grim and I were doing very little to suppress.

"Sit down, Merri, and control yourself. Now is not the time for any of us to drown in lust. We can save that for later." I softened my voice on the last, needing her to know I would give her exactly what she wanted once we dealt with the crisis at hand.

I could sense the war taking place within her. She was like a cornered cat, ready to bite and swipe her way out of an unwanted encounter. But she also knew that Lucifer's infiltration was not to be taken lightly. And Merri might be stubborn, but she wasn't stupid. She may not want to be in the middle of a lecture from Grim and me, but she recognized that there was no getting out of it.

She flounced past Grim and flopped beside me on the bed. "I don't know what you want me to say. He got in. And I'm pretty sure he'll do it again, because I have absolutely no idea how I'm supposed to keep him out."

"So that's it? You're just going to roll over and accept it? I thought you were made of stronger stuff than that."

The way she looked at me, as though I'd dealt her the most vile insult known to man, had me fighting a smirk. Bingo.

"No. I'm not accepting anything. But I don't know what to do."

I sat up, taking her by the hand and tugging until she was facing me. "Let me help with that."

"How?"

"Let me in. I want to see what I can find in those fragments of your dreams that are still in your mind."

Taking a long, slow breath, she nodded before locking eyes with me. "You might see something you don't like."

"I'm positive that will be the case."

"Great." The deadpan delivery didn't go unnoticed.

"Get on with it, you two. We need to see how far this has gone," Grim rumbled, taking a seat in the armchair nearest the fireplace.

"If you're going to stay, you'll be silent," I shot at him. "We've got enough to deal with at the moment, and the absolute last thing either of us needs right now is you riding our arses."

Grim's eyes seemed to shine with unholy light as the corner he sat in was suddenly overcome with shadow. "Just pretend I'm not here, then."

Merri let out a humorless chuckle. "Easier said than done."

"Eyes on me, hellcat. Don't look at him."

She obeyed like it was her job, and fuck if that didn't do something to me. Before I could respond to the way my heart stuttered at the eye contact, I fell into her subconsciousness, wading through memories and snippets of dreams as though it were the ocean.

Dreams were not like lived memories; they were fragments at best, which meant I was only catching whispers. Still, they were enough for me to be sure that Lucifer had, in fact, infiltrated Merri's mind. Even if I hadn't seen the tosser's face as he worked harder than an antibacterial wipe during a pandemic to seduce her, I'd have known it was him.

Slipping out of her mind and back to the present, I cut a glance at Grim, correctly assuming he'd want confirmation.

"And?"

"It was Lucifer. No doubt about it. I'm surprised he used his real face, though. That seems rather lazy."

"He probably didn't see any reason to hide. Besides, he always has been something of an attention whore. He'd hate it if she went and fell for someone other than him. He needs the credit."

"True," I mused, my gaze returning to Merri's pinched expression.

"I feel violated," she muttered, hands rubbing up and down on her arms like she was warding off a chill.

"You did nothing wrong. He is a master of lies and seduction.

There was no way for you to know that's who he was." Grim's gentle words surprised me, but he was right. Lucifer was so skilled at deception that he'd have you sacrificing your friends and family because he asked you to and then thanking him when it was done. I'd seen it.

"I almost . . ." The words died on her tongue.

"I know," I murmured. I'd caught the tail end of his last visit to her. "If he'd been successful, this would be over."

"But he wasn't." Grim stood, his shadows spreading out beneath him as his anger built.

Playing with one of her cuticles, Merri spoke low enough it was obvious she didn't think we'd hear. "Maybe I'm already pregnant, and it wouldn't have mattered."

Grim, as was his wont, did not give her the grace of pretending he didn't hear. "You're not."

Her shoulders slumped almost instantly. "Well, fuck."

"Yes. That about sums it up," Grim agreed.

"How do I keep him out? He's going to be angry if I make it obvious I know who he is."

My gut said we needed to keep her occupied at all times. One of us would have to be in her dreams, guarding her even when we weren't fucking. But the reality was, we didn't get to decide that. It wasn't us who visited Merri's dreams; it was her who visited ours. She ran the show.

My brain buzzed in the way it always did when I was on the brink of a new and, dare I say, brilliant discovery. There was something to Merri being in control of the dream realm. I just couldn't quite see it clearly.

"For the time being," I began, "you will need to play along with him. Keep him on the hook, and never let him get what he wants. I'm guessing he's already attempted to get your location and find out as much information as he can?"

Taking her lower lip between her teeth, she worried at it before answering. "Yes. Now that you mention it, he did seem to pry, but so

CHAPTER TWENTY-FOUR

MERRI

Moving through cobra and back into downward dog, I breathed through the stretch down my tight hamstrings as I lifted my ass in the air and did my damndest to create a triangle with my body. I hadn't been as diligent with my weekly yoga practice since being abducted by the grump brigade. And before you come at me, I know if I want to get better, I should be doing it every day. I'm sorry that I've been a little distracted by the world ending.

And by all the sex . . . though, honestly, I'm not really sorry about that one.

I let out an exaggerated exhale to reclaim my own attention—sort of the way you might clear your throat when trying to get someone's attention behind the counter when they're clearly ignoring you, except in this case, I'm the rude counter girl in question, and it's my mental health I'm ignoring.

My thoughts had been getting the better of me all afternoon, thus the yoga. I was attempting to find my zen. So far, it wasn't working.

Yoga was peaceful.

carefully it always made sense. I explained it away as my brain working through things."

I nodded. "Of course, because that's what he wanted you to believe. Not that I love to give the devil his due, but he's earned each of his monikers. He's had plenty of time to hone his craft."

She huffed out a breath. "So I just play along and let him lead me like a lamb to the slaughter? What if he catches on?"

"Then you force him out."

"How?"

"The same way you end any other dream. You wake up."

"I can't just will myself awake," she said with an incredulous laugh. "Can I?"

"I suppose the only way to know for sure is to try," Grim grumbled. "Just . . . take one of us with you when you do it."

"What do you mean? That's not how the dreamwalks work. I can't force people to just fall asleep and wake up at my whim."

I laughed. "Yes you can. You've done it more than once."

"No, I haven't. I have to seek out your subconscious realm"—she waved a hand as if we should all have a fully comprehensive understanding of said realm—"which is how I join you in your dreams. How can I do that if you aren't already asleep?"

"Merri," I murmured, placing a hand on her knee, "did you really never stop to consider that your seeking us out in that realm is what makes us fall asleep and join you there?"

"Well . . . no."

"All right, then. So the next time you dreamwalk, you will make the choice to end it at random. Control all aspects of how it starts and how it finishes."

"But it's not *my* dream. I'm not in control at all."

"Hellcat," I said with a chuckle. "I think we've just arrived at the crux of the issue. This whole time, you've believed that you are simply a passenger, but the truth is far more complex."

"But aren't I a passenger?"

"No, sweet girl. You're not just the one driving the car. You're the whole fucking vehicle. And the road. And the map."

"Really?" Her nose did that adorable thing it always did when she was uncertain. I wanted to smooth out the little ridges with the pad of my thumb. But not while Grim was here to bear witness.

"Tonight with Sin, test the theory. What do you have to lose?"

Determination flashed in her eyes. "Tonight."

CHAPTER TWENTY-SIX

SIN

Fuck, I loved a warm ocean breeze across my bare skin. Even if it was conjured by my own mind. Merri sighed and stretched, the black string bikini she was wearing doing wonderful things for her curves. A shaft of sunlight spilled in through the break in the cabana's curtains, hitting both my legs and Merri's, which were tangled together.

She picked up a fruity umbrella drink and took a sip. "This is heaven, and I never want to leave."

Reaching out, I tucked a strand of her hair back behind her ear. "We don't have to. Let's just ride out the apocalypse right here."

"Is that an option? Won't our bodies atrophy or something?"

I considered the question, realizing I had no idea, so I shrugged. "Worth it?"

"Probably."

I couldn't keep from kissing her, not when her soft lips were so close and I could smell the sweet vanilla of her lip gloss. Leaning in, I closed the distance between us and claimed her mouth in a slow and deliberate kiss. When she parted her lips, I used the opening to tease her tongue with mine and deepen it.

She melted beneath me, her luscious body cocooning mine as I readjusted our positions so I was mostly lying on top of her. My hands worked their way down her body until I was tugging at the flimsy string holding her bottoms together.

"You know, kitten, it's just us here. You don't need to wear one of these."

"You're the one who dressed me. The blame lies with you. I would've been naked if I'd been in charge."

A low chuckle escaped me as the fabric fell away, granting me access to her already wet pussy. "Missed me, I see."

"Of course."

"Well, I guess I should do something about it then," I said with an anticipatory smirk. Pleasuring my girl was quickly becoming my number one favorite quest.

Before I could part her thighs further and sink my fingers inside her, she tensed, one hand coming to my wrist.

"What's wrong, baby?" I asked, confusion swirling in my head. "Aren't we here to make sure you're fed and happy?"

"It's . . . I want to. I just . . ."

Concern replaced the confusion. She was stressed about talking to me. That wouldn't do.

"What is it? You can tell me anything."

"Malice gave me some homework, and if I don't do it right now, I'm going to get too distracted."

Annoyance replaced my concern. "Malice gave you homework for while you're with me? That interfering jealous fuck."

"No, no, it's not like that. It's because—" She cut herself off and readjusted until she was sitting up in the lounger. "He wants me to test the limits of my control while we're in these dreamwalks. He's trying to prove a point. Okay, maybe that's not totally fair. He wants me to learn how much power I have here."

She was being very deliberate with her words and purposely avoiding my gaze. My eyes narrowed with suspicion. "Why now? What aren't you telling me, kitten?"

Glancing around as though someone else was here, she shook her head. "I can't talk about it here."

"Merri," I warned.

"It's important. Trust me."

"Of course I do. You're the boss. If you need to do this *homework,* we can do it. I'm excellent at group projects."

Her smile was soft and sweet, and it was a potent aphrodisiac. My dick gave a happy jerk, begging for her attention. As discreetly as I could, I placed my hand on top of him. No need to distract her when she was trying so hard to focus. I could be patient. I was the most patient. No one had ever been more patient than me.

Lies.

All fucking lies.

I had the patience of a kid on Christmas morning. But it was just because I loved her so much, you know?

"Okay, what do I need to do to help?"

She frowned, her lips pursing as she considered my question. "I'm not sure. I think I just have to do it."

"Do what?"

And just like that, I was awake, in bed with the woman I loved, and back to real life. Rolling over, I found her looking at me.

"That," she said.

I'm the first to admit I didn't always understand the way Malice's mind worked, but I was struggling to see how Merri pulling us out of a dream—that we were in for the sole purpose of allowing her to safely feed and hopefully get knocked up—was a good thing.

"So . . . we're not in the dream anymore. Can you elaborate on the reason for this assignment the great and powerful Mal gave you? It really doesn't make a lot of sense to me."

Merri licked her lips, her eyes darting around nervously before landing back on mine. "We, um, sort of . . . well . . ."

"Just spit it out, kitten. There's nothing you ever have to worry about saying to me."

Releasing a heavy breath, she blurted, "Lucifer can infiltrate my dreams. He has been for weeks now."

Fury and panic hit me at the same time. "What?"

She held up a hand, effectively silencing me. "Malice wanted me to prove, mostly to myself, that even when I am in other people's dreams, I am the one in control. And that my strongest defense against Lucifer will be making the dream stop before he can manipulate me into anything."

"How do you know you'll be able to stop him? He can appear as anyone."

"He's been showing up as the same man in every dream I've shared with him. Mal saw him and recognized his face."

I sat up straight and dragged a hand through my hair. "Once he realizes you're wise to him, he'll stop doing that. Fuck, kitten, he could pretend to be me."

"No," she said, so emphatically it stopped me short.

"How can you be sure?"

"I know your signature. I could pick you out of a crowd of millions. Same with the others. There's no way he could ever make me think he was one of you."

I sort of loved that.

"My signature?"

"Yeah, like your personal mental print." She shrugged. "I'm not great with the terminology, but you get the idea. I can feel you . . . here." She pressed her palm to her heart and then did the same to mine with her free hand.

A smile twisted my lips as I rested my palm over hers. "Same here."

"Is it because you luuuurve me?" she teased.

"Yup," I said with an unrepentant grin. "Just like you love me."

"Guilty as charged."

The topic was the elephant in the room I knew we needed to discuss. Love wasn't an easy subject for either of us. It came with deep connections and ties we'd both been afraid of. Love meant I could be rejected. It meant we could lose everything. But it also meant we could gain so much. It had been centuries since I'd last even considered the big L. Horsemen certainly didn't have any need of it. But when Merri came into our lives, she changed everything.

Now, loving her was practically the only thing I thought about.

The intimacy of the moment washed over us. We may have already admitted our feelings out on the battlefield, but it was different doing it here when it was just the two of us.

"You okay with that?" she asked softly, reaching out to run her fingers along my cheek.

"More than okay."

"So why do you look like you just bit into a lemon?"

A bark of laughter escaped. "Well, I'm not gonna lie, kitten. I'm fucking terrified. I've never loved anyone but myself. Not once. What if I fuck it all up?"

"You might."

"Thanks for your vote of confidence," I said dryly.

"But so could I," she added with a one-shoulder shrug.

"I doubt it."

She snuggled closer until her chin rested on my shoulder. "You want to know a secret?"

"Obviously."

"Love should never be measured by its length. Only its depth. So, if you do go and fuck it all up, at least we will have this to remember it by."

I couldn't decide whether the right move was to shove her off the bed or pull her closer. I chose to believe the truth in what she said, that we had to live in this moment to moment rather than looking to a future we weren't certain existed. So, I pulled her to me and kissed her.

"You know," I said around the kiss, "we were supposed to try and knock you up in that dream. Maybe we should give the old-fashioned way a try and do it with our eyes open?"

Holding her as tight as I was, there was no missing the way she tensed.

"What's worrying you now?" I asked, not with judgment but genuine concern.

She peered up at me with worried eyes. "What if I can't get pregnant, Sin? Not in the dream realm or in the real world?"

"Why do you think that?"

"Because Grim said it hasn't happened yet."

I ran my fingers across her shoulder and down her arm to soothe her. "We haven't been trying that long. Some couples try for years before it happens."

"And sometimes it doesn't happen for them."

"We have time."

"Not a lot. And now that we know that Lucifer can find me in my dreams, we know he won't stop hunting me until he gets what he wants. At least until he realizes I'm no longer any use to him. And that won't happen until I get pregnant—"

Fuck. We were a bunch of insensitive assholes. Merri was so spun up, so concerned with getting pregnant, that she was a ball of stress. She was carrying the weight of ending the literal apocalypse on her shoulders as if she alone was responsible for the outcome.

"C'mere, baby. It's okay. I'm not going to let anything happen to you. If I have to come into your dreams every time you fall asleep, I will. Lucifer isn't going to touch you."

She held my gaze for several heartbeats, her fingers drawing invisible patterns on my skin. "Thank you."

"For what?"

"For being you."

"I haven't done anything."

"Not true."

I raised a brow. "If you say so, kitten."

"You're my hero, and I can say so if I want to."

Who was I to argue with logic like that? Instead, I wrapped her in my arms and snuggled her as close as possible. "I love you, Merri."

She hummed happily and pressed a kiss to my chest. "I love you."

CHAPTER
TWENTY-SEVEN
MERRI

The sky was still on fucking fire. It was cool at first, kind of like seeing the northern lights, but now? Now it was nothing more than a sign the world was ending and I hadn't done a damn thing to stop it.

I mean, logically, I recognized that I was only one person, and there was only so much I could do anyway. But also, I was the one with the fancy fucking womb and magic bloodline, so forgive me for feeling personally responsible.

Letting out a little huff of annoyance, I continued tromping up the path that led from the main house to Christian's cottage. I hadn't had a reason to venture out this way yet, but he'd moved back in a couple of days ago, so I wanted to check and see how he was faring. Luckily, the flowers I'd risked my life foraging for had been exactly what he'd needed to brew his healing potion or whatever. He'd needed a few days, but the man was mostly back to his usual self, if slightly altered personality-wise. He smiled less these days. Was a little less flirtatious. But who could blame him? He'd been on death's door. That would subdue anyone.

Knocking on the heavy wooden door, I waited for him to answer, nervous I was disturbing him.

The door swung open and there he was, complexion healthy, smiling, but eyes still slightly dull. That might never leave him. Trauma changes you, and never in a good way.

"Ah, mademoiselle, to what do I owe this pleasure?"

"I just came to check on you. The house seems emptier now that you've gone home."

He grinned, moving out of the doorway and gesturing for me to enter. "Come in, come in. This is such a welcome surprise. Would you care for something to eat? A drink, perhaps?"

Glancing around the cozy space, I took in everything there was to see. And by everything, I meant *everything*. The stone walls were lined with shelves, and dried herbs and flowers hung from the ceiling beams. Everywhere I looked, there were crystals, half-melted candles, pots, and vials. It was cottagecore chic, and I was more than a little jealous.

"You're living my bog witch fantasy, Christian."

He chuckled. "Comes with the territory, I'm afraid. Though I supposed if I lived among a coven, the herbs and other spell materials wouldn't be kept in my house."

"I guess kitchen witch is more apt, now that I think of it."

"I accept. Now, please have a seat. I'll make us some tea. I was just about to prepare some for myself, and I much prefer not to drink alone."

I sat in the overstuffed armchair that was positioned near the hearth, watching as he moved around the tiny but clean kitchen. While the cottage was crammed full of his belongings and supplies, there wasn't a speck of dirt or actual clutter. Everything clearly had a place.

"So how are you holding up, mademoiselle?" he called over his shoulder as he pulled two teacups out of a cupboard.

Sighing, I considered exactly how much information I should give him. Probably nothing, but he was as in this as anyone else.

"It's not great. Especially after the ward thing. I really messed up when I fell through."

He shook his head as he filled the kettle with water and then began heating it. "That wasn't your fault. If anyone should be upset, it's me. I sent you on that mission."

"And I was the clumsy idiot who triggered a mudslide." I waved my hand in dismissal. "It's fine. But the worry I caused them, then the attack . . . it just brought all of this forward about a million steps. Time is of the essence, and I'm frustrated."

He shot me an inquisitive glance. "Frustrated? That's an interesting word choice."

"How do you figure?"

"Well, I could understand if you were to say you felt anxious or scared. The world is on the brink of collapse, so those both make sense. But frustrated? That does not seem to fit the situation."

Well, when he put it that way, the man might have a point.

"Trust me. It does. You just don't have all the puzzle pieces."

Curiosity sparked in his eyes as he let my words sink in. "And . . . are you willing to give me any of them?"

"I'm not sure I can."

The kettle whistled, pulling his attention from me and breaking the tense moment. He turned away and prepared our tea with a practiced grace. I wasn't sure if Christian was going to push the issue of this conversation or if he'd let it go, and honestly, I didn't know which one I wanted. Carrying this around was weighing on me, and the horsemen were so close to all of it I couldn't really unburden myself to them.

Handing me a delicate cup and saucer before he sat across from me with his own, he offered a sympathetic smile. "Does this have anything to do with what I shared with you earlier? About their . . . contest?"

With everything that happened in the last week, I'd almost forgotten Christian was the one who spilled the beans. He'd risked a lot to tell me what he'd overheard. Just because I couldn't tell him everything didn't mean I couldn't trust him at all.

"Yes," I said, eyeing him over my cup as I blew on the steamy surface.

"I see. So you are a willing participant now?"

I blushed. "You could say that."

"So what's the problem?"

"I'm worried none of them will be successful."

"What a curious time to want to get with child."

He wasn't wrong. But only because he didn't understand the finer points of my situation.

I took a sip of my tea and then set down my cup, hands clasped in my lap as I lifted my gaze back to his. "It's extremely important that I get pregnant, Christian. I can't tell you why, but I need you to trust me on this."

A series of emotions washed across his face. First curiosity, then concern, and finally a somberness I was certain matched my own.

"Then I will help you."

Uh, what?

"I appreciate the offer, but the rotation is pretty full right now."

His cheeks went pink, and he spluttered on his tea. "No, no. Not like that. I can make you a potion to aid in fertility. My mother taught it to me. She was a powerful witch and served as our village's midwife until her death."

I tamped down the bloom of hope that had sprung at his words. "And this potion, it works on, um, not human people?"

"Why would I offer otherwise?" he asked, looking adorably confused.

I really appreciated that he took me at face value instead of slapping back with something condescending or mansplainy. Christian was a rare gem.

"Any side effects?"

"I would prepare for an increase in libido. But . . . I would not say that's typically a problem most complain about."

Now it was my turn to blush. "Right. Probably not."

I sipped my tea and let the floral flavor blossom on my tongue. Help wouldn't be a bad thing. Especially not with Lucifer so eager to find a way to beat the horsemen to the punch. Not even my mind was a safe place for me right now. It wouldn't be until I was pregnant, and if I was going to have a baby with anyone, it would be one of the four of them. Not the king of hell.

"Can I get back to you on your offer?"

"But of course. It will take me a few hours to gather the ingredients and prepare the potion. I could have it available to you by this evening, if you so choose."

"Good to know. Thanks, Christian."

"Happy to help. It is what I'm here for, and I do love feeling useful. It's so rare the château has guests."

"It must be lonely out here all by yourself." I was familiar with isolation, but at least I'd had Auntie Lilith to talk to every day.

He shrugged. "I get by."

Now this was the tea I was interested in. "Does that mean there's a Mrs. or Mr. Christian somewhere?"

He smirked. "Not at the moment. I'm a fairly solita—"

A soft chime preceded a soft violet light in the far corner of the room.

"*Mon Dieu!*" Christian jumped to his feet, tea splashing out of his cup as he hastily set it down.

"What's wrong?"

"It's an emergency alert."

"Like a bomb siren?"

He froze and glanced back at me. "Your mind is a very strange thing."

"You said it was an emergency."

Rushing to the spot where the light originated from, he snatched up an old leather-bound book and opened it. The light was so much brighter now, beaming up to the ceiling. A disembodied voice filled the room, unfortunately all in rapid-fire French, which I did not understand. Magic was pretty damn cool, and now that the grid was down, extremely useful.

When he closed the book, his face was pale and drawn.

"What was that?" I whispered.

"The Great Barrier Reef has died all at once. It has washed ashore along with the bones of thousands of sharks and other sea life. The ocean is nothing more than acid, eating through the hulls of ships and killing everything it touches."

"Shit," I murmured, dread collecting in my belly like a stone. It must be the sixth Prince. Every time one was released, there was a terrible natural disaster.

I stood so fast my chair nearly fell over.

"Mademoiselle?"

"Thank you, Christian. I have to go. I need to let the others know."

CHAPTER TWENTY-EIGHT

ASHER

I'd spent time in worse places, as far as hideouts went. At least this currently abandoned secret fight club Lilith brought us to had plumbing and central air. There was space for everyone too. And man, were there a lot of us. The wolf packs alone took up so much space I swore I could smell wet dog every time I walked by them.

I was pretty sure magic was at play here, both in regards to the amenities and the way we never seemed to run out of room for all of us. Lilith wouldn't admit it, preferring to play coy, but c'mon. I'd been to the secret rooms at *Iniquity,* and this had a very similar vibe. Minus the sexy dungeon aspect, of course.

All around me, groups of different species were clustered together, speaking in indistinct murmurs. I was most concerned about the Novasgardians and the shifters, if I was being honest. Both ran hot. Both were easily coaxed into conflict due to their natural inclination for battle. The shifters because of their animalistic, territorial natures. The Vikings because . . . well . . . Vikings.

"Do you really think we can all stay here, babe?" Remi said under his breath.

I shrugged. "I'm not sure there's any place else we can go. Not and stay safe."

"The tension is already so thick I can hardly breathe. It's a powder keg. If a vamp looks at a wolf the wrong way, it's going to be a bloodbath."

A snarl that was more animal than man ripped through the air as exactly that happened. West Blackthorne stood near enough to the wolf he'd been sizing up that he could've lost an arm, but Kingston was holding his packmate back, along with two other wolves.

"West, stand down," Thorne ordered, but his brother, arrogant and young but still old enough to know better, simply huffed a condescending laugh.

"I'm not doing anything. All I did was look his way."

"I'm not a blood bag, vamp. Keep your fangs to yourself," the shifter snapped, his body returning to a more human state as he calmed.

"Noah, maybe West needs to take a walk and get his head on straight?" Sunday suggested gently.

I knew him as Thorne, as most who were acquainted with Noah Blackthorne did, but my mate and Sunday both called him Noah. It had taken me a while to get used to the different moniker, though I understood the reason behind it now. The closer you were to him, the more real he was with you. I was not close with Thorne, and I never would be.

"I wouldn't stoop so low as to drink your gamey blood," West spat, anger making his eyes blaze.

Fucking hotheaded vampire royalty. He was going to get us all killed if he didn't rein it in right now.

Another snarl escaped the wolf, and this time, it was accompanied by a handful of echoes from his pack. This was turning sour and quickly. Funny, I really had my money on the Vikings.

Before I could say a damn thing, two impenetrable walls of shadow appeared in front of each group, barring them from sight.

Hades strode between the walls of shadow, blue fire glowing in his eyes from the power he was using. "All right, y'all, that's about enough. Who's in charge of this shitshow? Because I can tell you one thing. We aren't going to make it out of here if some law and order isn't established—and fast."

"Technically it's Lilith, I guess, since she's the one who brought us here and is in charge of this place," I said, looking around like I might spot her dark hair somewhere in the crowd. "But I haven't seen her all morning."

"Well, I can't keep them apart forever. We need leaders to keep things in line."

"I run a tight ship. Allow me to advise," Caspian offered from behind me, his arm around Dahlia as he gestured widely to the group.

"No." Hades shut him down so fast it was all I could do not to laugh. Especially when his pout looked so similar to Remi's.

"That's precisely why Lilith is gone," Caleb answered, joining our loose circle.

"Care to elaborate?" Hades asked, one eyebrow hiking up in annoyance.

"With this many factions banded together under one roof, she thought it might be best to re-establish the Council. Last I heard, she went off to collect someone she felt could be of assistance in that regard."

"The Council?" Kingston said, coming out from behind the wall Hades had erected. "Like *the* Council. The one made up of assholes who tried to convince us to k-i-l-l our little sunbeam?"

If Eden were still here, I was certain she'd be shooting around the room like a bouncy ball. That kid only sat still when she was sleeping. My lips twitched in the beginning of a smile. I couldn't help but wonder if our pups would be the same.

"One and the same," Caleb affirmed.

Kingston made a face. "Sounds like a bad idea. Besides, more than half the members are dead."

"That's why we want to re-establish it. Create a new Council with a new goal."

Hades nodded. "That's the best idea I've heard in weeks. It's the only way the gods ever achieved anything."

"Well, who are we appointing to this society of weirdos?" I asked.

"Oooh, we can call it the Hades Society," Remi suggested, grinning at the lord of the underworld like he was a delicious ice cream cone. "It has a nice ring to it. So chic, but also sort of sinister. It totally commands respect. Just say it. The Hades Society."

Hades smirked. "Well, I don't hate it."

Caleb sighed. "Call it whatever you want."

"Yes!" Remi whispered as he pumped his fist.

"What time is this Council meeting supposed to start?" I asked. Remi shot me a wounded look, and I immediately rolled my eyes and corrected myself. "Sorry, Hades Society."

"Good boy," Remi murmured, putting his hand in my back pocket and giving my ass a squeeze.

"First and foremost, we need to select members from each of the supernatural factions. That way we know who should be part of this Hades Society." Caleb turned to face the crowd of people we'd brought with us. "Everyone!" he shouted in his hellfire and brimstone priest voice.

"Oh, daddy," Remi said under his breath. "Take me to church."

I elbowed him, but he wasn't wrong.

Caleb continued, pure authority in his tone. "Choose amongst yourselves one leader to represent your species or realm. When called upon, this person will join us in the newly established Hades Society. You have one hour."

Nine of us sat in a circle in a room that felt a lot like a dingy, unused basement, the atmosphere heavy with the gravity of what we were about to do. It seemed equal parts futile and vital.

The door was still open since we were four members shy of our thirteen. Caspian was currently leaning against the doorway, arms crossed over his chest and a petulant pout on his lips.

"I still don't understand why *he* gets to represent all of Faerie. He's only familiar with one realm. I was the king of Ravenndel, which is a sovereign realm, I'll have you know. They deserve representation."

Kai, the *he* in question, looked around the room. "Remind me again, Cas, where is the Ravenndel contingent? Are they here, offering their support in the upcoming battle? No? Then kindly shut the fuck up."

Cas huffed, clearly affronted. "They are loyal to none but their realm. It's the nature of Ravenndel. Why else would it be the escape for those who wish to stay forgotten?"

The dragon shifter placed a large hand on Caspian's shoulder. "Go and see to our Dahlia. With two of her mates in here, she could do with a spare set of eyes."

"Or hands," Cas said with a lascivious wink. "Consider me convinced. As you were, dragon."

Crombie strode through the doorway Caspian had just vacated, his hair slick and shining, a black waterfall down his back, suit impeccable, and throat noticeably free of the gold collar I'd grown accustomed to seeing. He radiated power like never before, the promise of death, or at the bare minimum, violence if you fucked with him, following in his wake.

"Why haven't you got everyone here, Hades?" Crombie asked. "My Lilypad will be here momentarily, and you know how cross she can get when her time is wasted."

Hades, looking as unbothered as could be, simply shrugged. "Sit down and stop bothering me. I'm opening the portal now."

Crombie raised a challenging brow. "How convenient. Funny how the mice all scurry into position when the wolf appears."

Kingston glanced at Thorne. "Crombie's a wolf? I thought he was fae?" The shifter lifted his nose and sniffed the air. "He doesn't smell like a wolf."

"It's a metaphor, you absolute nincompoop."

"You don't have to be mean about it," Kingston muttered.

"Guys, did he say he was opening a portal?" Alek asked, his voice betraying the apprehension he always tried to hide. "The last time he did that, there was a . . . ghost."

"Christ on a bike, here we go again," Caleb muttered, pinching the bridge of his nose.

Before anyone could respond, Hades stepped forward and opened a shimmering portal at one end of the circle of chairs.

"Bossman! Fuckin' finally. Do you know how long Keeks and I were waiting out here? I peed on every fuckin' bush just to pass the time."

That little dog was talking again. It was almost like watching a cartoon come to life. I couldn't decide if I was fascinated or horrified. Not because I was afraid of tiny dogs, but because I'd watched a fuckton of cartoons, and the cute animals were usually always in the middle of serious shit.

"Oh, I love a super serious secret society. This is right up my alley. Saving the world, having a cool code name. Can I be The Editrix? You know, because I was an editor before I bit it?" Kiki, the most energetic ghost I'd ever seen, stood at the mouth of the portal, staying in her realm but fully in view of us all.

"No code names," Hades grumbled.

"Aw, c'mon, boss. You named the group after yourself. The least you could do is let us have cool names."

"Is she staying on her side the whole time?" Alek asked tightly.

"I don't have to. Want me to come over there and braid your beard, Viking?"

Alek jumped out of his seat and backed away until he stood in the corner, his index fingers held up in the sign of the cross.

"You've got to be fecking kidding me," Caleb groaned. "She's not a bleeding demon, Alek. Also, fingers offer no protection. You need a crucifix, not to mention genuine belief in the item."

"This is the guy they selected to represent the big bad Vikings?" Kai asked, both his brows lifted toward his hairline. "Are they sure he's the best choice?"

"Fuck you," Alek spat. "Ghosts are a hard line for me. I've been very clear about that."

"And we were clear on why we need her, Nordson," Hades reminded him. "If you can't play nice with Keeks, then we'll get your brother in here to take your place."

Kiki blew Alek a kiss from her side of the portal. "I don't bite. I promise. Well, sometimes I do, but only with consent! I'm decent like that."

"Pixie, how much longer are you gonna be?" a deep voice called from out of view.

Kiki looked to her left, her expression turning from irritated to absolutely twitterpated. "Not long. I'll be there soon, babe."

"Kiki and Bear, sittin' in a tree, F-U-C-K-I—" The dog was interrupted before he could finish his song. "Quiet, everybody. Mommy is here."

Everyone's attention snapped to the door where Lilith finally made her grand entrance, a man I'd never seen before one step behind her.

"Lovely, we're all here. Now we can begin." Lilith slinked into the room, her stilettos clicking seductively with every step. "Allow me to introduce our final member. This is Evander. He will be representing the celestial realm since Gabriel has not responded to any of my summons."

"He's an angel?" I asked, my own angelic blood humming in my veins. My contact with angels had been limited to Gabriel, and I'd seen him only once, under extreme circumstances.

"Yes," Evander said, pinning me with a startlingly emerald gaze.

"How's the ear?" Kingston said, pulling the angel's attention to him.

"I'm sorry?"

Thorne elbowed Kingston.

"Oof. C'mon man, it was low-hanging fruit."

Evander's brows pulled together as he assessed Kingston. "I'm afraid I don't understand what you're talking about. My ear, as you can see, is fine."

"Never mind. You ruined the joke."

Asshole laughed from his place at the portal. "I got it. I really thought you were too young to remember Mike Tyson's cannibal days. Good to see I was wrong. Maybe this generation isn't a lost cause."

Kingston pointed to the pup through the portal's shimmering surface. "You get all the dog treats, big guy."

Asshole puffed up his little chest. "Big dog energy, baby. Right, bossman?"

Hades winked. "Damn straight."

Lilith heaved a sigh before settling in a chair and crossing her legs. "Is everyone quite finished with the comedy hour? We do have a world to save, after all."

I couldn't stop my smirk. Lilith losing her cool was rare, but always entertaining. Unless I was the focus of her ire. Usually it was Remi, but then he made everyone lose their cool.

A soft growl of thunder rolled through the room, setting the hair on my arm standing on end. "The fuck?"

"That's quite enough, Drystan. They got the point."

Crombie's eyes were such a bright silver they almost appeared mirror-like. "Just reminding them of their place."

Kai glared at him from his seat in the circle. "Remind me why he's here? You don't exactly represent a court anymore, unless the rumors of your exile are false. And unless I'm mistaken, you're still top of the Hunt's most wanted list. So what is it exactly, Nightshade, you think you're bringing to the table here? Besides a whole host of trouble we do not fuckin' need."

Literal thunder crashed overhead, but it died down when Lilith put her palm out and Crombie took her hand.

"The Night Court is its own realm. Thus, it needs representation."

"I'll ask you the same question I asked Hook. Where's your contingent? I don't exactly see members of the Night Court coming to our aid."

Crombie's answering grin was pure evil. "I'm more than fae enough to get the job done alone."

"Is this how it's going to be? A bunch of posturing alphas volleying insults back and forth? If so, I can return to heaven and find more of the same," Evander muttered.

"We need more feminine energy. This is absurdly male." Lilith leveled a steely gaze at Hades.

Moira Belladonna, my favorite witch—which wasn't saying much since I fucking despised witches—cleared her throat. "Excuse me, I count for at least a dozen vagina-card-carrying members." She held up a finger. "One, I'm a witch. That's like ten points on its own. Two, I'm married to a woman, so like girl power."

"You tell 'em, sister," Kiki said, giving an approving nod.

"But where are the others?" Lilith asked, glancing around. "Surely after all they've done, they wanted a seat at the table where decisions were being made."

"None of them wanted the job," Caleb answered.

"I think Rosie's exact response was, 'I'm growing tiny humans, find someone else to do your dirty work,'" Pan said, smug annoyance stamped all over his handsome face. My brother had been sulking in the corner since we'd entered the room. He did not want to be here, but he'd been roped into it because he was the only one with any knowledge of demonkind and what we might be up against. Well, he and Lilith.

"Sunny said the same, plus 'I've done more than my fair share.'" Alek shrugged. "She's not wrong. And carrying Kingston's spawn has to be exhausting."

"Hey," Kingston said. "Well, yeah, you're probably right. We Farrells make big babies."

Lilith glanced at Kai and Hades. "I'm assuming it was the same for Dahlia?"

"Aye. She's worn down to the bone."

Kiki snorted. "The bone. That's what we're calling it now? You guys need to let my girl rest while she's growing your little parasite."

"Can we move this along? I have things to do," Evander asked, impatience written all over him.

"Yes, we should. There's no telling what the masses are up to without us in there," Hades agreed.

"All right," I said, slapping my hands together and rubbing them back and forth. "I call this first meeting of the Hades Society to order."

Lilith sighed audibly and rolled her eyes. "That's what I get for not being here to help name this collective."

"First order of business, introductions," Hades said. "I'll go first. I am Hades, lord of the underworld, mate of Dahlia, who is the daughter of the horsewoman Death."

And so it went, around the circle, as each member introduced themselves and the group they represented. Some were obvious choices, like Alek, Thorne, Kingston, and Moira, who'd inherited their parents' spots from the original Council. Others *were* original Council members, like Lilith and Caleb. Those two, along with Hades, now made up the "governing body" of the group, AKA they were the ones who would make and enforce the rules. The rest of us seemed to be selected mostly due to chance or our connection with the other group members. In other words, we were convenient.

Or at least, I guess that's why I was here. Since Lilith had hand-selected Evander to represent the celestials, I wasn't really sure what the fuck I brought to the table. I doubted it had anything to do with my hacking skills, and I was certain no one here was interested in the *human* point of view. This was a supernatural secret society, after all.

Finally, it was my turn to introduce myself. "Uh, I'm Asher. Half human, half angel, all hacker. Um, mate of Rosie, partner to Remi . . . and uh, to be honest, guys, I don't know why I'm here. I don't really represent anyone who hasn't already been covered."

Lilith laughed. "Oh, sweetheart, isn't it obvious? You're the heart of this whole thing. If not for you, none of us would be here right now. You were the one leading the charge and doling out information. It only stands to reason that you would continue in that vein. You've certainly earned your seat, if that's what you're worried about." She cocked one brow. "Also, have you forgotten you're the son of a horsewoman?"

I rubbed at the back of my neck, my eyes darting to Pan's lavender ones. "I guess we are, aren't we?"

"Don't remind me," Pan sneered. "She's dead to me."

"I mean, you did kill her."

"More's the pity it didn't stick," he muttered, wiping at an invisible speck on his pant leg.

"Unfortunately that is precisely why this group is necessary," Lilith said. "We will never be rid of them. Once we stop this apocalypse, there will be another one brewing."

Kingston groaned. "Are you for real?"

Lilith cut him a scathing glare. "Yes."

Caleb sighed and adjusted the cuffs of his sleeves. "There will likely be a quiet period if we succeed, just as there was the last time Lucifer nearly ended the world."

"Sounds a whole lot like it'll be someone else's problem," I mused.

Lilith cocked an eyebrow. "Don't be so smug, darling. That someone is likely your future children. Leave it to the humans to expect their progeny to clean up after them."

"It's not going to matter if we don't nip this one in the bud," Hades said, visibly irritated as his eyes burned with blue fire. "There won't be a world to clean up, so can we focus on the matter at hand?"

The air felt like it had been sucked out of the room as we all took a collective sigh.

"Does anyone have any news about number six?" Kingston asked, attention on Lilith since she was the only one among us who'd left the so-called safe house since we'd relocated.

"If you're referring to the release of the sixth Prince, that's part of the reason I brought Evander," she replied, gesturing for the angel to go ahead.

"Wrath has been released. The consequences of his arrival are far-reaching and devastating. Heaven won't be able to shelter the humans from the effects much longer."

"What do you mean, shelter?" I asked.

"The angels have been doing all we can to keep the humans from understanding the gravity of what is happening. We always have. Humankind has survived by the skin of their teeth countless times, and they've never been the wiser. Though arguably, they've never come quite this close to extinction."

Before any of us could give voice to the massive "what the fuck" that prompted, the angel kept going.

"The Princes are more than simply Lucifer's generals. They are seven of the fallen who rebelled alongside Lucifer. Stripped of their titles, they were cast out, their names struck from the collective memory when they were renamed for the sin they embodied. They've never been released from where they were imprisoned. Until now. We have hoped to keep it that way, but sooner rather than later, there won't be any way to shield the humans from the horrors the Princes are unleashing."

Alek shifted in his chair before raising his hand, eyes continually flicking toward Kiki in her portal as though afraid she was going to step through at any moment.

"Yes, Alek?" Lilith said, sounding increasingly impatient.

"How have you shielded them from anything? The sky is ablaze, and devastating earthquakes and volcanic eruptions have wiped out huge swaths of the United States. Entire mountains have sunk into the ground."

Evander lifted his chin, a defiant gesture I was very familiar with from living with Gavin. "As I've said, we have done our best. They see them as tragic natural disasters. Part of a life cycle. Some blame it on global warming. They do not realize it's the literal end of everything, and we want to keep it that way. Traumatized humans don't typically bounce back easily."

The rest of us exchanged uneasy glances. As one of the only humans in the room, not that Pan really counted since he'd only been one for the better part of a year, I wasn't sure heaven was as effective as they thought. I mean, people weren't stupid. Fire in the sky was a pretty big fucking indicator that shit had gone off the rails.

"So . . . you're gaslighting them into thinking this is all their fault because of pollution?" I asked before I could stop myself.

"No. We're helping them help themselves."

"Whatever you say, buddy."

"Hades," Lilith said, changing the subject with a segue as subtle as a slap to the face, "are you still in contact with the horsemen?"

"I was, but since the grid went down, I have no way to contact them."

"Hmm. My, my, we are in a pickle," Lilith mused.

I snorted. "You think?"

Moira caught my eye and mouthed, "What else is new?"

"Care to share with the class, Miss Belladonna?" Caleb huffed.

"Nope," she said with a smirk. "You're not my Daddy, I don't have to behave just because you glower at me. If you're looking for someone to punish, take it up with Sunday."

Kiki snickered from behind the portal, making Alek flinch.

Knowing that Moira was about as good as Remi at staying on topic, I interjected, "If we can't contact the horsemen, how are we going to do anything to stop this?"

"I can run it up the flagpole here in the underworld. See if anyone has a connection to Death. Maybe someone here knows how to contact him via the afterlife?" Kiki offered.

"Would that work?" Alek asked Hades. I had to hand it to the guy, for as freaked out as he was by Kiki's presence, he didn't dismiss her or her ideas out of hand. If anything, he took them more seriously than the rest of us.

Hades shrugged, expression going distant as he clearly thought through her suggestion. "It might. Never really needed to test it before, so I can't say for sure. The veil between realms is definitely thinner than usual, which would help matters. But depending on where Death is shacked up, he might be impossible to locate."

"That grumpy bastard has always been hard to pin down," Asshole added. "But hey, maybe if he's getting laid on the regular, he'll be more agreeable these days."

"It's not a bad plan. One that deserves looking into, but in the meantime, there is a surefire way to reach Merri." Lilith had that mischievous smirk on her lips again, the one that said she was up to something.

"Oh really? And you're only just sharing that now?" Pan spat.

"Yes, because it wasn't pertinent until now."

"Well, go on then, enlighten us," Hades prompted.

Lilith's smile stretched, making her appear like the cat who ate the canary. She held us in suspense for a few drawn-out seconds before finally revealing her plan. "Through dreams. Merri is a succubus. She can and does dreamwalk. All we need is a pathway in."

Kai leaned forward in his chair and focused in on Lilith. "You're a succubus too. By that reasoning, can't you do it on your own?"

"Unfortunately, no. Lucifer is paying far too much attention to my comings and goings. The last thing I want to do is lead him directly to the person I've tried so hard to shield." Her eyes flicked to Crombie's as another bout of thunder rolled around the room.

Apparently the Prince of Darkness was a touchy subject between the two of them. Fair enough. If the devil was Rosie's ex, I'd probably feel some kind of way about it too.

"So how do you propose we visit her dreams, and who exactly is our emissary?" Kai asked.

"Dahlia."

Kai growled low in his throat, but Lilith cut him off with a raised hand and continued.

"She knows Merri. A stranger won't do. Merri needs to hear from someone she trusts. Someone her subconscious will recognize immediately as a friend."

"Enemies wear friendly masks all the time," Thorne pointed out.

"True, but that's why having Dahlia relay specific information will be crucial. It will serve a dual purpose. One, it will prove that Dahlia is who she appears to be, and two, that she can be trusted."

"And how are we facilitating this, Lilypad?" Crombie asked.

"Moira will do it."

"I'm sorry. What now?" Moira's eyes were wide as saucers. "I will?"

"Yes, pet. Certainly you have a spell like this in your arsenal. The Belladonna coven is the most powerful witch coven in the world, isn't it?"

Moira sat a little taller in her chair. "We are. I suppose it's much like a basic traveling spell. We'll just need to fine-tune it so it will take someone to the dream realm instead of the earthly plane."

"Brilliant. Whilst Kiki attempts direct contact with Death, you take care of this spell. We'll work double duty and get Dahlia connected with Merri so all of our—what is it you Americans like to say—bases are covered."

As far as plans went, it wasn't great. We were hiding in a secret fight club/bunker, hoping that the four horsemen would knock up a succubus, and relying on ghosts and dreams to help us make contact with them. But what other options were there? It wasn't like there was anything I could do. Best to let the experts take the reins.

As for the rest of us? I guess we'd just have to wait and see.

Not seeing what else we could accomplish until then, I looked around the room and slapped my hands on my knees. "So, same time next week?"

CHAPTER TWENTY-NINE

MERRI

I pushed my index finger through the Scrabble tiles in search of my final two pieces.

"Are you trying to figure out what letters they are through osmosis?" Dahlia teased.

"Maybe," I said with a smirk as I plucked up an *A* and a *D* and then added them to the rest of my lineup. If Sin were here, he'd definitely have something to say about giving me his D.

"Well . . . I'm waiting." Dahlia sat back in her chair, her gentle smile only making her prettier.

Glancing around the day room, I frowned momentarily.

"What?" she asked.

"It's so empty. Where are the rest of the residents?"

She shrugged. "Probably off on some Blackwood-related excursion. You and I have more important things to do."

I laid out my tiles, beginning the game. "D-A-N-D-Y," I announced as each piece settled on the board.

"As in Yankee Doodle?" Dahlia snickered.

"As in tight pantaloons that do nothing to hide a bulge."

"Respect," Dahlia said, selecting her own tiles and setting them up vertically through mine.

"Soulmates?" I asked. "How did you manage to come out of the gate with that? Lucky bitch."

"How would I know? This is your dream."

It *was* a dream. This time it felt so real. I could even read the words we were spelling, and everyone knew you couldn't read or taste in dreams.

"E-X-I-L-E, *and* it's a triple word score. Booyah!" I pushed back from my chair, lifting my hands up and beaming with pride after getting to use that *X*. And against a writer too.

Dahlia's laughter filled the room. "Dramatic much?"

"These days, you've gotta take the wins where you find them."

In quick succession, Dahlia laid down her next word without saying anything.

"Destiny?"

"Yep."

Soulmates and destiny. Was I sensing a theme? Or was I reading way too much into words a romance author was intimately familiar with?

"D-E-A-T-H."

Dahlia blinked at me. "You trying to tell me something?"

"I dunno, are you?" I asked, watching as she spelled eternity with her next set of tiles.

Eternity. Yeah, it was her trying to tell me something. Especially with that look on her face. Dahlia Moore didn't play with words unless she wanted to send a message.

"Dahlia, why are you here?" I laid my hands on top of the table and looked her dead in the eye. "We both know it's not because you want to play a game."

"A mutual friend sent me."

"Who?"

She looked around the empty room and then shook her head. "The ghosts are always listening."

"So you came to pass along a message, but you're worried about being overheard? How does that work?"

Dahlia huffed out a breath. "I didn't exactly get a choice."

"Gee, thanks. It's great to see you too."

"No, no. I didn't mean that part. It's great to see you, obviously. I just mean, there's a lot going on, and right now I much prefer staying close to my mates."

There was that word again.

"It must be nice having mates."

Confusion flashed across her face, and she cocked her head. "You should know."

"What?"

"You've found yours, haven't you?"

The question brought me up short. I was falling in love with them; that was something I knew for sure, but that didn't automatically mean they were my mates. I didn't think succubi had mates. Did they?

"I can see you working this out in your head. There's no doubt they are your mates, Merri. Fate brought you together."

"Lilith did that."

"Just because there was a middleman doesn't mean it wasn't fate at work."

My chest felt tight and warm all at the same time. "They're only connected to me because of the dreamwalks. I'm not a shifter or vampire. We don't do mating bonds."

Dahlia inspected her nails before locking eyes with me. "Uh-huh. So would you say my mates and I aren't really bonded? None of them are vampires or shifters."

"Kai is a dragon."

"Not the same. He's a fae who inherited a dragon curse from his father."

"Tor?"

"Also cursed. But still not a vampire or a shifter."

She had a point.

"Well . . . I'd definitely call them your mates. But how did you know without the . . . you know, biting and stuff?"

Dahlia laughed. "Bonds occur in all kinds of ways. Just because a bite is the best-known way to solidify a mate bond, it's far from the only way. Cas and I forged ours during sex."

"Sex?" I snickered. I supposed if succubi did have mates, that would definitely be the way to seal the deal. As soon as the thought registered, all the hairs on the back of my neck stood on end as memories of my time with each of my men hit me.

"Yep. He started getting all glowy and literally levitated. It was pretty fucking amazing."

Glowing.

Oh. My. God.

Flashes of the dreamwalk with Grim in front of the fireplace ran through my mind. The way we'd been surrounded by tendrils of golden, glowing threads that seemed to pull us closer to one another. And that same golden glow had surrounded Chaos and me when we'd had our stolen moment by the lake.

Did that mean we were . . .

"And there's, you know, the way we can sometimes feel what the other is feeling, even if we're far away."

This time, my mind flooded with images of Malice. I'd always been pretty in tune with people's emotions, but there were points when I'd been with him where I would have sworn that his thoughts and his emotions were running through my body. Nothing tangible like his voice in my mind, but his influence all the same.

"We're stronger together, you know," she added, almost as an afterthought. "Which really came in handy when we faced off against my mother. Come to think of it, the same is true for Sunday and her mates. Rosie and her men too. That can't be a coincidence."

"What do you mean, Sunday and Rosie? Who are they?"

Dahlia smiled. "They're basically our cousins. Well, kind of."

"Our cousins?"

"My mother is Death. Sunday's is War. Rosie is mated to the sons of Pestilence." She reached out and took my hand. "That leaves you."

"My mother is Famine."

Dahlia nodded. "Don't worry. None of us will judge you for having a shitty mom."

I shook my head as so many different thoughts zoomed around in there, making it hard to focus. "I don't understand how having mates makes you stronger."

Dahlia shrugged. "Well, for us, it was part of a spell Kai came up with. Something that would allow one or all of us to sort of lend our power to another if they were in need. It doesn't work that way for the others. From what Sunday told me, each time she bonded with a new mate, she unlocked a new part of her own power. I have no idea how it works for Rosie."

I thought back to the fight with the demons and how I'd tapped into my inner horsewoman and taken them all out. Had it been because I was reacting to Sin getting hurt like the others suggested? Or was it because I'd unknowingly mated the four horsemen and, in doing so, unlocked my own horsey powers?

Or was it a combination of both?

Oh fuck.

I dropped my head into my hands and just breathed for a moment. Everything was so complicated. All the fucking time.

"This is a good thing, Merri. You are coming into your full power. You're going to fight, and you'll win. But you have to trust them."

"You want me to trust the Four Horsemen of the Apocalypse?"

I already did, but I just needed her to address the absurdity of the statement.

"If you can't trust your mates, who can you trust?"

"Women who visit me in my dreams, apparently."

Dahlia smiled. "I hope you trust me. I think you'd have eventually figured it out for yourself, but sometimes we just need a little nudge to allow ourselves to believe in something we didn't think was possible. For me, it was seeing ghosts. For you, it's visits from old friends in your dreams. You should feel lucky. Fate could have sent you the creepy ghosts." She shuddered, and her gaze flicked to the doorway as though she expected to see said ghosts. "Don't ignore your destiny, Merri. For all our sakes."

Before I could open my mouth to tell her I wouldn't, I was unceremoniously ripped from the dream, sitting bolt upright in bed and gasping for breath.

Don't ignore your destiny. The world was counting on me and my mates.

My mates.

As I let the word settle in my head and heart, I couldn't deny how very right it felt. The five of us were meant to be together, destined.

Throwing off the covers, I stumbled out of bed and snagged my robe, but my eye caught on the shadowy figure sitting on the edge of my bed.

"Jesus fucking Christ," I screeched as Grim stood to his full height.

"Where do you think you're going, wildflower?"

Grim

Merri, sleep rumpled and bathed in moonlight, might be my favorite iteration. She'd always had an otherworldly sensuality about her, but like this, there was a raw vulnerability to her that was undeniable. Few would ever get to see her this way, and I was one of them.

I didn't take that gift lightly. Which was probably why I was such a possessive and overbearing arsehole when it came to her. Not to mention undeniably horny. I'd spent my existence in a state of control which rivaled that of a monk.

Until her.

She stared at me over her shoulder, no longer startled. "Well, I was coming to find you and the others, but it seems your stalking predilection took care of the first part of my plan."

"You were frowning in your dream. Why?"

Her eyebrows snapped together. "Do you ever take a break from being a bossy pain in my ass?"

"No. What were you dreaming about? Was it Lucifer?"

"No."

"Are you sure?"

"Yes, Grimsby. I'm sure."

"How can you know?"

She threw her hands up in the air. "What's the point of asking me what I dreamed about if you won't believe me when I tell you?"

I narrowed my eyes and glared at her. "You're hiding something. Why?"

"I don't have to tell you every single thing. You're not my father."

"I damn sure am not. But you'll tell me because if you don't, I'll still have you over my knee."

"Doubtful. You wouldn't risk accidental skin touchage."

"Thanks to you, I've discovered the beauty of my shadow form. He's opened many new doors for me."

A flare of desire pulsed from her, but she averted her gaze. Something was wrong. This would not stand. How could I protect her if she kept things from me?

"Merri," I said, voice firm. "Tell me what happened."

"Not until I can tell you all."

Frustration, the likes of which I'd never known, radiated through my body. "Just tell me now."

"No, because then you're just going to make me repeat myself four times. I'm tired of having the same conversation over and over. It's my news, I'll deliver it how I want, and you'll shut the fuck up and let me."

I stared at her, my voice coming out as a dark growl. "Excuse me."

She wilted for a second, as if only just now realizing what she said, before straightening her shoulders and squaring off. "You heard me."

Balling my hands into fists, I stood and took a deep breath in an attempt to gather my composure so I didn't shout at her. "Fine. You have ten minutes. If you aren't in the library by then, I will come up here and haul you downstairs over my shoulder. Am I clear?"

"Crystal."

"I'm glad at least one of us knows how to be reasonable," I muttered.

"Can't wait for you to catch up to the rest of us," she called behind me as I headed for her door.

I shot a final blazing look at her over my shoulder. "Keep pushing, wildflower. See where it gets you."

Not bothering to close the door behind me, I stormed into the hallway. My shadow spread across the floor and up the walls, coating every surface near me in black.

"Malice! Sin! Chaos!" I bellowed from the top of the stairs, knowing that no matter where they were in the château, they'd hear me. "Library. Now!"

Chaos popped his head out of his room, rubbing a towel over the wet strands of his hair. "Why are you shouting?"

"Merri has an announcement."

He snapped to attention the way only a master of war could manage. "What happened?"

"She refused to tell me anything until all four of us were together."

"And you let her get away with that?"

I raised a brow. "What precisely would you have me do, Chaos?"

"Good point."

Sin stumbled out of his bedroom, hair tousled, shirt askew as if he'd just thrown it on. "What's wrong? Demons? Where are they?"

"Emergency book club meeting," Chaos muttered.

"Nope. I'm out."

Chaos leveled his gaze at Sin. "Merri called this meeting."

Sin's posture changed instantly. "Oh, well, in that case, I'll just go brush my teeth."

Malice was already standing in the foyer, a cup of tea in his hand. "You bellowed?" he asked as Chaos trailed me down the stairs.

"We're meeting in the library," I snapped, blowing past him.

"Goodie. You know how I love a meeting that could've been an email."

"Email doesn't exist anymore," Sin declared, jogging so he could catch up with us. "Besides, Merri picked the book this time."

"What?"

I took pity on Mal and said, "Merri has something to tell us. She'll be down momentarily."

Malice glanced between me and the others. "This feels like a lot of skulduggery for a simple announcement. Did something happen?"

What little was left of my patience evaporated. "How the bloody hell should I know? She refused to tell me a fucking thing. Now shut up and get your arse in the library so we can move this the fuck along."

There was dead silence as my three brothers stared at me in shock.

In a move that surprised no one, Sin broke the silence first. He whistled, long and low. "Wow. Somebody made Grandpa angry."

"Wouldn't you be if she was clearly distressed and refused to tell you why?" I snapped.

As soon as I reached the library, I stalked to the wall of shelves and began pacing. I didn't do well with uncertainty. Death was the one certain thing in life. I was inevitable. I had no room for what-ifs. Death came for every mortal creature without contest.

Not knowing what she was going to tell us had my heart in a vise, and it kept squeezing until I was sure it would be crushed to dust.

It was exactly sixteen steps in one direction before I was forced to spin on my heel and stalk back the other way. My focus was inward, but I felt the stares from the others. Malice appeared the most outwardly calm as he sipped his tea. Chaos was a bit harder to read with his furrowed brow, but I would bet he was just as unsettled as I was. Sin, as always, was an eager little puppy. He couldn't keep himself still.

"What do you think she's going to tell us? Do you think it's about Lucifer?" Sin blurted.

"Oh my God, it's not about Lucifer!" Merri shouted, exasperation clear in every word as she stood in the doorway.

Of course she looked like an angel sent from heaven. Hair falling down her back in long crimson waves, body clothed in a simple pair of sweatpants and one of her favorite well-worn T-shirts.

"Then what is it?" Chaos demanded.

"You guys need to settle down. Sheesh. I told Grim it's not about Lucifer." Her smile was soft and sweet as she approached us. "It's a good thing."

"Why didn't you think to mention that?" Malice asked me.

"She never said." Then I glared accusingly at Merri. "You never told me that bit."

"You were too busy jumping to conclusions to bother."

Something loosened in my chest, and I inclined my head in assent. "You're right."

Her eyes widened, but Sin interrupted any response she might have been about to toss my way.

"Well, what is it? We're all ears, kitten."

Nervous energy zinged through the room, most of it from me. I didn't have a wealth of experience when it came to good news. Things in my life could rarely be classified as good. I was actually more anxious waiting for Merri to share something she was clearly excited about than I was if she was about to drop something dire on us.

Dire I could handle. Had handled countless times before.

What the hell was I supposed to do with happy?

"I realized something while I was sleeping. It was the final piece of the puzzle I'd been missing since Lilith sent me to you."

"Go on," Chaos murmured.

She all but bounced on her toes, her eyes darting around the room to land on each of us as she spoke. "You four are mine. Not just my protectors or my bodyguards. You're my destiny. My mates."

The floor dropped out from underneath me. Of everything she could have said, nothing could have shocked me more.

Or garnered a more extreme reaction.

"Impossible," I spat before anyone else had a chance to so much as blink.

Merri's mouth dropped open, her face going pale. "I thought so too, but then I realized how everything just fi—"

"You're wrong."

Everything she was saying was so wrong. Merri wasn't my mate. She wasn't. I knew that as surely as I knew myself. The horsemen didn't have mates. We barely had anything that constituted a soul. Our kind weren't made for happily ever after. We were the antithesis of happily ever after. That's simply how it's always been and how it would always be. Period. The end. It didn't matter if one or all of us might wish differently.

"I'm not," she said, but her voice had lost all of its fire.

"You are. We are not your mates, Merri. We never will be. It is impossible."

CHAPTER
THIRTY
MERRI

Everything stopped, the room tilting on its axis as my heart fell on the floor at Grim's feet, only for him to crush it under his fancy Italian leather shoe. At least, that was how it felt.

Eyes darting from Grim to Chaos, then Malice, and finally Sin, I waited for one or all of them to protest. To tell Grim how wrong he was. None of them said anything.

I'd been so confident. So sure they would accept the truth for what it was. Not once had I doubted the connection between us after Dahlia had brought it to my attention and given it a name. Everything I'd noted but hadn't had an explanation for suddenly made perfect sense.

I was such a fool.

How could I ever think for a single second that these men would have been as happy about the news as I'd been? I was an unwelcome parasite in their lives; lust and love were only symptoms of my presence. None of this was part of some mystical plot. The bonds I'd been feeling were probably one-sided. A symptom of all the dreamwalks and my own silly need to be loved.

If I needed any proof of that, the others' silence was more than enough. Grim had never made me any promises, but Sin and Chaos both told me they loved me. Malice had merely promised me we weren't a casual fling. But that was a far cry from a declaration of love.

I never should have believed a single word out of their stupid, kissable lips. They were born liars. Masters of deceit and warfare. Skilled in manipulating people to accomplish their own end goals.

From the beginning, I had never been more than a means to an end.

"I see," I whispered, the words so rough they almost didn't make it past my lips. "Th-thank you for clearing that up for m-me."

Then I turned on my heel and bolted for the door. No one called out for me to stop. No one came after me.

It took all of three seconds for me to decide where I was headed. I couldn't stay here. Not while I was fully aware they'd lied and manipulated my heart in order to get what they wanted. I didn't care that the world was ending or that the devil was after me for his own nefarious purposes. At this point, I'd welcome his interference. At least then, I would have someone else to blame for my misfortune instead of my own foolish heart.

Bursting through the door to Christian's cottage without so much as a knock, I found the man himself standing at his kitchen counter brewing coffee.

"Merri?" he asked, concern etched through every kind feature. "Why are you crying?"

I reached up and touched my cheeks, surprised when they came away wet. "I . . . I didn't realize . . ."

He rushed over and wrapped an arm around my shoulders, ushering me to the sofa. "Here. Sit down. I'll make you a coffee."

"I don't need a coffee. I need . . ." The words died on my tongue as I processed through what I was about to say. If I did this, I was putting everything on the line. I would risk being captured by Lucifer. I'd ruin the plans between the horsemen and Auntie Lilith. But I knew how to use my power to my benefit now. I could yank the souls out of bodies and feed on them at will, sort of. If I did this, I would have to fight for my survival on my own.

But I wasn't the same girl I'd been when they'd taken me. In just a handful of weeks, I'd learned so much about myself and my abilities. I didn't need protectors anymore. If I did need protection, it was from them.

I could do this.

I *would* do this.

For once in my life, the person making decisions about my future was going to be me.

"Merri?"

Christian's question pulled me back into the moment. My gaze snapped up to meet his concerned one.

"Does that offer to get me out of here still stand?"

"*Oui.* Of course."

"You understand that when they realize you helped me run, you'll be in danger? They're more powerful than you know."

"Let me worry about that."

"But—"

"*Non,* Merri. I will be fine. You've taken care of me and worried about me enough. You focus on yourself now. I will deal with whatever fallout comes my way. I'm not completely helpless, you know."

I attempted to smile, but I don't think it was very effective because Christian's eyes swam with concern. Shit. I think I was crying again.

"Do you have a safe place to go?" he prompted.

Lilith and *Iniquity* flitted to my mind first, but I wasn't even sure it was still standing. Besides, that was the first place people would look for me. I couldn't go to Blackwood. It was decimated. I had no idea where Andi was, and now I wished I'd been more receptive to her offer of shelter. But Cole had given me everything I needed. He wouldn't turn me away, and no one would think to look for me with him because hardly anyone knew about him. They certainly didn't know the depth of our friendship.

It may not be a long-term solution, but it was a place for me to get my bearings and figure out my next step. That's all I needed to worry about right now.

What was that saying? How did you eat an elephant?

One bite at a time.

I didn't need to have everything figured out; I just needed to focus on my first bite.

"Yeah. I have a place in mind."

"*Parfait.*"

He turned back to the kitchen and rummaged in a cupboard, muttering to himself the whole time as he searched for what he needed. After a few minutes, he turned around with a bright green orb in his hand. It looked a lot like a bath bomb, if I was being honest.

"What am I supposed to do with that? Drop it in the tub?"

He grinned. "*Non.* Take this, and when you are ready, think of where you wish to go. Throw it on the ground and step through the portal, which will open immediately. *Et voilà*!"

"That sounds surprisingly easy."

"The best magic always is. Complicated does not mean better. It just means more things can go wrong with far greater cost."

I accepted the little ball from him, the weight of it on my palm making all of this feel far more real. I looked back at Christian, my lower lip quivering when I realized it might be the last time I'd ever see him.

"One more thing before you leave. The magic will only work outside of the wards on the property. You will have to cross the property line before you can activate the spell."

"They'll know."

"*Oui,* but they're going to figure it out soon enough anyway."

I released a breath before nodding. "You're right. So I guess it doesn't matter. This means so much to me." Rushing forward, I enveloped him in an embrace. "Thank you, Christian." The words didn't feel like enough, but they were all I had.

He let out a little huff of surprise, but his arms wrapped around me momentarily. "Go. Be safe, *petite fille.*"

The sentiment was laughable. If only because safe was probably the very last thing I'd ever be again. Especially once they came for me. And they would. I had no doubt.

But it wouldn't be for love. No, all my silly notions about them loving me were barely more than smoking embers. If I could see my heart, hold it in my hands, all it would be now was a pile of ash waiting to blow away.

The Four Horsemen of the Apocalypse were nothing if not dedicated to their calling. I had become that very thing. This time when they came for me, it would be to finish the job they started.

CHAPTER THIRTY-ONE

SIN

"What the hell was that? Seriously, what is wrong with you? I know you're emotionally stunted, but *that*"—I gestured dramatically to Grim—"is not the way you respond to someone who tells you that you are their soulmate."

Grim, the snooty fuck, looked completely unruffled. He had the emotional range of a mealworm. No, you know what, that was offensive to mealworms. He had the emotional capacity of a thimble . . . for ants. The guy could be doing bookkeeping or suffering from anal fissures, and no one would ever be able to tell the difference.

"I didn't see you speaking up," he answered calmly.

"You didn't exactly give any of us a chance. You just steamrolled right over all of us with your bullshit decree."

"And then you stayed silent."

"Because I was processing, Grimsby. Processing takes time. She just dropped a major life-changing bomb on us, and I needed a fucking minute." Raking my fingers through my hair, I loosed a heavy sigh as my frustration really came to a head. "We have to go tell her you are a dumb asshole and fix this."

"You will not," Grim snapped.

I looked at Malice and Chaos. “You two want to get in on this conversation, or are you going to stick to the statue impersonations?” I squinted at Chaos. “Weren’t you the model for a few of those?” I put my thumb and my forefinger super close together. “You and your micropenis?”

Chaos frowned. “There’s nothing micro about me.”

“Well, tell that to your itty bitty heart. Why were you so quiet? Do you really think she’s wrong?”

I couldn’t believe the way they were reacting. Like there was any possible reality where Grim was right and Merri wasn’t our mate. The moment she said it, my heart screamed, “Yes!” It was my head that needed a minute to catch up so I didn’t say something stupid, like “That’s impossible.”

“You better hope she forgives you,” I said, pointing a finger at Grim and then waving it at the other two for good measure. “I’m not going down with the ship. We found love in a hopeless place, and I’m not letting go of it.”

“I’m pretty sure part of that’s a Rhianna song,” Malice murmured, eyes downcast and expression completely shuttered.

“It is. And she’s right.”

Chaos pinned Grim with a look. “Is it even possible? What she said? Is there any way we could actually be her mates?”

“Absolutely not,” Grim said.

“Yes!” I shouted. We had both answered at the same time, so I spun toward him and demanded, “Why not? Why is it so impossible to believe? I mean, fucking Hades gets to have a mate, why not us?”

“Because Hades is more than his title! We are and will only ever remain chained to our purpose. Shepherd forth the end of days until we finally succeed.”

Bullshit. All of it was bullshit.

“Really? Then why the fuck did we agree to try and stop the apocalypse this time? If that’s all that matters, why do a damn thing to keep this one from sticking?”

“Because it wasn’t the right time. They cheated.”

"You are so full of shit."

Grim didn't answer, choosing instead to stare at me.

"The worst part of all of this is that I think you actually believe the crap coming out of your mouth. It's not just some put-on act."

Grim offered me a pitying look, and it took every bit of self-control I had not to deck him. This was insanity.

"You know what? You can lie to yourselves all you want. Take the chicken-shit way out and lose the greatest gift the universe has ever given you. But allow me to remind you of my power. You can't lie to me. Not when I felt your reactions to her words." And then, because I wasn't about to let a single one of these motherfuckers off the hook, I called them each out. "Hope." I pointed to Malice, who still wouldn't meet my gaze. "Joy." I pointed at Chaos, whose jaw clenched in response. "And fear," I snarled at Grim.

"Careful," Grim warned.

"Of what?" I snapped. "You just ruined everything that mattered already."

I couldn't look at them any longer. Not without trying to kill them.

"I need to go find Merri and fix what we all broke. While I do, do yourselves a favor and pull your heads out of your asses."

It was all just too much. I'd gone from feeling very little about anything to feeling everything all at once. I knew that was because of Merri and what she'd unlocked in me, and I wasn't stupid enough to resent her for it. It was sort of like that moment in *The Wizard of Oz* when Judy Garland wakes up in Munchkin Land and everything was in technicolor for the first time. Who the hell would ever choose grayscale when you could live in color?

I needed to tell her that. To apologize for not being able to find the words of reassurance when she needed them most. To explain that I might be new at this, and thus a little slow, but it didn't mean I loved her any less.

She was right. We were soulmates, and I was *not* prepared to lose her.

Furious with Grim for putting my relationship with her at risk, but also near to bursting with fear that I'd waited too long to speak up and she'd never forgive me, while also simultaneously filled with love for her . . .

It was just all too much.

"You know what?" I snapped, pausing on the threshold on my way out of the library. "Fuck book club. I quit."

"Didn't you do that already?" Malice queried.

"Yeah? Well, this time I mean it!"

Chaos

"Well, that was dramatic," Grim murmured.

"He wasn't wrong."

The words left my mouth almost without my permission. They were the truth, and simply put, I wouldn't lie. Not to them or to myself.

Grim looked at me, his eyes wide. "What did you say?"

"He's not wrong, Grim. I felt our souls weave together. She's mine. She's ours. I don't doubt it."

"No," Grim said, shaking his head.

"Deny it all you want. It doesn't make it less true."

Grim turned to Malice. "You agree with me, don't you?"

Malice took a second to collect himself before finally lifting his eyes. "No."

"No?"

"No, I don't believe I do."

A harsh laugh escaped Grim. For possibly the first time ever, he looked like a man on the brink. There was no hiding the emotion running through him. Even his hand shook when he ran it through his hair.

"You can't be fucking serious. Has everyone lost their collective minds? You do remember who we are, right? What it is we are supposed to do? There's no room for soulmates. We have one purpose. One. And Merri, as beautiful as she is, is not it." He braced his arms on the mantel over the fireplace and hung his head as another bitter chuckle left him. "I mean, I can't even fucking touch her. Death doesn't get a mate. It's impossible."

"You keep using that word. Maybe it doesn't mean what you think it means," I offered.

"Fuck off."

"Is it really so hard to believe?" Malice asked. "I know that you've spent your life believing a certain set of facts, but if science has proven anything, it's that our understanding of the universe and our place within it is always evolving. And when new evidence presents itself and proves that your understanding of the world has been incorrect, that isn't a poor reflection on the masses who believed incorrectly. It simply means there was more to learn."

I could see Grim unraveling, his posture changing as he realized none of us agreed with him. Striding across the room, I joined him by the fireplace before placing a hand on his shoulder.

"Malice makes a strong case for possibilities, old friend. After all, the earth was flat until suddenly humans realized it was round and they weren't going to fall off the edge and into oblivion."

"And if you need a more personal example, I never thought I'd be able to procreate until Odette got pregnant. Sometimes the best thing we can do is accept that we do not know everything. The world is filled with mysteries. Even from us. Maybe you were right, Grim. Maybe it was impossible for the four of us to have mates because it was before Merri existed. But with her birth, a new possibility was created, and with that, our next evolution."

"Stop talking science to me," Grim muttered.

I caught Malice's eye, and he shrugged.

"I tried," he said.

Grim was so close to the edge. I knew Death like I knew myself. He was stubborn and determined, holding tight to his principles, even to his own detriment, but eventually, he would see truth if truth was there to be found.

"You can touch her in dreams, Grimsby. You can have her just as we do. Tell me you didn't feel some sort of shift between the two of you. The rest of us have experienced it. I don't think you're exempt from that."

His only outward response was a visible shudder. He didn't want to admit I was right, but I could see plainly enough that I was. So I kept pushing.

"Fate found a mate that you could be with. Perhaps it's not in the traditional manner, but it's no less real. Would you really spit in the face of destiny after all you have been through? She is everything you ever wanted, right there, just waiting for you to accept her."

Grim shut down before my eyes. I'd been so close to reaching him, but my words backfired.

"I don't deserve a mate. Leave me. Go after her if you must, but I am not her mate. I never will be, and you three are fools if you think you will ever be granted a happily ever after."

I had one last card to play.

"You could lose her, Grimsby. Forever. Is that really worth risking?"

His knuckles turned white where they gripped the mantel, but he spun away, cloaking himself in shadow so no more of his secrets could betray him. "I never had her to begin with."

"You heard him, Chaos. Leave him," Malice said, standing and making his way to the door. "Let him cling to his lies. Perhaps the rest of us can mend some of the damage he's caused in the meantime."

"It wasn't just him," I pointed out. "Our silence didn't help."

“We are not normal men. Merri will take that into account.”

“Will she?” I asked, following him out the door.

“We can only hope.”

CHAPTER THIRTY-TWO

MALICE

Never in my wildest dreams did I think I'd end up on the side of . . . feelings. But here I was, fighting with Grimsby over a woman. The problem was, her statement had been so truthful I could taste it. She was my soulmate, even though Grim was right—that shouldn't be a possibility for any of us.

It made a twisted sort of sense. She was destined to be mine. Of course I hadn't been able to resist her. The fault wasn't mine; it was fate's. What a fucking relief. I'd been so stunned by the realization that I hadn't been fully present in the room until Merri was already on her way out.

I knew there would be hell to pay for that, but it was hardly the first time I'd had to make amends with my hellcat. We'd sort it out. Hell, I'd grovel if I had to. Can't say I'd ever done it before, but how hard could it be to figure out?

The thought of lowering myself to grovel actually made my skin crawl. I'd come close to it once, long ago, when I'd begged for Odette to let me have contact with my son. I had nothing to apologize for in that situation, so perhaps begging brought me lower than groveling ever would. For Merri, I was reasonably certain I'd drop to my knees, crawl across the floor, and kiss her pretty toes if it meant she'd forgive me.

Fuck.

A groveling expert, I was not, but I was fairly certain I shouldn't be hard at the thought of it.

Maybe I was picturing it wrong?

Shaking my head, I strode down the hall and back toward the main staircase.

"Do you really think she would have gone to her room?" Chaos asked, trailing behind me.

"No, probably not. She most likely wanted to get as far away from the four of us as possible."

"We should search the grounds, then."

"Agreed, but let's be diligent and check her room anyway. Just to be sure. Merri's contrary enough she could have popped up there for spite."

Chaos offered me a curt nod and took the stairs two at a time, leaving me in his wake. I might be eager to mend things with my succubus, but I wasn't in a rush to swallow my pride.

"She's not there. Don't waste your time," Sin said, emerging from Merri's room, shoulders slumped. "We really fucked up. I even checked under the bed and in the tub. No sign of her."

A knot twisted in my stomach at his words. Logically, I'd already surmised that would be the case, but hearing it confirmed made it real in a way I wasn't yet ready to deal with. The idea that Merri might actually be out of reach was too horrible to contemplate. But the wards hadn't been breached, I'd know. She hadn't left us.

Not yet, anyway.

"She wouldn't be wandering the grounds alone, would she? Not after the attack," Sin murmured.

I cocked a brow. "Have you met our girl?"

"We should split up like we did the last time she went MIA."

"Look at you go, G.I. Joe. Using your fancy soldier words," Sin said, slapping Chaos on the shoulder.

"G.I. Joe wishes he was as strong as me."

"As strong as *I*," I corrected, unable to help myself.

A low growl rumbled from Chaos, but I wasn't worried about him at present. I needed to ensure my mate was accounted for.

Your *mate. She's your mate now?*

The word felt right, even if my brain stuttered every time it was said. For as much as my words earlier had been for Grim, they'd been a reminder for myself as well. The horsemen might not have been made to have a mate, but that didn't mean our course couldn't be altered. Just because something had always been true didn't mean that it would continue to be. I was intimately familiar with evolution. Too familiar, in fact, to ever believe I was exempt from it.

One had to adapt to survive, and it would seem that Merri was crucial to that process. Did I want to reflect on how necessary Merri felt to my survival? No, I absolutely did not.

"I'll check in with Christian and see if he's seen her. She's grown rather fond of him over the last few weeks." I headed for the front door, not waiting for either of them to tell me their plan. I trusted them to handle it.

It was a short job to his cabin, and as it turned out, there was no need for me to knock on the door. As I approached, Christian was coming around the back, a pair of dirt-stained gardening gloves adorning his hands.

'"Ah, monsieur, what can I do for you?" He began removing the gloves as he drew closer to me.

"Have you seen Merri today?"

His eyes widened, mouth forming a little *O* before he shook his head. "No, I am afraid not."

"Damn," I bit out, frustration and panic spiking.

"Is something the matter?"

Glancing around, I searched for any hint of her. A flash of red, Merri-sized footprints, a dropped hair elastic. Anything would be better than what I came up with.

"I had really hoped she'd be here," I admitted.

"Did you two have an argument?"

"You could say that. Technically, I wasn't the cause of the issue."

"Ah, well, I wish I could help you, but I have been gardening all morning, and I have not seen her."

I blew out a breath and ran a hand through my hair as I recalibrated my options. "Right, well . . . I'll let you get back to it then. If you do see her, come find me."

Christian nodded, pulling the gloves out of his back pocket and shoving his hands into them. "Of course."

Where are you hiding, hellcat?

I glanced around the grounds, hoping inspiration might strike. Or better yet, that she'd come walking my way. I'd gladly accept her fury if it meant that she was safe in hand. Preferably *my* hand.

I'd only just left Christian and begun a search around the back of the château when I felt it. That hook tugging and twisting my insides.

I'd wanted a sign, but *this* was not at all what I'd had in mind.

"No," I whispered. "No, no, no."

Something just stepped through the wards.

"Merri!"

CHAPTER
THIRTY-THREE
MERRI

As soon as I left Christian's cottage, I bolted, running as fast as my legs would carry me toward the property's edge. The long driveway was the quickest path to the outside world, and I knew I'd leave tracks Chaos would be able to trace. My only hope was to be quicker than them, which meant it was now or never. The moment they realized I wasn't in the house, one or all of them would try to find me. If they caught me, I would never escape.

My feet pounded the gravel, each step sending shockwaves up my legs, the speed at which I was sprinting making my lungs burn. I might have been a succubus, but I was not a runner. I did yoga, for heaven's sake.

If not for what felt like the literal hounds of hell at my back, I don't think I would have made it. Between the fire in my lungs and the pain in my thighs, I was already struggling. And that had nothing on the ache where my heart used to be.

"Just keep going," I wheezed, seeing the gate come into view. Just a little further and I'd be in the clear.

All I had to do was push open the gate and step past. It wasn't locked. It was simply for show. But when I reached the ornate barrier, I hesitated, skidding to a stop and nearly falling on my ass in the well-worn gravel.

Biting down on my lip, I turned back toward the château, which I couldn't even make out from here. Wind whipped around me, sending my hair flying. If this were a movie, I knew I'd make a striking image. I also knew if I was watching said movie, I'd probably be shouting at the heroine. But would I be telling her to stay . . . or go?

If I did this, if I left them, that would be it. No coming back. No more Sin or Chaos. No Malice or even Grim. They each had my heart even after rejecting me, and whether they wanted to admit it or not, that wouldn't change. Once you found your soulmate, you couldn't just put them aside like they didn't exist. Or maybe you could. I'd heard about people rejecting their mate bonds before. It rarely ended well, but perhaps it was possible to move on and live without them. I guess I was about to find out.

Because I had to go, right? If I stayed, what was really left for me here? A life surrounded by men I'd fallen head over heels for who saw me as nothing more than an inconvenience? A fucktoy they could lie to with pretty words day after day just to keep me happy?

That would be death by a thousand cuts. Each interaction with them a reminder of what I'd thought I'd found and lost. Of how incredibly gullible I'd been. It would be rejection over and over again. I couldn't live like that, not without destroying a fundamental piece of myself I could never get back.

I deserved better.

I deserved a chance at a real life—short as it might be, given the circumstances.

But if the world was going to end anyway, I'd spend the time I had left on my terms.

Gripping the ball of magic tightly, I took a steadying breath and used my other hand to open the gate.

My entire body trembled as I stepped through the invisible wall of magic keeping the world outside hidden from view. I knew I'd been successful when the landscape changed and the decimated town beyond Malice's private island appeared. It was worse than before, and I didn't think it was due to this being a different area I was seeing. Most of the buildings were burned husks now, or simply piles of rubble. The streets were empty. But had the people evacuated to somewhere safe? Or had they been dragged to hell by demons?

I guess it didn't really matter; I wasn't sticking around to find out.

Pulling my phone from my pocket, I sent a quick thank you to past Merri, who'd kept the device charged by force of habit. I scrolled through my past texts with Cole until I found the address for his new location and took precious seconds to commit it to memory.

"Merri!" Malice's voice echoed in the distance, jolting me to action.

He'd felt me cross the wards.

With no time to spare now, I tossed the bespelled ball to the ground in front of me while murmuring the address aloud. The same street name and numbers burned in my mind's eye to help reinforce what I was saying.

I knew I'd done it right when a shimmering visage appeared before me. I could easily make out an idyllic house with a nice wrap-around porch through the portal's rippling surface. I didn't know if I'd be safer with Cole, but I had to go to protect my heart. If I had to spend the rest of my days on the run from Lucifer to keep him from getting his antichrist, so be it. Letting the horsemen have their way would destroy me in the long run.

With nothing left to do except get caught, I stepped through the portal and left the four horsemen behind.

CHAPTER

THIRTY-FOUR

LUCIFER

"It's your turn, Gabriel. Come on now, don't keep me waiting," I taunted as I held out the dice for the restrained messenger of God. "Oh, right, you can't use your hands. Silly me. I'll do it for you."

With a quick roll of the multicolored cubes, I smiled down at the low-scoring collection.

"Oh, that's too bad. Only a pair of twos. I got three sixes. How appropriate. I win again. What's the score now? Twelve to zero? You're really going to have to step it up if you hope to make some sort of comeback."

"You . . . always . . . get three . . . sixes." Gabriel's voice was weak and raspy. Delightful.

"I know. It's quite brilliant."

"You're . . . cheating . . ."

"Well, duh." I looked up at him with a surprised lift of my brows. "Why would I bother playing a game that wouldn't end up in my favor?"

"What is . . . the point . . . of this?"

Oh, how I loved it when he wheezed like that. Every time I won a round, I'd taken my victory out on his flesh. Last time it was with my whip. The time before that, a dagger drawn down his sides until his blood coated the stone floor like an area rug. But this time? I had quite the surprise up my sleeve for him. Literally.

"The point, dear brother, is this. You won't join me. I've given you ample opportunity to make the right choice, be on the right side of history, and yet you still decline. So . . . I'll take what I really need from you instead."

I was seated on the floor in front of him. One knee up, the other leg stretched out in front of me in a graceful sprawl. I might be sitting on a concrete slab, but damn, I made it look good.

Vanishing the dice, I rolled my wrist with a little flourish.

"I have something for you."

Gabriel blinked, his expression annoyingly vacant.

"I can see that you're dying to know, so allow me to put you out of your misery."

He opened his mouth as though he wanted to speak, but gave up before the words could come out. Oh, goody, he was nearly broken. I was so very skilled at this part. The destruction of will, the breakdown of one's personhood. Even an archangel was vulnerable to my tactics.

Using the same flourish I had to see to the dice, I manifested a heavy iron spike, approximately the length of my large hand. I balanced the square head on the tip of my middle finger while staring him down.

"You know what this is, don't you, brother?"

Recognition flashed in his tired eyes.

"Yes, I see that you do. Quite clever, am I right? What good is making you bleed when you heal instantly? Oh, don't get me wrong, pain for pain's sake is all well and good, but if I want to really make this count, if I want you to take me seriously, then I need to be able to do some real damage."

"Wh-where did you get th-that?"

For the first time, true terror showed on his face. As well it should. This was one of the nails used during *the* crucifixion. I was tired of fucking around and getting nowhere. One drag of this across his skin would spill not only his blood, but his angelic grace. I could pin him through the heart, drive this spike deep into his chest until it met the stone wall behind him, and take every ounce of power he had. Or . . . I could siphon it slowly. Painfully. And let him wear the scars of my torture for eternity.

Mmm, yes. I quite loved the sound of that.

"Let's raise the stakes. Each time I win, I will claim a vial of your grace. We'll keep playing until you either see reason and join me or until I steal every last drop. And between you and me, brother, I will have very little use for you after that. Not that I think you'll last very long without your grace to heal you. Do you? Shall we make a bet of it? See how long it takes until your body gives out? I'll even let you make your guess first, if you'd like."

"You know I'd become mortal. I'd bleed out and die."

"Yes," I said with a maniacal grin. "It would be quite poetic. Finally able to be the man your Ruby needs, the human who could actually be with her, only to die moments later."

"Fuck. You," he spat.

I laughed. "Oh, such disrespectful language. I expected better of you, your holiness."

"Why should I respect you?" he rasped. "You couldn't even keep Lilith under your thumb. Bested by a fae. It's laughable."

My eye twitched.

"Still omnipotent, I see."

"The Messenger of God knows all."

"Not all. You never saw this coming."

"That's what you believe. You're too full of yourself to see your own weakness."

I jumped to my feet and crowded his face with a snarl. "I have no weakness."

"You never change. You're a pathetic," he whispered. "Tragic. Attention seeker."

Rage burned through me, and I fisted the nail, ready to drive it through his belly so I could take what I was owed. I'd waited so long to take my revenge. To prove that I was not the prideful upstart who deserved to be cast aside. And what better proof was there than beating my father at his own game?

"I'd say this will hurt me more than it hurts you," I hissed, spittle flying into Gabriel's face, "but that would be a lie."

Pulling my arm back, I readied myself to take the first sample of Gabriel's grace, but before I lunged, a loud ringing pierced my ears. Gabriel was unaffected, but I couldn't ignore it. Someone was summoning me.

I cocked my head, trying to ascertain what I could about who needed me and where they were.

As the answers came to me, a smile stretched across my face. "Well, well, well, it looks like it's your lucky day. We'll have to save this for later, brother. It appears I'm needed elsewhere."

With a saucy wink, I left Gabriel where he belonged. Alone. Shattered. Disheartened.

Materializing in the foyer, I took a beat before answering the door. I needed to make sure I looked my best for this visitor. No need to scare them off because of a few rogue drops of Gabriel's blood.

Looking at myself in the mirror, I ran a hand through my hair, adjusted my appearance, and smiled wide before checking my breath once.

The doorbell rang, a shadowy figure visible in the frosted window next to the entrance.

Clearing my throat and beating away the butterflies in my stomach, I pulled open the heavy door.

"Cole?" she said, relief on her face when she saw the version of me I created especially for her.

"Merri? Oh my God, I'm so glad you're here," I said, adopting the voice I'd used for this persona as I stepped forward and swept my vessel into my arms.

At long last, Merri was here. With me.

"I'm so sorry to just show up like this." Her voice quavered slightly as she squeezed me back. Perhaps it was wishful thinking, but I would have sworn she held me like I was the only thing keeping her upright.

Reveling in the moment, I dipped my nose down to the top of her head and inhaled. Everything about her was perfect. The silk of her hair as it brushed my hand. The way she smelled. The fit of her against my body.

"If you don't want me here, I understand," she whispered.

"Don't do that. Of course I want you here."

I held her tight and fought the urge to laugh at the perfect victory I'd just won. Then I pulled back so I could look into her vibrant blue eyes. She was with me now, and I would never let her go.

"You're exactly where you belong."

The Mate Games: Apocalypse continues with Grim, coming soon. You can pre-order your copy here but in the meantime, Lucifer isn't quite done with you.

download your copy of Lucifer's bonus scene at www.themategames.com/MaliceBonus or you can download it on audio and listen to it at www.themategames.com/MaliceAudioBonus

The Mate Games Universe

By K. Loraine & Meg Anne

War

Obsession

Rejection

Possession

Temptation

Devotion

Pestilence

Promised to the Night (Prequel Novella)

Deal with the Demon

Claimed by the Shifters

Captive of the Night

Lost to the Moon

Death

Haunting Beauty

Hunted Beast

Hateful Prince

Heartless Villain

Apocalypse

Sin

Chaos

Malice

Grim

Lucifer

MORE BY MEG & KIM

Twisted Cross Ranch

A dark contemporary cowboy reverse harem

Sinner's Secret

Corruptor's Claim

Deadly Debt

Also by Meg Anne

Brotherhood of the Guardians/Novasgard Vikings

Undercover Magic *(Nord & Lina)*

A Sexy & Suspenseful Fated Mates PNR

Hint of Danger

Face of Danger

World of Danger

Promise of Danger

Call of Danger

Bound by Danger (Quinn & Finley)

The Chosen Universe

The Chosen

A Fated Mates High Fantasy Romance

Mother Of Shadows

Reign Of Ash

Crown Of Embers

Queen Of Light

The Chosen Boxset #1

The Chosen Boxset #2

The Keepers

A Guardian/Ward High Fantasy Romance

The Dreamer (A Keeper's Prequel)

The Keepers Legacy

The Keepers Retribution

The Keepers Vow

The Keepers Boxset

The Forsaken

A Rejected Mates/Enemies-To-Lovers Romantasy

Prisoner of Steel & Shadow

Queen of Whispers & Mist

Court of Death & Dreams

Standalones

My Soul To Take: A Forbidden Love Meets Fated Mates PNR

ALSO BY K. LORAINE

THE BLACKTHORNE VAMPIRES

THE BLOOD TRILOGY

(CASHEL & OLIVIA)

BLOOD CAPTIVE

BLOOD TRAITOR

BLOOD HEIR

BLACKTHORNE BLOODLINES

(LUCAS & BRIAR)

MIDNIGHT PRINCE

MIDNIGHT HUNGER

THE WATCHER SERIES

WAKING THE WATCHER

DENYING THE WATCHER

RELEASING THE WATCHER

THE SIREN COVEN

ETERNAL DESIRE (SHIFTER RELUCTANT MATES)

CURSED HEART (HATE TO LOVERS)

BROKEN SWORD (MMF MENAGE ARTHURIAN)

STANDALONES

Cursed (MFM Sleeping Beauty Retelling)

REVERSE HAREM STANDALONES

Their Vampire Princess (A Reverse Harem Romance)

All the Queen's Men (A Fae Reverse Harem Romance)

About Meg Anne

USA Today and international bestselling paranormal and fantasy romance author Meg Anne has always had stories running on a loop in her head. They started off as daydreams about how the evil queen (aka Mom) had her slaving away doing chores, and more recently shifted into creating backgrounds about the people stuck beside her during rush hour. The stories have always been there; they were just waiting for her to tell them.

Like any true SoCal native, Meg enjoys staying inside curled up with a good book and her fur babies . . . or maybe that's just her. You can convince Meg to buy just about anything if it's covered in glitter or rhinestones, or make her laugh by sharing your favorite bad joke. She also accepts bribes in the form of baked goods and Mexican food.

Meg is best known for her leading men #MenbyMeg, her inevitable cliffhangers, and making her readers laugh out loud, all of which started with the bestselling Chosen series.